Henry Theophilus Finck

The Pacific Coast Scenic Tour

From Southern California to Alaska, the Canadian Pacific railway, Yellowstone Park

and the Grand Cañon

Henry Theophilus Finck

The Pacific Coast Scenic Tour
From Southern California to Alaska, the Canadian Pacific railway, Yellowstone Park and the Grand Cañon

ISBN/EAN: 9783337189495

Printed in Europe, USA, Canada, Australia, Japan

Cover: Foto ©Andreas Hilbeck / pixelio.de

More available books at **www.hansebooks.com**

PREFACE.

Books on California and Alaska exist in abundance, if not superabundance; but the intervening States of Oregon and Washington have been comparatively neglected in a way which seems surprising when we consider the remarkable scenic and climatic attractions of those States, their industrial resources, and the great future which doubtless lies before them. The present volume is an attempt to give a general and impartial view of the whole Pacific Coast, from San Diego to Sitka. Covering such a vast territory, it cannot, of course, make any pretensions to exhaustiveness, but is simply an endeavor to reproduce the local color of each State, by describing a few typical and important localities in each. I have naturally chosen the most favorable specimens, as every author or other mortal does in showing samples of a thing with which he is in love. I am in love with the Pacific Coast, because after living on it eleven years, at various times, and twelve years on the Atlantic Coast, I have found the scenery so much grander and the climate so much more delightful and exhilarating on the western side of our continent than on the eastern; and climate and scenery, in my opinion, make up fully one-half of human happiness. Scenery, indeed, requires some æsthetic culture for its appreciation, but climate affects all alike; and where the sky is habitually overcast with clouds, and the air humid and sultry, the millionaire suffers from habitual depression of spirits just as much as the beggar.

If the enthusiasm which pervades these pages should prove contagious to some of the readers, I do not fear that any of them will chide me hereafter for having induced them to emigrate to the West,—least of all, those who are in comfortable circumstances and wish to spend their last days amid bright and cheerful surroundings, and in a climate which favors longevity. It is my solemn determination to build a chateau somewhere on the Pacific Coast for myself some day, — if I can manage the "comfortable circumstances." Tourists, however, I must add, may possibly take the Pacific Coast Scenic Tour described in this volume and come back more or less disappointed. This will probably be the case if they visit Southern California in July, the Yosemite in October, Oregon and Washington in August, and Alaska before July or after September; for they will then find the temperature uncomfortably high in Southern California, and the water-falls reduced to a minimum in the Yosemite; while in Oregon and Washington they will probably see nothing at all, on account of the dense smoke from forest fires; and in Alaska the mountains will be obscured by mist and rain. But just as a prudent sight-seer does not visit Switzerland except between the middle of June and the middle of October, so we have a right to expect of him that he will plan his trip to the Pacific Coast for the most favorable season. This may seem difficult, on account of the great distance to be covered, and the variety of climatic conditions; but as a matter of fact it is the easiest thing in the world. Indeed, this trip can be taken in such a way that each locality as described in succession in this volume can be seen under the most favorable conditions possible. If an excursion agent had planned the climate of the Pacific Coast, he could not have made things more delightfully convenient for tourists. All you have to do is to follow spring northwards. Leave the East in the abominable winter months and spend a few months in Southern California, which from January to April is a paradise. If the Southern Pacific or Atlantic and Pacific railroads are taken, there will be no danger of a snow blockade, the temperature will be comfortable, and the scenic attractions abundant. Early in May, when vegetation fades in Southern California, the Yosemite should be visited to see its water-falls at their best. San Francisco and Tahoe also are most attractive in May. Continuing northward, we find Oregon and Washington still in their spring garb in June, while the snow-peaks are not yet concealed by smoke. July and August may be devoted to the sea-coast and to Alaska, and in September the return trip may be made across the Canadian Pacific, with its three mountain chains and the National Park as its chief attractions; or the Northern Pacific, which among its attractions includes the Columbia River scenery, the snow-peaks of Oregon and Washington, Lake Pend D'Oreille, and the Yellowstone National Park; or the Union Pacific, which includes the Sierra Nevada, Lake Tahoe, the stupendous scenery of the Rio Grande, Salt Lake City, Denver, and the Rocky Mountains, — three routes between which it is difficult to make a choice.

To complete the American Scenic Tour, we must of course take in one of the Great Lakes, Niagara Falls, the Thousand Islands and Rapids of the St. Lawrence, Lakes Champlain and George, and the Hudson River, —

scenes which have been too often described to be touched upon here. I have seen parts of four continents, but am still looking for a tour equal to the one outlined in this volume with the addition just named. It includes the grandest water-falls, the largest lakes, the finest river scenery and geysers, the most stupendous glaciers, and some of the most superb snow-peaks and ranges in the whole world; while the Yosemite and the Grand Cañon are absolutely unique and without rivals anywhere.

Most of the illustrations in this volume are by courteous permission reproduced from photographs in the excellent collection of Messrs. Taber, San Francisco, Haynes, Yellowstone Park, B. C. Towne & Macalpin & Lamb, Portland, and Pierce & Blanchard, Los Angeles.

H. T. F.

Tokio, Japan, August, 1890.

THE PACIFIC SLOPE—FROM MEXICO TO ALASKA.

CONTENTS.

CONTENTS.

xiii

LIST OF ILLUSTRATIONS.

I.

LOS ANGELES COUNTY.

TWENTY-THREE years ago, when the first transcontinental railway was commenced, the possibility of not only its success, but of its very construction, was almost universally doubted, and the San Francisco bankers who advanced money for the enterprise had to do so secretly, in order not to create a panic among their depositors. To-day there are five transcontinental lines, or six, if we count the Oregon Short Line separately, and the tourist or invalid can pay· his money and take his choice, according to the season, — the Canadian Pacific, Northern Pacific, or Union Pacific in summer; the Atlantic and Pacific or Southern Pacific in winter. The last-named is less interesting scenically than some of the Northern routes, but to invalids leaving the East in winter it presents the advantage of plunging at once *in medias res*, so far as semi-tropical climate is concerned.

Of the southern United States, this side of the Mississippi, one gets a rather unfavorable impression from the railway window, as the greater part of the distance from

1

Washington to New Orleans, and some hundred miles beyond, seems little else than one boundless swamp, with moss-covered trees, an occasional low mountain range, corn and cotton fields, and beggarly huts, as the only scenic features.   Montgomery seems a sleepy country village; and although New Orleans has sights worth seeing, it requires courage and a taste for roughing it in order to get at them; for the streets (naturally inclined to be muddy, because the city lies below the level of the Mississippi) are so horribly paved that even a New Yorker must lift up his hands and thank Heaven that he does not live in such a city.   Without any exaggeration, a Swiss stage-road in the midst of the mountains is not so rough and jolting an affair as the street-car tracks in New Orleans; and what the roads are beyond the paved streets may be inferred from the fact that in January I found it absolutely impossible to reach the City Park (where the Exposition was held some years ago) on foot, from the terminus of the street cars. Some of the gardens on the way were ornamented with orange-trees laden with ripe fruit, but both trees and fruit presented a sad contrast to the luxuriance I beheld in Los Angeles three days later; and equally great was the contrast between the moist, warm, enervating atmosphere of the Louisiana marshes, and the dry, cool, mountain and ocean breezes of Southern California.

If you leave New Orleans, say, on Wednesday noon, you will be at Los Angeles on Saturday evening before ten.   A good supply of reading-matter is desirable, as there is little to see for a day or two, except cactus bushes, a few painted Indians, and bleak mountains, some of them across the Mexican border.   At El Paso, which calls itself "the Paris of the Southwest," and claims twelve thousand inhabitants, the train stops long enough to afford a chance to drive across the river into Mexican soil. The El Paso papers try hard to induce the passengers in quest of health to stay there, and have a very poor opinion of California. The *Herald* which I bought, editorially described the "recent terrific rain-storms" in that State, and found it difficult to decide which was a worse place for invalids, "Holland with her damp marshes, or the Golden State." The editor probably mixed up that State with Arizona; for on arriving in California we discovered there had not been a drop of rain for several weeks, while in Arizona we found the deserts, as far as the eye could reach, one vast plain of shining, semi-liquid mud, interspersed with large temporary lakes. The rain poured down in blinding torrents and with true tropical violence, forming channels several feet deep across the desert, and whirling aside thirty-feet iron rails like straws.

The spectacle of this rain-storm in the desert was so weird and sublime that we gladly in return accepted the fate of reaching Los Angeles twelve hours behind time; for the train, owing to the numerous washouts and soft places, could only creep along, and beyond Tucson we had to wait five hours for daylight, as the engineer did not dare to proceed farther in the dark. Such storms and washouts are obviously frequent in this region, for ties and rails are scattered all along the road for emergencies. Nature, provoked by the "soft thing" which the Southern Pacific had in building this level road, seems to have taken this means of getting square with it. At Colton, California, the scenery becomes snow-mountainous and interesting, and remains so as far as Los Angeles.

During my first visit to Southern California, in 1887, I was amused to notice the vast contempt with which the fifty thousand inhabitants of the city of Los Angeles looked down on the three hundred and fifty thousand benighted denizens of a certain northern village known as San Francisco, and on other places that have the effrontery to grow rapidly, and to claim special advantages of climate, situation, and commerce. The Los Angeles *Herald* informed its admiring readers that —

"Pasadena and Los Angeles will be one city in a brief period, and form a continuous municipality from the Sierra Madre to the sea — an extent of thirty miles in length by at least six in width, with five hundred thousand people contained therein, and will be the capital of the richest State in the Union. The claim of New York as the Empire State is already in dispute, but the dispute will soon be settled by the pre-eminence of South California."

It must be admitted that much had happened to justify this Los Angelic grandiloquence. Seventeen years ago the City of Angeles had only ten thousand inhabitants, no street cars, and only one railway. To-day it has at least sixty thousand inhabitants, electric street cars, and more than half-a-dozen railways, with about seventy-five daily trains. Orange-trees have increased in the county from twenty-five thousand to a million or more ; grape-vines from three millions to twenty millions ; and other agricultural products in proportion.

Its very disadvantages have proved advantages to Los Angeles. For instance, the fact that coal, like wood, is expensive, made the city the first in the country to adopt a general system of electric street-lighting. It has seventeen masts one hundred and fifty feet high, fourteen masts sixty feet high, and hundreds of private lights. The electric railroad is also being rapidly extended. The cars run at the rate of ten or twelve miles an hour, which can be increased to twenty outside the city limits. The road's capacity is said to be four times that of a horse road, and its cost only one-half, while there is no torturing of poor horses in the hot noonday sun. A ride or a walk along the streets of Los Angeles conveys the impression that the city is quite as large and as "metropolitan" as it claims to be; the natural bustle and activity being increased by the winter visitors from the East.

In every country the smaller cities are apt to take after the metropolis. Thus, Rouen constantly suggests Paris; Linz, Vienna; the English cities, London, etc. Similarly, Los Angeles suggests San Francisco in many details, — the appearance of the stores, hotels, Chinese shops, and the gardens, although the gardens have a more decided semi-tropical aspect, and there is a general appearance of more open-airness, if the word be permissible. The city is surrounded on all sides by high mountains and buried among groves and gardens. Orange, lemon, "pepper," and fig trees adorn the gardens everywhere, side by side with many luxuriant shrubs and flowers, dwarfed apologies for which are often seen in Eastern gardens. In size and brilliancy of color these California flowers are incomparable, but the same causes which tend to give quinces, for instance, a less pronounced flavor than they have in the East, appear to impair the fragrance of some flowers. This fact has often been commented on, but I believe that too much emphasis has been placed on it. Repeated experiment has convinced me that the verbena and heliotrope, and perhaps the geranium, have a less delicious fragrance in California than in New York, at least in October; but the same is not true of roses and pinks and lilies; and the countless varieties of wild flowers that adorn the hill-sides in spring have a most intoxicating fragrance, wherewith they allure so many bees that honey can be sold at four cents a pound.

The present ambition of the Los Angeles people is to surpass all the rest of the world in as many things as possible. In one thing certainly they were pre-eminent, a few years ago,—in the number of real-estate offices that decorated their town. Neither San Francisco nor any mining town ever had so many saloons to the number of inhabitants as Los Angeles had of these land offices; and the day after my arrival I heard a mother scolding her baby for putting a handful of dirt in its mouth — doubtless because she thought real estate was too valuable to be thus wasted in luxurious living. Almost every landowner, whether he had a sign over his door or not, was willing to part with some or all of his property for a consideration — not a slight one, by any means; and the whole county was affected with this epidemic, there being places of only a few thousand inhabitants where corner lots were sold almost at New York City prices.

One day, driving along a country road about twenty miles from Los Angeles, I noticed half-a-dozen well-dressed men resting under a tree. My companion informed me they were doubtless a syndicate looking about for a place to locate a new town. At Fullerton, a few miles from Anaheim, I saw one of these new towns. It consisted of the framework of a large hotel and of a few hundred yards of elegant cement sidewalk, not in front of the hotel, but in another part of the "town." Elsewhere towns get pretty large before any one begins to think of a sidewalk, even of the most primitive kind; but the residents in Los Angeles County of course would not be satisfied with a sidewalk in any way inferior to that in front of Mr. Vanderbilt's house in Fifth Avenue. I may add that since then Fullerton has grown up into quite a little town.

Having built his sidewalk and his large hotel (with real-estate office) in place of the saloon which usually is the pioneer building in Western towns, the Southern Californian begins to cast about for a supply of water; not so much for domestic use — since wine is almost as cheap as water — as for the irrigation of his garden and fields. If a river or brook is near by, a water company is formed, ditches are dug, and each shareholder, after paying his dues, may have his water " on tap " whenever he wants it. In the absence of a river, wells are made to supply the water. Sometimes these wells are bored horizontally into the mountain side, thus creating an artificial spring; but, as a rule, the wells are vertical, from eighty to five hundred feet deep, or even more, although at one hundred to two hundred feet the water is generally obtained in abundance. A windmill is then erected over the well, which pumps the water into a large, high tank, whence it is easily conveyed to the garden or field by hose. There is no lack of wind to drive these mills; for the charm of Southern California's climate lies in this, that although the sky is commonly cloudless, and the sun warm, winter and summer, there is almost always a brisk breeze to temper the solar rays, and deprive them of their sting.

This is true especially of Los Angeles County, which

is situated between the deep sea and an imposing circular range of mountains, that send their breezes down over the valley as soon as the ocean breezes cease; and although at some seasons both these air-currents, near their source, would be unpleasantly cold for invalids, they are almost always mellowed and warmed by the sun's rays before they reach the centre of the valley. The morning — till about two o'clock — is the warmest part of the day; but in the autumn the morning heat is tempered by a daily fog, which remains till about ten o'clock. It is not a depressing fog, and is rather enjoyed by the natives, as a temporary change from the everlasting sunshine. In fact, sunny monotony is the gravest charge that can be brought against the climate of Southern California. In the autumn and spring a few rainy days afford refreshing variety; but summer and winter are alike in their cloudless skies, warm sunshine, and alternating mountain and ocean breezes. As a physician at Anaheim remarked to me, the seasons do not differ in character, but only in flavor, like the differences between severals kinds of apples. He also informed me that, although the temperature sometimes rises above a hundred in the shade, he has never seen a case of sunstroke — thanks to the dryness of the air and the almost incessant breezes. Yet, like all southern climates, it fosters indolence, mental and physical; and he would not recommend it, therefore, to young persons, except for money-making purposes. But for invalids and for elderly persons, it is the best place in the world. The somnolence brooding in the air (except in Switzerland I have never slept so soundly in my life as here) would cure the worst case of Wall Street insomnia; and the incessant sunshine and constant life in the open air can hardly fail to add ten years or more to the life of old men or women who desert their over-heated and ill-ventilated Eastern homes for the open air and winter sunshine of Los Angeles County.

The general irrigation now resorted to, and the numerous green oases which have in consequence sprung up amid the deserts of prickly cactus, have already exerted some influence on the climate, and there is reason to believe that rain will be more abundant in the future than it has been in the past. A potent factor in producing this change will be the groves of trees that are being planted everywhere. There are some poplars and locusts and other trees that appear to flourish tolerably well, but the two species that most triumphantly defy sunshine, dust, and drought are the red-pepper-tree and the Australian eucalyptus, both of them beautiful to behold. The red-pepper-tree, with its gracefully drooping branches, resembles a weeping willow, but its growth is more luxuriant, its dimensions larger, and it is adorned with bunches of beautiful small red berries. The leaves, when bruised, have a strongly pungent cayenne odor, whence the name of the tree. The leaves and fruit of the eucalyptus have a still more objectionable odor when crushed (very much like assafœtida), but the tree has a most stately appearance, and its marvellously rapid growth — a seed becoming a large tree in a few years — causes it to be raised on a large scale for fuel and for shady avenues.

But although Los Angeles County can raise the Australian eucalyptus and the pepper-tree, there is a point at which the climate draws the line further south. Thus, the banana and the pineapple, although they can be raised here, do not usually thrive well, and the same is true of the almond. Yet the Los Angeleños do not despair on that account, as they have a superabundance of other fruits to fall back on. Of the vast and fruitful orange and lemon orchards of this region every one has read. Figs grow abundantly and are in good demand, especially those of the Smyrna variety, which are now displacing the others. The demand for California olive oil is greater than the supply, and it is equal in quality to the best Italian oil. English walnut-trees yield a profitable crop. Peaches are so abundant that they are fed to the cows, and some varieties (but not all) are equal in flavor to the New Jersey and Delaware crop. Ears of corn a foot long, with twenty rows to the ear, can be seen in the market, side by side with gigantic twenty-horse-power onions, and potatoes weighing from two to five pounds. Sugar-beets are on exhibition, weighing fifty pounds, and pumpkins of one hundred and fifty to one hundred and seventy-five pounds. Pumpkins, melons, tomatoes, and other creepers grow wild, without any care, and may even become a weedy nuisance. If a Chinaman eats a watermelon under a tree along the road, the chances are that a crop of wild melons will be found in that neighborhood the following season; and on one farm I saw a volunteer tomato plant which the owner said he had ploughed down twice, but when I saw it, it measured at least twelve feet square, and had thousands of small red fruit on it of the kind which is only used for preserves, although, like the little yellow ones, it is of a much more delicate flavor than the large tomatoes, which alone, for some inscrutable reason, are ever seen on our tables.

This list is very far from complete and is being constantly extended; for California is still largely in an experimental stage of development. The experiment with ostrich-farming near Anaheim has resulted successfully, and other farms have been started near Los Angeles. I visited the original farm near Anaheim. The keeper, an Englishman imported from Africa, showed me a fine lot of healthy birds and some beautiful specimens of feathers, naming prices which, if they were advertised by a New York house, would create a riot among "bargain"-seeking women; for it is to be hoped that women, having abandoned the vulgar fashion of wearing stuffed bird-corpses on their hats, will return to their old love, the delicate plumes of the ostrich, the wearing of which involves no cruel massacre of innocents. And California has another kind of plume to which the attention of women should be directed, the product of what might be called the vegetable ostrich, — pampas grass. Nothing more exquisite for a vase or for a (fan-shaped) wall ornament could be imagined than these bushy white (or colored) plumes, which in Los Angeles County attain the height of thirty-six inches, not including the stem. Formerly, when these plumes were imported from South America, florists charged a dollar or even a dollar and a half apiece for them; now the retail price is twenty-five cents, and the wholesale price three or four cents. Vast quantities are being exported to Europe, and Southern California is able to supply the demand of several continents, as the pampas grass, like most plants, grows there like a weed.

A dark cloud has, however, lately risen, and is for the moment casting an ominous shadow over the cheerful prospects of California. All the products so far mentioned are, of course, subordinate in importance to the grape crop; and the California grape-vine has been for several years threatened by an enemy more dangerous, because more obscure, than the phylloxera. A few years ago some of the grape-vines in Los Angeles County suddenly began to die out. Among these were some of the oldest vineyards, eighty years old or more. Indeed, the old Mission grape was the first to be attacked. Then followed other varieties, always in the same order in each vineyard. The disease begins at the tip of the vines and slowly spreads downwards, the roots being affected last. The second season the crop is a comparative failure, and the third the vineyard is a graveyard. One lady told me she had dug up and used for fuel as many as eighty thousand of her vines within a few years. The disease is said to be not phylloxera nor mildew; nor have the chemical experts who have examined the vines been able to throw any light on the matter, except by attributing the decay to a kind of cellular degeneration. Various theories are being discussed, and the owners of the vineyards meanwhile console themselves with the statement that a similar mysterious disease affected the grapes of Sicily and Madeira at one time, and disappeared after a few years, allowing the young vines to grow as before. What causes them to look with comparative indifference on this temporary (as they hope) interruption of business is the fact that there has been an over-production of grapes, in consequence of which the price of wine has fallen to unprofitable figures. An interruption of a few years in this excessive production would raise the prices, and thus pay for the losses now sustained.

In the meantime the wine-growers would do well to ponder the fact that quality is of much more value, financially and gastronomically, than quantity. Labor is

OSTRICH FARM—SOUTHERN CALIFORNIA.

scarce in harvest-time, and, to save trouble, too many of the small growers neglect to pick out the green and sour grapes, which therefore vitiate the juice of the whole bunch; or else they intrust the cleaning of their old barrels to ignorant Chinamen (the Indians have all disappeared), with equally disastrous results. Too many Eastern people have contracted absurd prejudices against California wines, because chance threw some of this sour wine into their cellars. But it may be safely stated that the average California claret and white wine and port are superior to the wine that may be bought for the same money in France and Germany and elsewhere. The *labels* of famous French wines and Cognacs are for sale openly in the show-cases of country stores in Los Angeles County! These honest folks are practically compelled to use this stratagem. They would much prefer to sell their best wines under California labels, in order to build up their reputation. And if California wine-growers used the same caution as those of Europe, this subterfuge would no longer be necessary. I have tasted old Zinfandel equal to the best French château wines, because made with the same care, and it fetched almost as high a price in San Francisco as foreign wines.

Whatever may be the outcome of the present vineyard epidemic, Southern California will have plenty of other things to fall back upon. A few years ago it looked as if all the crops were to be neglected, comparatively, and a specialty made of building hotels for invalids and tourists. Among the special attractions for tourists is quail-hunting in the foothills. The physician already referred to kindly took me out on an afternoon hunt. We drove in a tough two-horse buggy, up and 'down hill and along the dry bed of a brook, carefully dodging the bristling cactus bushes, which are apt to make a deep impression on "tenderfoot" visitors, less by the grotesque manner in which their fleshy leaves are stuck on one another at odd angles than by their fish-hook-like spines. These prickly leaves are so arranged that nothing larger than a quail or a rabbit can get under their protecting shadows. The dogs give them a wide berth, and the quail can only be shot on the wing if they are alarmed and fly from one group of cactus bushes to another. The result of an hour's buggy-hunting was nine quails, three pigeons, and two rabbits.

II.

SOUTHERN CALIFORNIA IN WINTER.

IN 1887 all the hotels in Los Angeles were over-crowded, the post-office almost unable to get through with its business, the city growing like an asparagus stalk after an April shower, and the demand for labor so great that the workmen could practically dictate their own terms. The smaller towns and would-be towns had also caught the infection, and were building huge hotels, cement sidewalks, and street-car lines; not because it was supposed that towns of two thousand inhabitants needed such things, but in order to be able to advertise in the Eastern papers and in real-estate circulars that the place had street-car lines, cement sidewalks, and hotels "with all the modern conveniences." Each town printed a special illustrated pamphlet in which its unique attractions, as compared with all rivals, were set forth, culminating in the claim that its township was the "Italy of America" or of the West; while San Diego brought matters to a climax by styling itself "the Italy of Southern California."

In 1889, when I made my second visit to Los Angeles

County, I found everywhere evidences that the boom had collapsed. The street-car lines in the small towns barely paid expenses, though it was regarded as an act of local patriotism to ride on them; and the cement sidewalks, which had been prolonged far into the fields, had failed to charm into existence the rows of houses that had been looked for. In the metropolis itself, work-men were grumbling at insufficient employment, merchants clamored that their rents were fifty per cent too high, many store windows were pasted with closing-out notices, real-estate offices were no longer as abundant as saloons, and the bookstores, more wretchedly supplied than those of any town of ten thousand inhabitants in the United States, were even selling the twenty-cent paper novels at "cut rates." The newspapers of Northern California, of Oregon, Washington, and other Western States as far east as Kansas, which had long been jealous of the prosperity of Southern California, and desired a boom of their own, crowed loudly over the "busted boom" of Los Angeles, while the papers of that city, no longer compelled by the pressure of real-estate advertisements to add two or four extra pages to their issues, had daily elaborate editorials to disprove the allegations of their envious rivals.

An unprejudiced observer, interested only in the climate and the scenery, and not in the real estate, of Southern California, could not but admit, from the signs just noted, that these "envious rivals" were right in insisting that the boom had collapsed; but the inferences drawn from this fact, that Southern California had been overpraised, and that its road was to be down hill in the future, were absurd. Southern California cannot be overpraised, and, in my humble opinion, its pros-

pects are brighter than those of any other portion of the
United States. To a large extent the late boom was
nothing but a huge gambling scheme, an epidemic of
wild land-speculation, which carried along in its rush
thousands of thoughtless victims, like the mad stampede for Oklahoma. Southern Californians knew better than others that the sudden rise in their land prices
were artificially stimulated and would be followed by a
reaction; but they were bound to make hay while the
sun shone, and found to their delight that the sun shone
longer in California than elsewhere, in the metaphorical
sense as well as in reality. At last the storm came, and
swept away many of the " tenderfeet," or late comers,
and their new buildings, whose débris is now lying
about, so to speak, and is pointed at as a terrible warning and lesson; but the only lesson it does teach is that
people should avoid real-estate gambling. The fragments of the ruins will soon be cleared away, and then
it will be found that, although many individuals have
suffered during the storm, the State as a whole has
been benefited by it.

In many cases the large, useless hotels built in the
small towns have already been secured at a bargain for
school buildings, and in the larger cities many public
works have been provided which, without the artificial
stimulus of the boom, would have been postponed to the
indefinite future; as, for instance, the long flume, costing almost a million of dollars, which now provides San
Diego and vicinity with abundant pure water, and will
do more to develop the resources of the county than
the discovery of several gold mines. Los Angeles
made the great mistake of not building a sewer to the
sea during flush times, and now suffers under the dis-

advantage of vitiated air, which, if not remedied, will destroy its reputation as a health resort.

In other respects, Los Angeles is already recovering from the effects of the collapse. Fine new buildings are again going up, the streets are always animated, and the cable-car tracks have been lately prolonged into the picturesque hilly region behind the city, which affords the finest imaginable sites for suburban cottages, with superb views of the mountains, and a glimpse of the Pacific Ocean, fourteen miles away. Though founded in 1781, Los Angeles had less than five thousand inhabitants in 1860, and only thirteen thousand in 1880, while to-day it has sixty thousand or more. Thirteen years ago no railroad connected it with other parts of the world, while to-day it is one of the greatest railroad centres in the West. And as it still remains, what it always was, unsurpassed by any city in the world for climatic and scenic advantages, it has every reason to look forward to a prosperous and brilliant future.

Southern California includes five counties, — Los Angeles, Santa Barbara, Ventura, San Bernardino, and San Diego, — embracing, as General N. A. Miles points out, "a territory nearly the size of the State of New York, and with natural resources of ten times its value." This seems a big statement, but its truth can be realized, without the use of figures, by considering that these five counties are capable of supplying the United States with all the figs, raisins, prunes, wine, olives and olive oil, oranges, lemons, nuts, and canned fruits that are now imported from France, Italy, and Spain; most of them, with proper care, equal in quality if not superior to the imported articles. Although large quantities of all these fruits are already raised, they are a mere trifle compared with what the soil is capable of yielding to a larger population. It has been proved over and over again that ten to twenty acres of good irrigable land are all that is needed to support a family, and there is therefore room for hundreds of thousands of immigrants. However, it is candidly admitted that Southern California is a land of more promise to the farmer who has at his disposal a capital of a few thousand dollars than to the emigrant who brings with him little but a team and a pair of muscular arms; for improved land, with bearing vines and fruit trees, costs from one hundred to five hundred dollars an acre, while unimproved land, though it may be had for one-fifth those prices (twenty to one hundred dollars), yields no return for several years, unless grain is raised; for all of the semi-tropical fruits above named require from three or four to ten years before a profitable crop is yielded.

And yet personal observation has led me to believe that there are special opportunities in this region precisely for the farmer with limited means, if he is willing to curb his ambition and content himself with dairy farming and the raising of poultry on a large scale for the market. The farmers now settled in Southern California are so ambitious to become orange, olive, or vineyard kings that they entirely neglect the farmyard, and have hardly enough milk and butter and vegetables for home consumption. It is almost impossible in any part of Southern California to get a good piece of beef or mutton, and chickens are imported by the carload from Kansas and other " Eastern " States, and sold at absurdly high prices at Los Angeles, although in this mild climate it is easy to raise chickens all the year round, and I have myself seen splendid broods of young ones grow up in about half the time they need in the East to reach a marketable size, the simple precaution being taken of providing them with dry housing during rainy nights. If this is not done, their growth is remarkably retarded, and many of them become diseased, and, if not killed or isolated, will infect a whole yardful of poultry.

Cattle-raising, too, must prove profitable in a region where the animals can feed on the green foothills and valleys all the "winter," and in summer eat the sun-dried grass or clover which covers the whole country. The wild, clover-like alfileria, which furnishes most of this natural hay, grows in profusion along the roadsides and in the meadows, and even fills up the empty patches in the cactus fields. After the spring rains it attains a height of ten to fifteen inches, with a dozen plants to the square inch, and is so juicy and tender that one can mow it down with a cane or with the hands; and a week later it is as high as if it had never been cut. It looks so luscious and sweet as to almost make one long to be a cow or a sheep, in order to be really "in clover" for once. Again, the cultivated clover, or Chilian alfalfa, if sufficiently irrigated, yields half-a-dozen or more crops of hay a year, which makes the sweetest butter and meat in the world. Yet the Southern Californians, as I have just said, import most of their butter and meat; consequently, if some farmers should undertake to supply the local market with home-made products, fresher and cheaper, because with no freight charges on them, they would have a sure source of prosperity before them. It is probable that the drought of 1863–64 discouraged the cattle business; but there has been none since that time, and with the present railway facilities and a reasonable foresight in storing hay, no disaster need be feared in the future. Moreover, one of the best and cheapest kinds of cattle food, pumpkins, as large as beer-barrels, can be raised here by the thousand with hardly any trouble or expense. Sometimes they lie in a field so densely that one might walk over it without touching the ground; and I saw several fields in which hundreds of fine pumpkins, for which the farmers had no use, owing to the scarcity of cattle, were left to rot on the ground.

Before purchasing land in California of the South, it is well that the investor should have made up his mind in regard to what branch of agriculture he wishes to devote himself. For although it is one of the chief advantages of this soil that it can be made to produce most of the fruits of the temperate and semi-tropical, and some of the tropical zones, yet each township or locality has its special adaptedness for this or that product, and to ignore this is to labor under disadvantages. Thus, Riverside and vicinity have been found most favorable to the culture of the orange, because the destructive scale-bug does not flourish here as it does nearer to the coast. Of lemons, the finest specimens are grown near the Mexican border, in San Diego County, which also furnishes some of the best raisins and olives. Santa Barbara County yields the finest pampas plumes and the best walnuts, and Los Angeles County is still the wine centre of the South, notwithstanding the ravages of the mysterious vine disease. The conclusion, too, is being gradually reached that for vineyards the foothills are the best localities, since in Europe all the best vines are raised on the hill-sides. Plants of a distinctly tropical type, also, like tea, bananas, etc., might perhaps be successfully raised on the lower foothills, which have an immunity from the light frost that occasionally, in winter and spring, visits the lowlands near the ocean. And besides these facts, it is well to know that in the same locality the soil often presents great differences, so that in a twenty-acre field one half may be well adapted for the orange or olive, while the other half needs a different crop. Above all things, "tenderfeet" should beware of buying land immediately after the spring rains; for then the whole face of the country is covered with a rich carpet of grass and flowers, so that it is difficult to distinguish the good land from the sand-bottomed site of a former river bed, useless for anything but cactus.

Finally comes the most important of all questions, — the facilities for irrigation. Grain, if sown in winter or early spring, ordinarily needs only the regular rains of the season to reach maturity, and there are localities where many other crops can be raised without irrigation; but these are the exception, and as a general thing the semi-tropical fruits which constitute the specialty of Southern California, need water for profitable culture. So well is this now understood that it is a favorite joke of the natives to say that if you pay for the air and water, they will throw in the land gratis.

Fortunately there are no fewer than six sources from which crops are supplied with water, if we include rain. For small vegetable or flower gardens sufficient water can be raised by means of windmills, which are kept in brisk motion every afternoon by the sea-breeze in the whole region within twenty or thirty miles of the ocean, except during two or three of the "rainy months," when they are not needed. These mills also supply the kitchen, and it is curious to note how cold the water

FRUIT FARM IN SOUTHERN CALIFORNIA.

remains in the large tanks exposed all day long to a semi-tropical sun. Much of the water used in town and orchard is supplied by artesian wells, which, however, occur only in certain belts, especially in Los Angeles and San Bernardino Counties, although none of these, I believe, equal one dug in Sonoma County last winter, which is one hundred and fifteen feet deep, cost only two hundred dollars, and yields almost half a million gallons every day.

Rivers of the size of the Sacramento, or those of Oregon, Southern California has none, but there are some smaller rivers and a large number of creeks, fed by the mountain snows, which are tapped in two ways for irrigating purposes, — on the surface and below the bed. The surface water is often carried many miles in ditches ; and wise is the community which lines its ditch at once with cement, else in summer it loses almost two-thirds of its water supply by absorption on the way. The Santa Ana River, which is quite a respectable stream in winter, and after rains becomes a formidable torrent, liable to overflow its banks and change its channel (thereby causing boundary disputes), is in summer tapped so freely that its bed becomes dry, and not a drop reaches the ocean.

Much more curious than this surface tapping, however, is the tunnelling, by means of which the water which has buried itself beneath the sandy river bed, as if to escape the merciless pillaging of the hot sun and the greedy farmers, is brought to the surface again and utilized. It is in this way that the Santa Ana River is despoiled of its last drop, and the value of this procedure may be estimated from the statement made by the San Bernardino *Times*, that "the Ontario Land Company has driven a tunnel in under San Antonio Creek, a distance of nearly eighteen hundred feet, at a cost of about fifty-two thousand dollars, and they have about two hundred and fifty inches of water, worth a quarter of a million of dollars." As it hardly ever rains during the summer, all the water thus drawn off the rivers in the irrigating season comes from the springs and the melting snows in the mountains. This is just about sufficient for the present needs of the population; but no fears need be entertained for the future, since, as the rural population increases, it will become profitable to expend large sums in building reservoirs in the cañons to store the abundant winter water which now runs to waste in the ocean. In this way the mountains can be made to yield an absolutely unlimited amount of water, sufficient to support tens of millions; and the lesson taught by the Johnstown disaster will prevent the dams from being carelessly constructed.

III.

THE GREAT AMERICAN PARADISE.

THAT there could be no better way of investing capital than by building reservoirs is shown by the fact, recently pointed out by the California State Board of Trade, that ten years ago the lands of Frenso sold at from three dollars to twenty dollars per acre, while now, with water on it, the same land sells at from seventy-five to seven hundred and fifty dollars per acre. Equally great is the gain from an æsthetic point of view. Without water, four-fifths of Southern California is a dreary cactus desert during the greater part of the year; with water, it is a veritable garden grove. Nothing could be more delightful than to watch the effect of water in this magic climate, when the first rains fall in October or November. Up to that period everything except the irrigated garden and orchard oases wears a parched yellow and brown aspect; but hardly has the rain penetrated a few inches into the soil, when the grass turns green, and before the eye has become accustomed to the change, gaudy flowers, gradually increasing in variety and abundance, spring up on all sides, even on land which appeared to be pure sand, but which on closer examination proves to be rich in decomposed vegetable matter. The irrigated gardens have an abundance of choice flowers all the year round, and the garden of the house where I lived, though without the slightest pretensions, had in full bloom, in January, petunias, calla lilies, violets, honeysuckles, geraniums (six feet in height), stock, California poppy, hyacinths, smilax, heliotropes, nasturtiums, red, white, yellow, and *green* roses, etc. In February a frost nipped the leaves of the bananas, heliotropes, and nasturtiums, but in a few days they were out again; and of the three or four subsequent frosts none was heavy enough to injure them, while the other flowers mentioned grew uninjured all the " winter." This was at Anaheim, twelve miles from the sea and twenty-eight miles south of Los Angeles, and gives a better idea of the climate than columns of statistics. Nor was it an exceptional year; for there are orange-trees in the State over eighty years old, and at the San Fernando Rey Mission olive-trees over a hundred years old, proving that in all this period there has been no frost sufficiently severe or prolonged to injure these sensitive trees. In 1880 a little snow fell in Los Angeles County — just enough to astonish the young folks, who had never before seen any; nor have they seen any since. The only time when ice ever forms (never more than a quarter of an inch in thickness) is immediately before sunrise, and hardly has the sun risen above the horizon when it disappears again.

To this short duration of the occasional frosts is attributed the fact that they do not kill the semi-tropical vegetation, as happens occasionally in Southern Europe ; and at nine or ten o'clock the California farmers may be seen ploughing for their winter wheat, in shirt-sleeves.   Hence sufferers from pulmonary complaints who cannot endure cold will not know that the thermometer ever reaches freezing-point if they remain in bed till the sun has been out for half an hour.   Immediately after sunset they will again need the protection of the house, or of a spring overcoat, as the temperature at that time suddenly drops ten to thirty degrees.   But while the sun shines, they cannot afford or desire to lose its rays for a single minute.   It is the very luxury of existence to walk, ride, or hunt in the Southern California February sunshine.   The oldest inhabitants, used to it as they are, cannot help muttering every morning, " What a fine day ! "   January, February, March, and April, the very four months which are the most disagreeable of the twelve in the East, are here the most perfect: the sky of the deepest blue, the air neither cold nor warm, exhilarating and laden with the perfumes of orange blossoms and wild flowers. There are, of course, some disagreeable days, but they are few and far between, there being but twelve to twenty rainy days in Los Angeles County during the whole " rainy season " from November to May, so that invalids hardly ever miss their sun-bath. Dr. C. B. Bates mentions, in the *Southern California Practitioner*, the case of a consumptive who kept a record of the weather at Santa Barbara, and found that in a year there were but fifteen days upon which he was confined to the house, ten of them being rainy and five windy ;

and another case of a lady who, without any other than a brush shelter, spent all of eighteen months, except nine nights, in the open air.

This will appear the more remarkable in view of a certain peculiarity of Southern California rains. Elsewhere people often exclaim, "If we only had fine weather in the daytime, I shouldn't care how much it rained at night!" Here this wish is fulfilled, for most of the rain falls at night. Some will be ready to cry out against the "eternal monotony" of this sunshine; but on arriving on the ground they will find this objection purely theoretical, and will be only too glad to know that they can make projects for work or pleasure, for picnics or excursions, weeks ahead, with an almost absolute certainty of having fine weather. Still, there are a few day-showers to break the "monotony," and they make up in profusion what they lack in frequency — a fascinating spectacle to the senses, and still more to the imagination, which evokes pictures of prosperous grain-fields and lovely flower-meadows. Surely that must be pronounced an ideal climate for an invalid and valetudinarian where every rainy day, even during the so-called rainy season, is regarded as a special dispensation of a kind Providence, is commented upon in jubilant editorials by the journalists (who had for some time predicted "better weather," *i.e.* rain), and is recorded in telegraphic tables noting the daily rainfall in every town, to the hundredth of an inch! And be it admitted that there is ground for this jubilation; for in three years out of ten the rainfall is insufficient, and then the crops suffer, except where irrigation is practised.

In this immunity from rain-storms, Southern California

possesses a great advantage over other winter resorts for invalids, but it is only one out of half-a-dozen advantages which may here be briefly touched upon. The first and most important is the dryness of the atmosphere, which favors the rapid radiation of the earth's heat, so that the nights are always cool enough for refreshing sleep, even in midsummer; and sleep is the best of all medicines. So dry is this air that strips of beef can be jerked in it by simply letting them hang outdoors till desiccated. And the strangest part of it is that the sea-breeze, which always blows during the hottest hours of the day, is a dry wind, too — a circumstance which some have tried to account for by considering it a sort of undertow, or a wave of air which came from the dry desert lands to the eastward, and returns thither, absorbing but little moisture during its brief contact with the ocean. But whatever the cause of this dryness, it is a great hygienic factor, which this region can play out as one of its highest trumps against Florida and Italy. No enervating, malarial swamp winds, no sultriness, such as often makes suicide a welcome thought in the East, will ever oppress any one in this Western sanitarium, not even during the rainy spells. Nor has California ever suffered from yellow fever, like Florida, or from the cholera, which is a frequent menace in Spain, Italy, and Sicily. Again, on the shores of the Mediterranean, in Europe as well as in Africa, the invalid will find it almost impossible to obtain comfortable lodgings and proper food, except in the large cities, while in California he can find home comforts in any village and many farmhouses in the midst of the wildest scenery and purest air. Never will his nostrils be offended here by the pestilential odors which poison the air within a radius of several miles of Italian and Spanish cities; nor will he ever be compelled by the muddy condition of the streets to take his walks all winter long on the roof of the hotel, as the proprietor of the Continental at Tangier told me some of his invalid winter-guests did. What a life compared with the floral walks, the hunting, fishing, and picnicking on the dry ground and under the blue, rainless sky of Los Angeles or San Diego County! Surely, Southern California is destined to become the sanitarium, not only of America, but of Europe as well.

What makes the fulfilment, of this prophecy the more probable is the circumstance that California is an all-the-year-round sanitarium, and not one of the mere winter resorts which compel the unwilling invalids to pack up and seek a new clime, when May is gone. No one would dream of spending the summer at Malaga, Cannes, Naples, Palermo, Algiers, or Jacksonville, exposed to a sultry, malarial atmosphere, and the danger of deadly epidemics; whereas California has countless places where summer and winter are alike, or rather alike unknown, the only season known being an eternal spring. Many residents in our Eastern and Middle States have often wondered what has become of the spring, which used to form one of our seasons. It has followed the general tide of immigration, has gone West, and may now be found in riotous exuberance along the coast and the foothills of California. Not that all parts of Southern California are as exempt from a summer season as they are of winter. On the contrary, there are many most desirable winter resorts which invalids and tourists will be only too glad to abandon in June, such as Riverside, and other places too far in the interior to get the benefit of the afternoon sea-breezes. Even so near the sea as Los Angeles, it is by no means pleasant to be exposed directly to the rays of the July sun; yet, owing to the dryness of the atmosphere, — which, moreover, increases as the heat increases, — 100° is not so oppressive here as 90° in New York. Besides, in the East there is no refuge from the all-pervading heat, except in a cellar; whereas here one needs only to step in the shade to find relief, the difference between the sunny and the shady side of a house running as high as 30°. Finally, as Southern California has an average width of only forty miles, it takes only an hour or two to reach the sea-coast, where it is always pleasant; and cool mountain resorts are equally accessible everywhere, as can be seen by a glance at the map, which is blackened by groups and chains of mountains, attaining in the San Bernardino range a height of over eleven thousand feet. No wonder that camping is the favorite pastime of the Californian in summer, and not only of the wealthy; for as the farmer does all his work in winter, he can lie fallow in summer, like his somnolent fields, and pitch his tent along any beach or cañon he chooses; and camp-life is so inexpensive, especially when rod and rifle are available, that the poorest can indulge in this luxury during the warmest months.

Surely, when the human race cuts its wisdom teeth, it will no longer crowd into dirty, noisy, malodorous cities, but will seek health and fresh air all the year round. Southern California will loom up more and more as an ideal place for building up a vast city in the country, so to speak, — a city in which each house will be surrounded by ten or twenty acres of irrigated land, capable of producing all the fruits and vegetables, eggs and poultry, needed by the family, and shaded by one of the fifty varieties of eucalyptus-trees already imported from Australia, or by the spacious pepper-tree, and a small orange, peach, and fig orchard. Such a city could be built up in a few years, with shade and all. Elsewhere when people plant trees, they do so for the benefit of posterity; here a row of the eucalyptus will grow in a few years large enough to afford abundance of shade. / Noiseless electric railways will traverse this country town in every direction, bringing the scattered population to the business places and centres of amusement. But they will not crave the artificial excitements of city life as they do now; for when there are no excursions to the sea or the mountains, the fascinating care of the orange groves and flower gardens will absorb all the leisure moments. What novel, what theatrical play, could afford so much amusement as the daily irrigation of a flower-bed, and noticing how the plants grow visibly and in a few weeks develop into exotic wildernesses of tropical and semi-tropical flowers of the most gorgeous colors and unheard-of size? Or watching a rose-bush as it gradually intertwines itself among the branches of an orange-tree, which some morning will present the bewitching spectacle of a tree bearing red roses, white orange blossoms, and golden oranges all at the same time? Or sitting under this orange-tree in February, listening to a mocking-bird perched on its branches, and reading in your paper about the blizzards and storms of the East, and the tornadoes and cyclones which you know will never visit your home? Why should our novelists lay the scenes of their tales in Andalusia when we have an Andalusia of our own here on the Pacific

Coast? At one time it formed part of the so-called Great American Desert, but in the next century it will be known as the Great American Paradise.

Yet let not the coming population of the Pacific Andalusia fancy that they will be spared all the trials and annoyances of life. Even Southern California has its disadvantages,—quite enough to prevent it from degenerating into a Utopia. Thus you will some morning be standing in your garden admiring your favorite banana bush. Suddenly it will tremble and sink into the ground a foot or two. Earthquakes are not unknown in this region, but they don't "strike in one place" like that. No, it was one of those irrepressible gophers, the terror of the rural Californian. They will eat the roots of your fruit trees and choicest flowers, regardless of expense; and though cats and traps will catch them, and irrigation drowns them, the neighboring fields always furnish a fresh supply; and what is worse, their subterranean passages from these fields serve as tunnels which carry off your water, and make you pay twice as much for irrigation as you would have needed but for those holes. Then there are scale-bugs of all colors, which attack your orange-trees and have to be sprayed off; and a mysterious disease which kills your vines and small green insects which eat up your flowers and buds so that you need a whole drug store to combat them. Rabbits will eat your vegetables and grape-vines, and the quails will feed on your grapes; and, to add insult to injury, the Los Angeles sporting clubs have succeeded in passing a law which prevents you from shooting these birds at a time when it would do most to protect your crops. However, if you are a sportsman, you will forgive and observe this law, which enables you at other times to shoot at a flock of quail in your own vegetable garden, though you live in a town of two or three thousand inhabitants.

The desolate appearance which all the unirrigated parts of the country present after May must also be reckoned among the disadvantages of this climate; for a sensitive soul can hardly help feeling pity for the drooping, parched vegetation, especially after having noticed how eagerly it drinks in the first rain of the autumn, with as much evident enjoyment as a Bavarian emptying his mug of beer at a draught. Nor can one help admitting that the orange groves and eucalyptus avenues, delightful as they are, cannot entirely atone for the absence of green forests; for Southern California, except in the foothills, is as treeless as Spain — which it resembles in so many other respects, — and a single oak-tree has more than once furnished the nucleus of a town. The higher mountains are as bare of trees as the valleys, but this is compensated for by the consequent greater clearness and variety of the sculptured outlines, and by the snows which fall during every rainstorm, sometimes extending almost down to the foothills. In the clear southern atmosphere these mountains, though they be fifty or sixty miles away, seem to be almost within stone's throw; and as they are visible everywhere, they constitute one of the greatest charms of Southern California. Once in a while, however, this view is spoiled for a day or two by one of those desert winds and sand-storms which are the most annoying feature of this climate, and are known as the Norther, or the "Santa Ana" wind, as the Anaheimers call it, in order to give a hated rival town a bad name. Without being a hurricane, or even a gale, this wind reaches a considerable velocity, is as dry and warm as if it came from an oven, and raises clouds of dust which obscure the sun and mountains as effectually as the smoke of the forest fires does in Oregon, and a film of which even lines the waters of the Pacific to a considerable distance from the shore. If I finally mention that this dust, even when it lies quietly on the ground two or three inches thick during seven or eight months of the year, is by no means a desirable thing to have about, I shall have mentioned all the serious blemishes that I could discover on the face of this fair country; and they are so insignificant compared with its attractions that I have given them the advantage of having the last word in this chapter, confident that they cannot essentially modify the opinion therein expressed as to the future of Southern California.

IV.

THE HOME OF THE ORANGE.

AFTER enjoying the sights of Los Angeles, including the palms and orange groves, the cable-car scenery, and Chinatown, which have been often enough described, it will repay the tourist to devote a week or two to a round trip through that part of the State which lies south of Los Angeles as far as San Diego and Tia Juana on the Mexican border. Take a ticket to Riverside, via Orange, and stop over a day at Anaheim, which commands a specially fine view of the snow-capped San Gabriel range and the giant San Bernardino. Anaheim is known as the "mother colony," having been founded as early as 1858 by a party of fifty Germans from San Francisco, in search of a pleasant site for homes and good soil for raising Rhine wine. To-day the population is no longer exclusively German, nor is wine-making the chief industry; for Anaheim enjoys the sad distinction of being the place where the destructive vine disease originated, and now there are few good vineyards left in the vicinity, though the cellars of the hospitable families are still well stocked with a Riesling that unmistakably betrays its legitimate descent from the celebrated Johannisberger stock on the Rhine. Undaunted by their misfortune, the Anaheimers have dug out their dead vines and planted in their place oranges, walnuts, pampas plumes, and figs, which in a few years will bear as rich fruit and as big profits as the former vineyards. The fields and orchards are supplied with water through a ditch from the Santa Ana River, sixteen miles long, and lined all the way with willows. A drive along this ditch is interesting, as is a visit to the ostrich farm, two or three miles from the town. If a longer stay is contemplated, there is excellent hunting of wild goose, ducks, and other water-fowl, all the way from Anaheim to the ocean, while in the cactus fields around the town may be found quails and pigeons, and the sportive jack-rabbit abounds. In hunting him, you not only satisfy the craving for murder of some sort, which still lingers as a relic of savagery in the gentlest human breast, but you do a great service to the farmers, who are sometimes obliged in self-defence to organize rabbit drives, at which two or three thousand of the long-eared, fleet-footed robbers are killed.

Rabbit-hunting in cactus fields is a sport quite *sui generis*. The moment you catch a glimpse of Jack, he is apt to catch a glimpse of you and dodge behind a cactus bush; and if you follow him too quickly but unwisely, you will suddenly find your nether limbs pierced with a thousand fish-hook-pointed thorns, requiring an hour or two of hard and bloody work for their extraction. Unless you kill him on the spot he will crawl into a cactus bush, where neither dog nor devil can get at him. You know just where he is, but he might as well be at the bottom of the Pacific so far as you are concerned. But the loss is not great; for three out of four of these rabbits are not fit to eat, and are therefore usually chopped up for chicken food. Whether it is that in their flight they run against a thorny cactus leaf or that they carry off part of a load of shot, the fact is that the meat is generally diseased, being filled with a granular jelly-like substance like tapioca pudding. Tourists will do well to avoid hare when they find it on a Los Angeles bill of fare, as there is little reason to believe that the huge piles of jacks seen in the market there have been carefully sorted. But there is another much smaller rabbit, the cotton-tail, which affords equally good sport, and which is always good to eat; the younger ones tasting somewhat like chicken. Near the towns they are shy, active dodgers, and hard to shoot unless you sneak on them; but in less frequented hunting-grounds they graze complacently along the roadsides and look upon passing buggies as calmly as cows. Bang! goes the gun; Nero jumps out and brings the victim; and in this way dozens can be bagged in a few hours, before sunset, without once leaving the buggy; so that even invalids and cripples can go rabbit-hunting in Southern California. But there are stranger things still.

Did you ever see a cow eat oranges off a tree? That was one of the sights I witnessed in Anaheim. Not satisfied with the basketful of windfall seedlings which she received every day, our Millie, like Eve, cast longing eyes on the fruit tree near her open stable, and one day she broke loose and had a regular picnic before she was discovered. Her daughter, too, a promising young Jersey of six weeks, after one or two suspicious trials, became very fond of oranges, and having eaten three or four, would baah for more. The children of our Mexican neighbors, seeing all this fun, would come in to buy some for themselves, and received a liberal dozen for five cents.

These seedling oranges make delicious orangeade, and have a certain value because they ripen later than the finer sorts and produce larger crops; but they are rather sour and thick-skinned, and therefore fetch only a dollar or even seventy-five cents a box on the tree and two dollars at Chicago, while the best budded variety brings two dollars and a half to three dollars on the tree and four dollars to four dollars and a half in Chicago. Consequently the seedlings are no longer set out to any extent, while the demand for Washington-navel-trees was so great last winter that the nurserymen could not supply the demand, and young trees had to be imported from Florida. The Washington-navel is by far the best of all California oranges. It is a Brazilian orange, imported in 1873, and seems specially adapted to the climatic conditions of California. Riverside is its chief home, and Riverside navels are so highly valued that even in Los Angeles you get only three or four of them for a quarter of a dollar. They are very large, and, like the Spanish blood-oranges, almost always seedless, have a thin skin (with a small, navel-like formation or even a tiny orange at one end), and a sweet and most delicately flavored juice. I have squeezed as many as twenty teaspoonfuls of juice out of a single one of these oranges — a feat which I have never succeeded in accomplishing with a Florida orange. (I may add in parenthesis that to eat an orange with a teaspoon is to lose two-thirds of its flavor.)

The town of Orange, between Anaheim and Riverside, already gives warning of the neighborhood of the State's orange centre. The station, in the springtime. is piled up to the ceiling with boxes of oranges, and near by a number of men are busily at work wiping the golden fruit with wet rags and rolling it down inclined boards to dry, preparatory to packing. The fruit is generally bought on the trees by the packing companies. who send round their men with ladders, and sacks suspended around their necks, from which the fruit is transferred to boxes, to be repacked afterwards, the bruised or imperfect ones being thrown out, so that three boxes (of the seedlings at any rate) yield only two for the market. Orange-picking is painted by the imagination as the most poetic of all agricultural employments, and nothing certainly could look more picturesque than the boxes of luscious fruit scattered through an orchard, under the dark-green, fragrant trees ; but the orange-tree, like the rose-bush that loves to twine around it, bristles with thorns which cry for blood, and make orange-picking about as exciting and perilous a pursuit as rabbit-hunting amid the cactus bushes.

The town of Orange belonged till lately to Los Angeles County (a separate Orange County was formed last year with Santa Ana as its capital), but before reaching Riverside we have entered San Bernardino County, the largest in the United States — "about the size of the States of Connecticut, Delaware, Maryland, and Massachusetts combined." The counties of Southern California are very much larger than those of the central and northern part of the State, and as the population increases they will doubtless be further subdivided. But it is doubtful if San Bernardino County will be divided very soon, for the greater part of it is comprised in the irredeemable Mojave Desert. The region west of the Bernardino range, however, is one of the most valuable in the State, experience having shown that it is the chosen home of the orange. Los Angeles County has many fine and luxuriant orange groves, and more of them than San Bernardino County; yet to see California orange culture in its highest perfection, one must go to Riverside. Nowhere else do the orchards seem so luxuriant and so well cultivated, or the fruit and trees so glossy and clean. Here the oranges do not need cleaning with a rag, owing to the absence of the black scale which elsewhere often gives the leaves and fruit a dirty appearance. The white scale-bug, too, which destroys the trees, has thus far spared Riverside groves, and in the business street of the town a notice is posted warning purchasers of orange-trees not to import any from infected counties. The orange is not indigenous to California, as it is to Mexico and Florida; it does not flourish here without some care, and becomes remunerative in proportion to the amount of care bestowed on it. A glance at the well-ploughed, weedless, carefully irrigated orchards of Riverside at once explains the enormous profits realized by local growers; and an incident that occurred at Anaheim throws further light on the matter. Noticing a couple of malodorous freight-cars on the side track, I asked a man what they contained. "Manure," he replied, "from the numerous sheep corrals in the neighborhood, and bound for Riverside," adding that this had been found the best manure for oranges, and that in a few years the Anaheimers, who now foolishly sold their treasure, would be importing it from elsewhere at an exorbitant price. Rows of cypress-trees are planted along the edge of every orchard, and sometimes even traverse the orchard in several places, to serve as windbreaks; for though there are no hurricanes to provide against, the desert wind is sometimes sufficiently boisterous to shake down bushels of unripe fruit and break the heavily laden branches unless thus protected.

The best way to see the Riverside orange groves, and marvel at their extent, is to ride or walk along Magnolia Avenue, doubtless the finest avenue in America. It is laid out a distance of twelve miles, and seven miles are now finished. Between the road and the houses on each side are four rows of tall eucalyptus and spreading pepper-trees, and two rows of fan palms, ten to twenty feet in height, and growing more beautiful every year. Nor is this fine avenue a monopoly of carriage-owners; for the poorest can enjoy its sights by paying ten cents for a ride in the street cars, which have their track under a row of pepper-trees, without interfering with the broad carriage-drive. In this way Riverside spreads itself out, covering a territory, orchards included, of fifty-four square miles, and almost realizing the ideal of one of those California "rural cities of the future," sketched in the last chapter. The grounds of some of the elegant villas which line this road are thrown open to the public, and one of them, which I examined, with its extensive stables, shady walks, hammocks, tennis grounds, and notices of club meetings, and *al-fresco* teas, had an air of hospitality and sociability, recalling the life on

ORANGE GROVE, SOUTHERN CALIFORNIA.

Southern plantations before the Civil War. The large adobe house, a relic of the Spanish occupation, was deliciously cool on a warm day, and the owner said he did not find it unhealthy. He showed me through his extensive orchard, and with a large table-knife cut open specimens of more than half-a-dozen different kinds of budded oranges for me to taste. They were all sweet and juicy, but he had to admit himself that the differ-.ences in flavor were not so pronounced as the differences in the original homes of these varieties led one to expect. California fruit-growers doubtless attempt too much in seeking to raise oranges from so many different countries in the same field without losing their characteristic flavor. This difference in flavor is due to differences in soil and climate, and can only be preserved and reproduced in a similar soil and climate. As California fortunately has an infinite variety of climates and soil, it is probable that the problem of raising Italian, Spanish, Mexican, and Florida oranges all in the same State will yet be solved, but not in one and the same orchard. The Spanish blood-orange, for instance, the most delicately flavored of all oranges, is rarely seen in California; and when I asked why, I was told that it was inclined to sport and lose its characteristics. There is a fortune in store for the man who finds out under what conditions this variety flourishes in Spain, and seeks out a similar locality for it at home. Another excellent variety, the Florida russet, I never saw on the Pacific Coast. Its appearance is against it, and it is difficult to teach people to select their fruit for the palate rather than the eye.

Riverside is a little too far inland to get much benefit from the ocean breezes, but it is surrounded by mountains, snow-capped till summer, which to some extent atone for this disadvantage, and which make Riverside, from a scenic point of view, one of the most attractive places in the State. This, combined with its horticultural prosperity, causes it to grow rapidly, and among the new comers and the old there are a large number of English families, who, of course, endeavor to bring their household gods and customs with them. Foremost among these is the fox-hunt; but as there are no foxes to be hunted, the simple-minded plebeian jack-rabbit has to take the place of his astute, bushy-tailed colleague. There are no fences to jump or fields to destroy, and everything is in plain sight; but as the riding is much faster than in England, there is no lack of excitement. To come home from one of these hunts with a pair of rabbit ears in her hat is the chief pride of the English damsels at Riverside. Besides, these ornaments take the place of a parasol, much needed here sometimes. In midsummer, no doubt, Riverside is a good place to get away from, but in winter it offers special advantages to invalids, provided they are willing to submit to being treated like children, in being told what they may drink and what they may not. Riverside is a prohibition town. So I discovered at the hotel when I asked for a pint of claret. I have never been drunk in my life, and I find that a few glasses of pure claret aid my digestion, and moreover I like it, and am able to pay for it. Yet here I, who am supposed to be a free citizen in a free country, am placed in a position where I cannot indulge in a harmless and useful pleasure which concerns no one but myself, without breaking the law. Of course I broke the law, as anybody but a fool or a coward ought to do. A few words in private to the waiter, and the wine appeared on the table. Of course, when I asked him how much it was, he said he wouldn't charge for it, — he had merely brought it " to oblige me "; and of course I asked how much he paid for it, and then left that amount, plus a suitable fee, on the table. A resident with whom I conversed subsequently on the subject gave me some instances of capital withheld and capital withdrawn from Riverside in consequence of the prohibition law, which unfits it as a residence for people who like to be free and law-respecting at the same time. A friend in Los Angeles had previously explained to me how Pasadena was damaged by the local prohibition law (which I believe has since been repealed), and gave an amusing account of the visit of the city fathers to Mr. Raymond, who continued to serve wine to his tourist and invalid guests after the law had been passed. Mr. Raymond quietly informed them that if they would not allow him to run a first-class hotel in their town, he would pull it down and rebuild it elsewhere. As the Raymond is one of the largest hotels and chief resorts on the Pacific Coast, the city fathers got alarmed, took their leave, and never molested Mr. Raymond again.

One more instance: Until within a year or two the owner of Catalina Island would not allow any beer or liquor to be sold to the thousands of campers on it; whereupon, an enterprising man hired a barge, moored it a hundred yards from the shore, put canvas over it, filled it with drinkables, and hired a boy to ferry his customers over and back. Mr. Shatto thereupon refused to allow the steamer to land anything for this man on his pier; but the latter got around this, too, by simply having his beer-barrels lowered directly from the steamer to his boat. These are illustrations of how prohibition prohibits in California.

It is not necessary to stuff your pockets and valise full of oranges on leaving Riverside for the South; for you will find just as good fruit, and plenty of it, in San Diego County. Backing up to a station called Citrus, a few miles north of Riverside, you wait for the train which leaves Barstow on the Atlantic and Pacific, or Santa Fé, Railway, for San Diego, and which, soon after you have boarded it, enters the county of that name, — a county not quite as large as San Bernardino, but still, according to the guide-book, covering as much ground as Massachusetts, Connecticut, Rhode Island, and Delaware combined. It forms the southwestern corner of the United States, and owes much of its local color to the proximity of Mexico, or Lower California, — a peninsula which a large number of educated people in the East are in the habit of mistaking for "Southern California." The branch of the Santa Fé road referred to is known as the California Southern Railroad. Between the Bernardino range and the ocean it traverses a region where the spring vegetation, though almost as abundant as in Los Angeles County, is not so luxuriant, owing to the diminished rainfall. Three-fifths or more of the vegetation which carpets the fields seems to consist of Compositæ, and the predominant color is yellow — as if to hint at the fact, which has long since been demonstrated, that there is more gold to be got out of the surface of California soil than out of all its subterranean mines.

One never tires of looking at these gaudily colored fields, especially when bordered by foothills, whose green garb is ornamented with red, yellow, brown, and blue patches, like a "crazy-quilt," varying in shade and atmospheric effect with the time of the day; or when, as on this route, there is a background of high mountains, with their snow caps drawn half-way down their treeless foreheads as late as May. The two chief mountains are too long-drawn-out to be imposing sculpturally, but the great mass of snow on them gains in charm by contrast with the surrounding blue sky and warm sunshine. The best point of view is from Perris, the junction for the short branch road to San Jacinto.

Soon thereafter the Laguna is reached, also known as Lake Elsinore; but if the tourist expects to see one of those picturesque mountain lakes for which the State is famous, he will be grievously disappointed. The Laguna is a commonplace, dreary old pond, with steep hills on one side and flat on the other. There are ducks on it, but no cover to approach them. In May, 1889, it was sixteen feet higher than two years previously, and it has a habit of getting very low till the real estate on its banks has been claimed, whereupon it roguishly rises and submerges it for a few years. But the soil in the vicinity is credited with marvellous properties.

We now enter the region of Indian missions and reservations, and expect to see some of the redskins loitering about the stations, as they do at Yuma and elsewhere; but not a single one is to be seen at any of the towns. Those who make pilgrimages in the tracks of novel heroines may find something to interest them hereabouts with their "Ramona" as a guide; but otherwise the region is dreary and desolate, its only apparent attraction being the snow mountains just described. A pleasant change is afforded by the passage through the Temecula Cañon, in which it is refreshing to follow along a creek, though it be but a few inches deep and two or three feet wide. It cools the air and lines the bank with pretty bushes.

Presently smoke-like mists begin to rise from the water, as if it were on fire; scattered pools with bul-rushes and flocks of birds, and the russet color and rank monotony of the vegetation, indicate the approach to the ocean. A cool saline breeze strikes the cars; the windows of the more sensitive passengers are lowered, and at the same moment the Pacific comes into sight — to many of the tourists their first view of the king of waters. But the outlook is limited, for a few miles at sea hovers a fog-bank which looks as opaque and solid as if a Krupp gun could make no impression on it. For the rest of the way to San Diego the ocean is almost constantly in sight, and new varieties of plants and flowers occupy the attention. Conspicuous among the flowers are a white morning-glory, larkspurs, and lupines in several colors, the ice-plant with red flowers and leaves that seem to be covered with icicles, and a flower-ing bush which at a distance resembles the alpenrose.

V.

OVER THE MEXICAN BORDER.

ALTHOUGH San Diego has no lack of hotels, most of the tourists cross the bay which separates the city from the thirteen-mile-long peninsula known as Coronado Beach, and take up their abode in the Coronado hotel, covering more than seven acres, — the largest in Southern California, and second in size and elegance only to the Del Monte at Monterey. Porpoises sport about the ferry-boat, almost within arm's reach, and excite the appetite for sea-fishing. On the peninsula, a steam-dummy connects with the ferry and conveys those passengers for whom the coaches are too slow to the hotel. Coronado affords an excellent instance of what can be done in this region with irrigation. A few years ago this whole peninsula was a desert, while now there are numerous villas and stores, and good roads, and avenues of young trees, which in a few years will afford welcome shade. The hotel is surrounded by flower-beds as monstrous in proportion as itself, crowded with enormous double stocks, petunias, large pansies, marguerites, etc.. etc.: and another superb flower-garden takes up the interior court. Dining-room, parlors, and dance-hall are sufficiently spacious for all emergencies, and simply though tastefully decorated. It may seem a disadvantage that, owing to the position of the dance-hall, there are few rooms facing the ocean; but as it is always cool here, day and night, summer and winter, the site of rooms is not so important a matter as on the Atlantic Coast.

No other part of California has so perfect a climate as Coronado and San Diego, the mean difference in temperature between summer and winter being only 12.3°, with an average of only five days a year when the thermometer rises above 85°; and, what is still more remarkable, only twelve days a year when it rises above 80°. As only ten inches of rain fall in a year, — just one hundred inches less than at Sitka, the other extremity of our Pacific Coast, — and clouds or fogs of more than a few hours' duration are rare, it may be inferred that the sun shines almost perpetually, even in winter. When an invalid who proposes to make the Coronado his home for awhile reads in the rules and regulations pasted upon his door that a single fire costs a dollar, he is relieved to be told that cold weather is as scarce as fuel, and that, according to official government records, during the ten years from 1876 to 1885, there were only six days on which the temperature fell below 35°, two on which it fell to 32°, and none below that point! I had also read somewhere that mud is practically unknown, since the little rain that falls sinks into the soil immediately, so that it is safe to lie on the ground a few hours after a shower. I was therefore surprised, on picking up a local newspaper, to see an editorial headed " Too Much Mud." But on examination it proved to be a political, not a meteorological article. On politics climate has no effect.

The Coronado beach is well adapted to bathing, which is indulged in all the year round, there being only about six degrees' difference in the temperature of the water, winter and summer. When the ocean is too rough, or the tide unfavorable, the bay affords a safe bathing-ground, as at Fire Island. That the ocean is rough sometimes is evinced by the sad havoc it has made with the plank walks between the hotel and the water, and, as at Coney Island, it seems to be encroaching on the hotel premises, and will soon thunder against its very foundations. It is interesting to walk along the beach towards Point Loma, on which a lighthouse is picturesquely situated. Entertainment is afforded on the way by the water-fowl, which stand inside of the breakers waiting for a big foaming wave, into which they plunge headlong, emerging calmly swimming on the other side, with a fish struggling in the beak. Twenty miles at sea, to the southwest, are the Coronado Islands, the haunt of seals, occasionally visited by yachting parties. There is always something that appeals to the imagination in the meeting of two countries, and the fact that these islands belong to Mexico makes them doubly interesting.

Twice a week or oftener opportunity is given the guests at the Coronado to put foot on Mexican soil. A steam-dummy, with open cars, starts from the hotel, goes down the peninsula and up on the other side of the bay, as far as National City, and then branches off, first to the great Sweet Water Reservoir, and then to Tia Juana. It would be difficult to imagine a more delightful excursion than this seventy-mile round trip in open cars.

The cool, fragrant air is free from dust, and the country is so picturesque that one keeps on choosing one place after another as an ideal site for a cottage and an orange grove. On reaching the Sweet Water Reservoir, which covers seven hundred acres, it is difficult to believe that it is not a natural lake, so prettily and cosily does it rest at the foot of the surrounding hills. Yet here, where now the wild ducks disport themselves, stood several farmhouses a few years ago, surrounded by green fields. The dam which created this lake is about four hundred feet long at the top and forty-six feet thick at the base, built of solid rock; and the reservoir holds six billion gallons, sufficient to supply National City and San Diego with water for consumption and irrigation for three years, though not another drop of rain should add to its volume. A flume seven miles in length carries the water to the two cities, which now, with abundant and cheap water, can amend their arid, treeless appearance, which at present is their least attractive feature.

After visiting Sweet Water Lake, the train faces about and turns towards old "Aunt Jane," or Tia Juana, in Mexico, passing through the town of Chula Vista, a characteristic Southern California enterprise. A tract of five thousand acres has been subdivided by a land company into five-acre lots, with avenues and wide streets through which the steam-motor passes, and ornamented with thousands of evergreen trees. These lots are sold only to purchasers who will agree to build on them houses costing not less than two thousand dollars within six months from date of purchase; and by way of providing models and starting the ball, the company itself has erected a number of cottages. Such an attempt to force a town by hot-house methods would fail anywhere else: here it will probably succeed. Every time the train stops, a handful of real-estate circulars is thrown into each car, setting forth the unique advantages of that particular locality; while the fine appearance of the residences, with their lovely gardens and orchards, contributes its share towards advertising the region. For the convenience of the scattered settlers, the train-boy throws the daily papers into the yards from the flying train. Near the boundary line are some yellow pools, in one of which a water-snake darted out its angry tongue at a whole carload of tourists and then dived out of sight. A few minutes more and we were on Mexican soil; and though sufficient of the Mexican element lingers in Southern California to form a gradual transition, the change is distinctly perceptible. Characteristically enough, the first thing I saw after leaving the train was a young burro, with silky hair and no larger than a Newfoundland dog. In Spanish countries, where the railroad ceases the donkey begins. One side of Tia Juana is American; the other, Mexican. The dividing line, where the Estados Unidos meet Mexico, is occupied by a restaurant which bears the modest title of "Delmonico." Opposite is a cigar-store which has the suggestive sign of "The last chance." There are more saloons in Tia Juana than buildings. This may seem a paradoxical statment, but it is true; for some of the saloons are in tents, open in front, with a counter in the centre and empty beer-barrels for seats. The sight of the town is the Custom-House, with its polite but pistolled officials, and the rooms filled with rifles which parties crossing the line had to leave behind to await their return. There are also a few curiosity stores, conducted with a truly Spanish lack of enterprise. Almost every tourist wants to buy a memento of his hour in Mexico, but there is nothing to be had except some very crude pottery and a few tiny, hideous clay gods. Nor does the proprietor's knowledge of English go beyond the ability to say twenty cents or thirty cents.

Looking beyond Tia Juana, nothing is to be seen but lone, low mountains, — not a house or hut anywhere, — and we gladly return to civilization with the train. On the way back, the conductor pointed out to me the place where the famous Bonnie Brae lemons are grown. I had previously eaten some at San Diego, and found them large and juicy, with fewer seeds and a much less thick and coarse skin than other California lemons. This variety seems destined to retrieve the reputation of the California lemon, which is not equal to that of the orange, or of foreign lemons. But I doubt if any kind of lemon will have much of a future in this country. At San Francisco lemons are not valued nearly so highly as Mexican limes, which are gradually taking their place. The lime has a tougher skin than the lemon, and does not break so easily in the squeezer. In fact, it can be easily squeezed by hand; and besides, there is more juice in a small lime than in a lemon twice its size and twice or three times its cost. Its taste, after a few trials, is more agreeable and piquant than that of any lemon, and I believe that Eastern cities will soon follow the lead of San Francisco in this matter. The lemonade of the future will be made of limes.

VI.

SANTA CATALINA ISLAND.

EASTERN people have no idea how fast things grow in California. Everybody, of course, has heard the story of the farmer who in the morning planted watermelon seeds in his field, and in the evening found that the vine had grown to his kitchen door and deposited a ripe melon on the steps. But this is nothing compared with the way in which the cities grow. Thus, on page 216 of Drs. Lindley and Widney's valuable work on "California of the South," we read of "San Diego's fifteen thousand inhabitants," while on page 218 (and it surely cannot have taken more than a day or two to write these two pages) they say that "San Diego is growing with most wonderful rapidity. Its population is doubtless twenty-five thousand." Most wonderful indeed! San Diego did seem quite a lively place when I saw it, although this may have been partly attributable to its being the headquarters of the miners going to the Santa Clara mines in Lower California. 'Tis an ill wind, etc.; and the losses of these duped miners were the gain of the San Diego merchants, who sold almost a hundred thousand dollars' worth of victuals and tools to the gold-hunters. The temptation to follow the latter and get a glimpse of a genuine California mining-camp was great; but on hearing of the hardships to be endured, of the two hundred dollars' duty laid by the Mexican government on a single wagon and team crossing the border, and the taxes on provisions equal to their full value, which raised the cost of food in camp to figures considered fabulous even by miners accustomed to starvation prices, — not to mention the tropical rains just then prevalent, which made tenting an invitation to catarrh, rheumatism, and pneumonia, — I concluded to move northward sixty miles or so, and spend a few weeks instead on Catalina Island.

Before leaving the Coronado I had an opportunity to note a curious way of settling urban questions in California. It had long been in dispute whether or not Coronado Beach belonged to San Diego, so it was determined to settle the matter on election day. There being a law that no liquor may be sold in San Diego on an election day, the barkeeper at the Coronado hotel was instructed to keep open, for which he was promptly arrested. This was to compel the courts to decide the question at issue. What the decision was, I do not know, as I left the next morning. Retracing my steps as far as Oceanside, I took the California Central direct back to Los Angeles. This road continues to skirt the ocean as far as San-Juan-by-the-Sea (a few miles from the famous San Juan Capistrano Mission), where the tourist bids good-by to the Pacific, not to see it again till he reaches San Francisco, unless he takes a branch road to one of the numerous seaside resorts of Los Angeles or to Santa Barbara.

San-Juan-by-the-Sea was called by Dana, in his " Two Years before the Mast," " the only romantic spot in California," which is probably the most absurd statement regarding California that has ever got into print. But it certainly is one of the most charming points on the coast for those who love solitude, and all tourists ought to stop over at least between two trains and see it. If they decide to spend the night at the "hotel," I wish them better luck than befell me. Early in the morning, having paid the (really) big sum of one dollar for supper, lodging, and breakfast, I went down to the beach, about half a mile from the station, across an immense field of wild mustard, buried completely in a sea of fragrant yellow flowers waving over my head, and then had to cross a lively little creek on a narrow plank, — a creek which enjoys the satisfaction, rare in this region, of reaching the ocean without being tapped, or absorbed by the thirsty sun. The view from its mouth contrasts delightfully with the uninterrupted, flat sandy beach all the way up from San Diego. A high, precipitous rocky shore rises abruptly, and presents itself as a bulwark against the restless waves. It leads up to hills from which fine views may be enjoyed, and which give room for daily varied rambles which one misses so much at a flat place like Coronado Beach. As there is a fine beach a short distance below, it would be a splendid place for a hotel, and is already much frequented in midsummer by campers. When I was there, a deserted hut was the only visible evidence of human agency, and the solitude was emphasized by four monstrous pelicans sitting motionless and majestic on an isolated rock half a mile at sea. Below the precipice, where the waves in low water tumble gently over the rocky débris jutting far out into the sea, may be found quantities of shells, not dead and deserted specimens lying bleaching on the beach, but shells and cockles alive and wide awake, and moving about like little pagodas with wheels and clockwork.

On the way back to the station I cut off one of the tallest mustard plants, — bushes they might well be called, so thick and tough are the stems at the base, — and asked the station master how high he thought it was. He measured it and found it eleven feet in height! Then for the first time I felt convinced that the narrative of an Anaheimer, who told me how thirty years ago he once got lost *on horseback* in a wild-mustard field on the fertile soil near where Fullerton now stands, was not a " California story." To-day many of these fields of wild mustard are mowed down, yielding a crop which is the more profitable as there are no expenses for ploughing and sowing. I cannot see why there should not also be money in the castor bean, which, elsewhere cultivated in gardens as an ornamental shrub, is here a weedy nuisance hard to exterminate when it once gains a foothold. I have seen it grow as high as a second-story window in Los Angeles, side by side with a fuchsia *tree*, so to speak, still higher; while roses often cover a whole house, roof and all, and would aspire to the moon if there was a connecting link.

To reach Catalina Island we take the train at Los Angeles for its old harbor town, San Pedro, whence a steamer makes trips to the island three times a week. San Pedro is considered good fishing-ground, has numerous duck-ponds in the vicinity, and appears to be the headquarters of all the sea-gulls on the Pacific, the beach being completely fringed by them at times. The chief article of import seems to be timber, the wharves being covered with acres of boards and planks, brought from Humboldt County and from Oregon and Puget Sound. A part of the town lies in a hollow which forms a complete kettle, and must be an ideal breeding-place for typhoid fever. Hotel accommodations are very primitive, but the Southern Pacific is completing a hotel near the lighthouse, where the sea-breezes can never fail. The little steamer *Hermosa*, specially built for the traffic between San Pedro and Catalina, is new and comfortable, but has the great fault of rolling on the slightest provocation. However, the distance is but twenty miles, so that even those inclined to seasickness need not dread the passage. Santa Catalina Island is the second in size and the most interesting of the large number of islands which lie along the coast of California, beginning with the Coronado group, just below San Diego, and ending with Santa Cruz and Santa Rosa, off Santa Barbara. As it is the only one which has steam connection with the mainland, it has for many years been visited every summer by thousands of campers, and the hotel erected there lately has added to its popularity, although for sanitary and scenic reasons the site chosen for it is not the best that could have been found. The island is visible from the mainland all along Los Angeles County, even far in the interior, as it has mountains which rise to a height of about three thousand feet. Indeed, as the boat approaches, we see that it consists entirely of mountains, being a sort of floating highlands, like a section of the Coast Range rising abruptly out of the ocean, without any gradual slopes or foothills ; presenting a solid front of perpendicular rocks except in a few places where the wall is broken by a little cove or harbor, with a pebbly beach, as at Avalon, where the hotel stands. A study of the map of Southern California leaves no doubt in the mind that these islands at one time actually did form a part of the Coast Range, being connected with each other and constituting a peninsula extending from Point Conception to below Coronado, with a wide channel or sound between (like that which now extends for about a thousand miles from Olympia to Sitka), and navigated by the Pineugnas Indians, who in the time of the early Spanish voyagers inhabited Catalina Island, and were noted for their fine physique and skill in shipbuilding. Though they are now widely separated and scattered, these Channel Islands continue to affect the climate of Southern California by breaking the force of the wild Pacific waves and winds.

This fact can be vividly realized by climbing the hills on Catalina till the Pacific is sighted, dashing its huge billows against the naked rocks that rise perpendicularly to two thousand feet or more above it, the home of eagles that build their nests in these inaccessible heights, — monstrous birds, measuring sometimes twelve feet from wing to wing. In striking contrast to this turbu-lence on the west side is the calm of the eastern side, which is hardly ever disturbed, even in stormy weather. Here the campers and hotel guests bathe in the bay every day in the year, the temperature of the sea-water in August being about 66°, and only four degrees lower in midwinter; while in Rhode Island, for example, the difference between midwinter and midsummer temperature is about 35°! The Kuro Siwo, or Japan current, three to four hundred miles in width, which is deflected by the Aleutian Islands southward along the coast of Washington and Oregon, becomes so far cooled off by the time it reaches San Francisco as to make sea-bathing in that neighborhood unpleasant even in summer. But this current is deflected again by Point Conception; and between the Channel Islands and the mainland south of this cape there is a return ocean current from the south, which partly accounts for the higher temperature of the water at Catalina, as well as along the main shore of Southern California.

The temperature of the air on Catalina Island hardly ever rises above 85°, and, thanks to the twenty miles of water which separate it from the mainland, it is never visited by the hot, parching desert winds. Yet, though thus surrounded by a vaporous sea, fog is almost unknown, being shut out by the mountains, and, what is stranger still, the air is said to be drier than on shore. With such conditions and with constant sea-breezes and an immunity from dust as complete as on shipboard, it is no wonder that Catalina is beginning to be looked upon as standing to Southern California in the same relation as Southern California does towards other States. I met several invalids afflicted with rheumatic or lung troubles who had failed to find relief at Los Angeles or Santa Barbara, but found it at once on Catalina Island; and convalescents make more rapid recovery there than elsewhere. He must be fastidious indeed who is not satisfied with the climatic conditions of this island, and notwithstanding its mountainous structure, I am convinced that before the end of another decade it will be covered with hundreds of handsome cottages and several hotels and supply villages. There is room for a considerable number of health and pleasure seekers; for the island is about twenty-three miles long, and from one to seven wide.

A few miles from its northern end, Catalina presents a curious contrast to its usual appearance. Here the mountains terminate abruptly, and the island becomes reduced to a narrow isthmus, about half a mile wide, on one side of which are the turbulent Pacific breakers, on the other the calm sound. Here are the ruins of government barracks, erected during the Civil War and now deserted, but no other signs of human habitation, though a hotel will doubtless be erected before long. The only way of reaching this interesting point is by an occasional excursion on a little tug-boat stationed at Avalon, the only village on the island at present. It consists of the Hotel Metropole (what a name for a hotel in such a position!) and a row of shanties, half wood and half canvas, in which bread and provisions and shells can be obtained. The hotel is built on the site of an old Indian burial ground, which is not a pleasant thought to those who know that invisible ghosts in the shape of typhoid-fever germs have been exhumed from European graveyards which had been undisturbed for several hundred years. For this and other reasons the hotel ought to be removed part way up the hill, just south of Avalon, whence a fine view of the island and the sound can be obtained.

But do not fancy that from the top of this hill, or the higher one to which it leads, you will catch sight of the illimitable Pacific. The higher you climb, the higher do

the mountains, that were previously hidden from sight
by the lower intervening crests, loom up and shut out
the view westward.   But these curved ridges, rising one
behind the other, like seats in a cyclopean amphitheatre,
are in themselves a fascinating sight, especially in
spring, when the hill-sides are green with high grass and
abundant shrubbery.   Looking down from this hill, we
can see the large fish swimming about in the crystalline
water, several hundred feet below us.   To lie here on
the grass, in the balmy sunshine, taking in the view and
inhaling the ocean breeze, mingled with the floral perfumes that rise around you, is the very luxury of existence, and every deep draught of this air is a day added
to one's life.   Thanks to the breeze, no shade is needed,
and thus all the healing virtues of the sun's rays can be
utilized.

Should the labor of climbing this steep hill be
dreaded, equally romantic spots may be found by following up the cañon or gulch which leads from the
hotel into the midst of the hills by a gradual but steady
ascent.   The road follows a dry brook-bed, which probably once in a while becomes a torrent, though heavy
rains are rare here, even during the "rainy season."
An endless variety of shrubs and flowers lines this road,
becoming more rarely beautiful in color and shape the
higher we rise.   Climbing up one of the side gulches, I
was frequently obliged to cut my way with my cane
through bowers most gracefully built by the poison ivy
(or oak), which is so abundant throughout California,
afflicting some people, if they only pass near it, with a
painful swelling of the face, while to others it is as
harmless as is real oak or ivy.   From one of these lovely
bowers a humming-bird arose and darted up into the air

as fast and straight as a rocket, till almost out of sight;
then down again like a lump of lead; then circling in
a wide curve about me, humming all the time like a
spinning-wheel. To an observer who stands perfectly
motionless, these birds afford no end of amusement by
their wonderful swiftness and curious caprices. Often,
when I watered my flowers during the winter, one of
them would hover over the stream from the hose, take
a foot-bath for a minute, then alight on an orange-tree
for a second, and return to the sport again and again.
They are very abundant in California, these butterflies
among birds, as if to atone for the rarity of real butterflies, which is one of the most curious defects of this
State; for one would think that a country so crowded
with wild flowers would be the very paradise of butterflies. Another kind of bird very abundant on Catalina
Island is the quail, which, even without the advantage
of color, vies with the humming-bird in beauty. Being
seldom hunted, the quail are much tamer than on the
mainland. One couple had a nest in a cactus bush not
more than a hundred yards behind the hotel, where they
remained undisturbed till a heartless young idiot from
Los Angeles killed them with his shotgun. Walking
up the cañon, one or two pairs repeatedly ran along
leisurely in the middle of the roadbed, not a hundred
feet ahead of me. At other times I came within a few
yards of them before they saw me, for the ground in
many places is covered with a velvety kind of grass,
noiseless and delightful to walk upon. Far up the
gradually narrowing gulches we come upon patches of
lovely maiden-hair and other ferns, guiding us to tiny
brooklets of clear cool water. Water is not abundant
on the island so far as explored, and last summer only

one of the springs near Avalon — that which supplies the village pipes — was alive. But it would be easy to secure all the water desired by damming up one of the gulches.

The most serious drawback to the delightful rambles on Catalina Island is that one always has to keep an eye on the possibility of running across a "rattler." The first evening of my two weeks' sojourn I was sitting on the hotel piazza, drinking in the salubrious night air, when the conversation of a group of men attracted my attention. Two of them were representatives of an English syndicate who were trying to buy the island, and have since succeeded, I believe, in bagging it for six hundred thousand dollars. The reason why one of these ubiquitous English syndicates (who seem to "want the earth" at present) coveted Catalina Island, is, according to the Los Angeles papers, to be found in the fact that it abounds in silver ore, which, though not rich enough to be worked in this country, where labor is so expensive, might be carried as ballast in vessels returning to England, and profitably reduced to metal there. The agents were interviewing a resident as to the advantages and disadvantages of the island, and one of them, *inter alia*, asked about snakes. "Not a snake on the island," was the answer. This was such curious and interesting information that I jotted it down in my notebook. Next morning after breakfast I took a walk up one of the hills, and just after passing a little wooden building, I came across a young Englishman in a white flannel suit, who was cautiously prying along the road on both sides. "Lost anything?" I asked. "No," was the reply; "I am looking for rattlesnakes. Killed one a few days ago right here, and don't like them quite so near my house."   He was greatly amused when I told him how his countrymen had been "stuffed" at the hotel on the preceding evening. "The island swarms with snakes," he said. "They have never been interfered with, and have been allowed to multiply for several centuries, until they have become as abundant as ground-squirrels. Only the other day a party moved their tent away from a spot over on that hill because a snake family had established a previous claim on the neighborhood. However, you need not be afraid of walking along the cañon or up the grassy sides of the hills, for they avoid the grass and haunt only the naked rocky hill-sides, exposed to the full glare of the sun, where they can be easily seen."

I soon found that the simplest way to steer clear of rattlers is to hunt for them. I spent several hours looking for them in the most likely places, because I wanted to study the nature of the beast and get a few rattles, but not one did I see. There is no doubt, however, that they exist in large numbers, and the sooner they are exterminated, the better for the future prospects of the island as an all-the-year-round health resort. However, it must be said that there are few instances of men having been killed by snakes in California, while the dreaded scorpions, centipedes, and tarantulas are hardly more dangerous than hornets. According to Dr. Weir Mitchell, who has made a special study of this subject, a rattlesnake bite in the extremities rarely causes death in this country, and he has known of nine dogs being bitten by as many different snakes, and but two died. He considers them a much-maligned animal, and says they have always seemed to him averse to striking. This agrees with what the late T. S. Van Dyke says in his "Southern California": "At least a dozen times I have either been about to step directly on one, or have stepped over it, or else have set my foot directly beside it. In no case have I been struck at by them, though I have made them strike very savagely at a stick." "Hunters take no precautions against them, and children run bare-legged through the bush everywhere without thinking of them." Still, the nervous might carry in their pocket some permanganate of potash, which Dr. Mitchell considers the most potent external antidote, that has saved many lives.

It might be worth while to introduce on Catalina Island some of the "road-runners" so common on the mainland, — a bird looking somewhat like a large pheasant, which runs along the roads, seldom rises on its wings, and is said to live on snakes, lizards, centipedes, and similar delicacies, and is nevertheless pronounced a good gastronomic morsel by those who have the courage to eat it. It might also be good business policy to import a few of the Arizona cowboys, who, after making the rattlers strike, catch them by the tail and swing them like a whip till the head flies off. But cowboys are objectionable neighbors on other grounds, and it would be better, all things considered, to give the freedom of the village to a dozen pigs, who would soon make rattlers scarce about camp, and who might be allowed to run wild and clean out the whole island.

There would be a precedent for this in the wild goats which were turned loose by Vancouver on this and other Pacific islands, a hundred years ago, and which have now multiplied to thousands. These wild goats form one of the most characteristic attractions of Catalina. They are hunted on horseback, and are often seen in large herds, feeding along the hill-sides. It is not very easy to get near enough for a shot, but still one or two are generally brought back as the result of a morning's ride; and the next day there is always "venison with jelly" on the hotel bill of fare. If it were a little more juicy and less insipid in taste (the young ones only are eaten), it might deserve that name. Barring an occasional hunt, these wild goats lead an ideal life, which the happiest mortal must envy them, — no wild beasts to prey on them, and plenty of grass-grown hillsides to climb and browse upon. They are more fortunate than their cousins, the wild goats and half-wild sheep on the neighboring island of San Clemente, which, though almost as large as Catalina, is more barren, and is said to have no water at all except the heavy morning dews which the animals sip in with their breakfast of wild clover. Imagine a goat living on dew-drops and clover leaves! What becomes of *Puck* and the tomato-can theory?

To those who find goat-hunting on horseback too arduous and risky a sport, Catalina offers a variety of entertainments in its bathing facilities and the rare opportunities for botanic, mineralogic, and archæologic research, besides fishing, watching the pelicans and flying-fish, and visiting the seal rocks. Bathing in the placid bay lacks the excitement given by plunges into foaming breakers, and it must be admitted that small pebbles do not make as agreeable a beach as sand. Yet those who can swim will enjoy a bath here as much as anywhere. There is a drawback in the thought that only sixty miles to the south, at San Diego, a young man, while in bathing a few years ago, suddenly disappeared, being doubtless carried off by a shark. However, no shark has ever been known to eat more than one man at a time, so that if several go in together, each one has a fair chance of escape. Small sharks are occasionally seen in the bay of Avalon, but no accident has ever happened. Bathers are occasionally stung by a kind of animal called a stingaree, which causes a wound that must be cauterized, and is said to be almost as dangerous as a rattlesnake bite. But then we cannot expect to have everything arranged to suit us.

The charms of Catalina's flowers to lovers of beauty and botany I have already referred to, but I must not forget to mention that the thrill of delight on coming across the first Mariposa lily will mark an epoch in their experience. Amateur mineralogists may go prospecting for silver ore. In some places they will find patches of coal-black soil, besides igneous rocks in abundance, and other evidences of former volcanic agency. But the greatest treat awaits the archæologist, who may dig in the site of the graveyards, or the former village, part way up the main cañon, for Indian relics. The objects most frequently found are the pestles and mortars of various sizes, in which the squaws ground their grain and acorns, and strings of shells. These shells were used by the Indians as money, and Catalina Island was the place where most of them were found. The Yankee, who has succeeded the Indian at Avalon, still makes money out of these shells. There are a number of varieties strewn along the beach; but the largest and most beautiful is the abalone shell, the inner surface of which is often equal to the finest mother-of-pearl, while the outer surface can be made equally attractive by persistent polishing. The professional abalone-hunters, who have their stores at Avalon and ship large quantities to the East, to be made into buttons, jealous of competition, will tell you unblushingly in spring that these animals are only caught in the winter; but after a low tide you may see them rowing in with a whole boat-load of them. It is interesting to watch these men at work. One of them plies the oars, and the other has a long pole to stick under the unsuspecting abalone, which he twists off the rock and hauls in; whereupon the search for another begins. The Californians seem to consider the abalone possibly useful as well as ornamental; for there is a tradition (probably manufactured by an ingenious Catalinian) that a Chinaman, one day while bathing, put his foot under one of these shells, and was held till miserably drowned by the returning tide. If this story becomes known at Sacramento, a law will probably be passed forbidding abalone-fishing. Besides serving as a trap for Mongolians, the abalone has also a gastronomic use; for it makes the finest soup I have ever eaten, — superior to the best terrapin.

Of the fish which abound here the best flavored are the large sardines, of which a whole boat-load is easily caught with one haul of the net. There are literally miles and millions of them along the coast, and it would doubtless be a profitable industry to can them, although the oil would have to be imported, for California olive oil is too much in demand and too expensive to be used for such a purpose. But there is a serious objection to these sardines, — they spoil the fishing; for the large fish have their sardinian breakfast so handy that they refuse to bite unless tempted by a special delicacy, such as a piece of lobster. In April even this ruse often fails; for then the water is filled with spawn, and when a fish has spawn to eat, he turns up his nose even at lobster.

To one solely intent on catching the fish, it must be most provoking to see hundreds of them, of all sizes, swimming about his tempting crawfish bait without paying any more attention to it than if it were a pebble.

But the lover of nature can here enjoy scenes which make him oblivious of the ignoble excitement of catching fish. Catalina Island has one of the most enchanting salt-water aquariums in the world. Row out into the ocean a few hundred yards, and you will get a glimpse of a submarine garden more wonderful than anything to be seen on shore. The water is calm and as clear as crystal, showing objects fifty or seventy feet below as distinctly as if you could touch them. Kelp, anemones, and seaweeds, green, purple, and yellowish, and of various forms, wave about slowly in the current. Abalone shells cling to the rocks, and jelly-fish float along, expanding and contracting rythmically. The waving seaweeds are covered everywhere with a bluish mass looking like jelly. It is the spawn, the favorite food of the hundreds of fish in sight, whose life, swimming calmly to and fro, seems to be a perpetual picnic, like that of the goats on the green hill-sides. But they have their enemies everywhere, — in the water, in the air, and on shore. When the spawn is gone and the sardines have migrated, the fisherman and the tourist cast their hooks and pull in dozens in a morning; although once or twice an hour they are surprised by a twenty or thirty pound monster who swallows the hook and simply walks away with it, heedless of the tiny line which seeks to hold him. The chief excitement of ocean fishing lies in this, that one never knows what kind of fish one is going to land next. More than twenty varieties are caught here, including rock-cod, sheepshead, whitefish, barracuda, mackerel, etc. The most fascinating of all is a bright red fish which haunts the rocks; as beautiful as the Chinese goldfishes kept in glass globes, but very much larger. It is almost too beautiful to kill, but it has an ugly mouth, and is good to eat, so up it comes *en route* to the frying-pan.

The fisherman is the least formidable enemy of these fish. The pelican and the seal are wholesale butchers in comparison. The large pelicans, with their huge, ugly bills, with which they can scoop up a dozen sardines or smelts at one fell swoop, are very abundant at Catalina Island, but at the present rate of extermination by tourists they will soon be scarce. Their wing-bones make good and novel pipe-stems, and their skin, with the soft white and gray feathers, is ornamental; and that settles their fate. They are very stupid birds, and slow, and not a bit afraid of human beings, which makes them easy victims. Tourists kill them from the beach or on boats, and after skinning them, throw the carcass overboard, where it is immediately pounced upon and disputed by a dozen greedy gulls. The seals occasionally visit Avalon Bay on their fishing excursions, ingeniously swimming a dozen abreast in a semicircle, and driving the fish before them till they are cornered. Sometimes the terrified fish, in their eager flight, jump on the beach, where they may be picked up alive. No one should fail to pay a visit to the seal rocks and see these creatures "at home." The rocks are at the southern extremity of the island, about six miles from Avalon, and can be reached by row-boat, or by the steam-tug which almost daily takes down a party. A row-boat is preferable, because the seals allow it to approach

nearer than a puffing tug. On the way down observe
the splendid precipitous rocks, to the sides of which
some wild goats may occasionally be seen clinging like
flies. The boat passes projecting rocks and rugged
promontories, on which a few pelicans and seals are
basking; and between them are several large curved
beaches of smooth pebbles, three or four feet high, and
fifty feet wide, to which every winter's storms add a
foot or two. As we approach the southern end of the
island, the swell of the outer Pacific becomes perceptible, and at the same time the seal rocks rise up before
us. The hundreds of sea-lions lying on them appear
to be fast asleep; but suddenly a sentinel raises up his
head, watches us a moment, and then utters a cry of
alarm. Immediately the whole army are awake, and
gradually assume an erect position, barking hoarsely as
we approach them. Among them are some formidable
monsters, large and heavy as oxen, and were they not
known to be perfectly harmless, it would seem a most
hazardous undertaking to row right up to them. With
every stroke of the oars they become more excited and
noisy, and finally, when we are within forty or fifty feet
of the rock, they plunge headlong and pell-mell into the
water. For a moment they are invisible, and then they
are seen collecting in a body in a sort of pool between
the rocks, sticking up their snake-like necks and heads,
and barking louder than ever, the younger ones bleat-
ing just like sheep. But gradually, as we move away
a little, and throw out our fishing-lines, they become
convinced that our intentions are honorable, and then,
with many a groan and snap at their neighbors, they
climb back clumsily to the summit of the rocks, the
biggest ones securing the best places. Seal rocks are

always good fishing-ground; but why is it that the fish do not learn to avoid places where they hear the loud barking of their voracious enemies? In this respect their instincts appear to fail them.

VII.

SANTA BARBARA AND THE YOSEMITE.

A DAM UNDER A RIVER-BED — BEANS AND CULTURE — AN ÆSTHETIC TOWN — BEAUTIFUL GARDENS — SPANISHTOWN AND CHINATOWN — THE MOJAVE DESERT — ON THE WAY TO THE YOSEMITE — A FINE STAGE RIDE — FLORAL WONDERS — THE SIERRA SNOW-PLANT AND MARIPOSA LILIES — RESEMBLANCE TO OREGON SCENERY — DISCOVERY OF THE VALLEY — THE YOSEMITE AND BRIDAL VEIL FALLS — RAINBOW SPRAY — EL CAPITAN AND MIRROR LAKE — ORIGIN OF THE VALLEY — YOSEMITE AS A LAKE — GLACIER POINT AND OTHER EXCURSIONS — THE BIG TREES IN THE MARIPOSA GROVE.

THERE are two ways of reaching Santa Barbara from Los Angeles (or San Francisco), — either on a coast steamer or by the new railway branch from Saugus, about twenty-five miles north of Los Angeles, which was completed two or three years ago. For scenic reasons the latter route is preferable, as it takes us in succession over the lovely San Fernando Valley, through a mountain cañon, and lastly, for almost thirty miles, along the edge of the ocean, thus exhibiting Nature in her three principal phases. Near San Fernando, which is a pretty and inviting place, may be seen one of the greatest curiosities in the State, showing what strange methods are sometimes resorted to in Southern

California to secure water for irrigation. It is a granite dam, fifty feet deep, which brings to the surface the water of a subterranean river. Only three feet of the dam are above ground, the rest being sunk down to the bed-rock, so as to force up into the surface-pipes a stream of water fifteen feet deep and forty feet wide. Another curiosity of San Fernando is a small boy who, while the train stops, walks up and down with a basket on his arm, shouting incessantly, "Nice sweet oranges, five for a nickel, *eight* for a dime!"

Soon after leaving San Fernando the train plunges into a cañon, where we get a near view of the foothills and mountains which had so often aroused our curiosity and a desire to make their acquaintance. They are of the most diverse forms and colors, now rugged, gray, and forbidding, and again femininely rounded, green, and handsome. At Newhall and beyond we greet the sight of beautiful oak groves on the foothills, — real, natural, unirrigated shade trees, with cows resting under them. The ocean is reached at Santa Buenaventura, which is getting to be a seaport doing a considerable export business in grain, oil, pork, flaxseed, honey, and, above all, beans. The region between this town and Santa Barbara is remarkably favorable to the growth of beans, 113,700 sacks having been raised in 1887, as compared to only 35,000 sacks of corn, the next highest item; and we are not a bit surprised, therefore, to read in the guidebook that "Santa Barbara prides herself on being more æsthetic and cultured than her somewhat plebeian sisters, San Diego and Los Angeles." Hereafter it will be impossible to doubt the Boston-baked-beans theory.

There is unquestionably an air of refinement and good taste about Santa Barbara which impresses one as favorably as the scenic and climatic attractions. It is a substantially built, most picturesquely situated town of four or five thousand inhabitants, traversed by a long, wide business street in which are many elegant stores which at once indicate it to be a great resort of tourists; and what predisposes one especially in favor of this place is the clean and noiseless asphalt paving of the streets, which promises rest and refreshing sleep to the victims of nervousness and insomnia, — a pavement which if introduced by legal enactment in every town and city in the country, would reduce the income of physicians twenty-five per cent. But as there are few but physicians who know this fact, we of course hear very little about it. The Arlington is one of the most comfortable and best managed hotels in California, and from its cupola a good view of the town and surroundings may be obtained. To the west is the Pacific, bounded by the semicircular harbor, which is invaded by a long pier, — the coolest place in town. Then, in a wider semicircle, comes the town, half buried amidst the Peruvian pepper and other fine shade trees, extending up to the foothills, behind which rise the green and gray snowless mountains.

Santa Barbara is not a commercial place, there being no large ships in the harbor, and its trade only local. More than any other place in Southern California it gives the impression of being merely a town of quiet homes and a pleasure and health resort for tourists and invalids. Though Indian remains must be scarce by this time, there are here, for the benefit of this class of visitors, a large number of curiosity stores, whose goods are probably manufactured in San Francisco, like the "Indian relics" and curios sold in Alaska. The old Mission, however, is genuine, and attracts many visitors.   A pleasant resort is the free library, well stocked, and the reading-room, which is always cool, but has the objectionable feature of commanding so fine a view that it requires a special effort to prevent the eyes from constantly wandering away from the pages of the books.

The gardens of Santa Barbara are probably the finest and most varied in the State, and nowhere else did I find myself so frequently obliged to stand still and peep over fences at some new species or varieties of flowers or flowering shrubs and trees.   Persia itself can hardly excel Santa Barbara in roses, three hundred varieties of which are found here.   " At one of our annual rose fairs we have seen one hundred and fifty-six varieties of roses, all cut from one garden that morning," says the Rev. A. W. Jackson; in "Barbariana"; and the wonderful cosmopolitanism of California soil and climate is indicated by the assertion that " trees native to Peru, Chili, Australia, China, Japan, New Zealand, North Africa, South Africa, Southern and Central Europe, Southern and Western Asia, and our own Southern and Northeastern States, are found growing in it side by side."

There are years when the thermometer does not rise above 85° or sink below 35°, and for this climate Santa Barbara is partly indebted to the four mountainous islands (similar to Catalina) which lie twenty miles or more to the westward and shut out the cold trade winds. Fogs, however, are abundant in spring, and there is an occasional scorching day or two, or a dust-storm; but these blemishes, as Mr. Jackson cheerfully remarks, amount to no more than " the freckles on the face of a young lady, who is beautiful and delightful notwithstanding."   Like every other town of over two thousand in this part of the State, Santa Barbara has its Spanishtown and Chinatown, but with this difference, that there is said to be a remnant here of the better class of Spaniards who formerly owned the State and lived in large adobe houses, while in other towns little now remains but a handful of the poorer classes, aptly characterized as " Greasers." Though poor, they are not always honest, according to report; and I have myself seen young girls enticing a neighbor's chickens with a handful of wheat into their house, whence they never issued again; and sometimes they catch them with fish-hooks. The men make a precarious living by taking care of cattle and horses or doing some agricultural work. They speak a very corrupt Spanish, and live in a most primitive way in one-room shanties raised a foot or two above the ground. The children run about barefooted all the year round, and the women are ignorant of the uses of flannel, their dress consisting simply of a calico wrapper: hence it is not surprising that, as a prominent physician informed me, a large proportion of them succumb to the sudden changes of temperature, and die of consumption, — the very disease against which this climate, with proper precautions, is so potent.

It is a significant fact that although an American occasionally marries one of these Mexican women, it hardly ever happens that an American woman marries a Mexican. Thus disease, emigration to Mexico, and intermarriage are gradually decimating the Mexicans, and in two or three decades few will be left in Southern California. It is a sign of the times that at Santa Barbara the Chinese are gradually invading Spanishtown. Say what they will, the Californians at harvest time are glad of all the Chinamen they can get; nor are there many who refuse to patronize the Chinese vegetable man, who is a feature of every place. Every morning he comes round with a wagon-load of assorted vegetables which he sells at such an absurdly low price that even farmers find it more economical to buy than to raise their vegetables. Five or ten cents will supply a family of three or four with choice vegetables for two meals; and the man always throws in a bunch of celery or some other thing which in the East would cost as much as is here paid for the whole. But John can afford it. All he asks of life is his daily ration of rice, a portion of a room to sleep in, and a brisk sea-breeze to fly his musical kite, which he watches and listens to by the hour with an expression of genuine enjoyment.

In coming to Santa Barbara, the last fifty miles were made in the darkness, so that the saline breeze alone gave evidence that for almost two hours the train skirts the ocean. In returning, we take the morning train, to connect at Saugus with the north-bound Los Angeles train for Yosemite, and thus get a chance to enjoy this ride along the ocean, which is very different from the stretch between San Diego and Oceanside, — there, a level, sandy beach, and the mountains at a distance; here, a mountain chain with its foot in the breakers, leaving hardly room enough for the train to wind along, the piles occasionally lapped by the waves. Between Saugus and Mojave numerous large bee ranches can be seen from the train, though there seems no superabundance of flowers.

As we enter the Mojave Desert, — which is a real desert, by reason of its sandy soil, and not simply in appearance, owing to the lack of irrigation, — the most conspicuous objects are the large *yucca* cactus-trees, rising to a height of forty feet and more, with large, thick branches, which furnish fibre for paper. On all sides isolated, naked hills, and clusters of hills with curious vertical water-furrows, rise as abruptly out of the level, sandy floor as Catalina does from the Pacific. By and by darkness closes in, and we miss the experience of passing through the seventeen tunnels and seeing the famous " Loop," where the train crosses its own track about eighty feet above. All that we remember of this region is the dismal howling of the desert wind, which is cold enough to make blankets comfortable even in a Pullman sleeper, though in the daytime the temperature in this region may have been anywhere between 100° and 120°.

At 3.30 the porter wakes us, and at 4.10 we are dropped in the midst of a prairie, a quarter of a mile beyond the Berenda station, whence a branch road is to take us in the direction of the Yosemite Valley. The short ride to Raymond, the terminus of the branch railway, is over a level region densely inhabited by jack-rabbits, who are used as targets by pistolled tourists in the freight car. Perhaps it is hardly correct to say that this region is level; for there are thousands of curious little round hills several feet high and fifteen or twenty in diameter. They are locally known as " hog-wallows," but their origin is unknown. At Raymond, those of the passengers who had been wise enough to telegraph a week in advance for outside or box seats on the stages take possession of them with a feeling of proud superiority over their less prudent fellow-travellers. But there are stages and stages, and an inside seat in a new stage, with good springs, is preferable to an outside seat on an old rickety stage, at least for those who would rather lose some of the scenery *en route* than be "seasick" all the way, as not a few ladies are; for the road is rough and the pace rapid, regardless of holes and bumps. Four horses are attached to the stage, which are changed seven times before we reach the Valley, next day at noon. In the height of the season this company employs three hundred horses. The ascent begins at once; mountain air and scenery surround us, and become more inspiriting and inspiring in a gradual *crescendo*, till the climax is reached at Inspiration Point, just above the Valley. The vegetation changes every few hours and becomes constantly more fascinating. Large, stately oak-trees are everywhere, adorned with pendent branches of mistletoe as large as beehives. The stage passes under some of these, which leads a passenger to remark that it is lucky for young ladies that this route is not open during Christmas week.

Grub Gulch is the suggestive name of a small place we stop at for a few minutes; and further on, while the horses are being changed, passengers have a chance to inspect the reducing works of the Gambetta gold mine, the flume of which, conducting water from an enormous distance, runs along the stage road for hours. We stop for lunch at Grant's Sulphur Springs, a wild, romantic mountain resort, the proprietor of which built a stretch of road costing twelve thousand dollars, on condition that the stages should pass his way and stop for lunch. Supper is served at the Wawona Hotel, where we spend the night. This place has its own attractions in the shape of a fine water-fall, a lake, a trout-stream, Hill's picture gallery, and an Alaskan bear in a cage near the river.

It may seem strange that a bear should be imported from Alaska to the Sierra, which has plenty of its own. But they are less easily caught here, and avoid the haunts of men. We saw none on the way, nor any other animals except squirrels and a few birds, among which the pretty but unmusical bluejays predominated. One passenger said that he caught a glimpse of two deer, but could not prove his assertion. Scenery similar to that of the preceding day, only grander and more of it. There may be mountains in other parts of America to match these, but nowhere such a bewildering profusion and unique beauty of flowers, shrubs, and trees. The driver showed no disposition to stop and give us a chance to pick these floral novelties; and wisely, for we should have never reached the Valley if he had. An amateur botanist, on foot or on horseback, would require a week to get there. It is not only those fringing the road that can be enjoyed from the stage, but those at a distance, too; for they grow in large blue, yellow, white, or red patches, looking like irregular garden beds, resting cosily under a shade tree, or exposed on a sunny ledge or hill-side, where they sometimes present the appearance of gayly colored rocks. Even Southern California has nothing to match this; for although there may be a still greater profusion of flowers, there are not so many varieties as here. Bleeding hearts, larkspurs, and lupins in all colors, yellow and white violets, snapdragons, fragrant California lilac, honeysuckles, tiger-lilies, etc., etc., carpet the ground with the luxuriance of weeds. Fortunately those that are most peculiar to the region are also the most abundant; namely, the Indian pinks (with fringed scarlet petals, looking like groups of tiny Japanese parasols),

Indian paint-brushes, Mariposa lilies, and snow-plants. The long-stemmed, tulip-shaped, white and yellowish Mariposa lilies are especially numerous; and when one of the passengers jumped out as the stage climbed up a hill and brought back a handful, two of the ladies exclaimed simultaneously, after glancing at the curiously marked downy inside, " Why, they look just like butterflies ! " — which shows that they are well named; for mariposa is Spanish for butterfly.

But the gem of the collection is the Sierra snow-plant, which is of such striking and unique appearance, that even those who do not ordinarily care much for flowers cannot repress an exclamation of rapturous admiration when they first see one. It is called snow-plant because it grows only at an elevation of from four to eight thousand feet, while the last snow-patches are melting: but the name is misleading, as one expects from it a white flower; whereas, the small, bell-shaped flowers, as well as the scaly, brittle, thick stems around which they cluster irregularly, in great profusion, are all one red blush of blood color. They push themselves like mushrooms out of the ground, displacing the layer of dry needles under the fir-trees; and the mode of their growth and origin is, I believe, still something of a mystery to botanists. Of the shrubs I will mention only the dogwood, whose blossoms are as pure white and as large as in Oregon ; the tough leather-plant, with yellow flowers, similar to those of the dogwood; and the manzanita, so called from its berries, which look like little apples. On account of its beautiful, smooth, brown rind, marked like alligator skin, it is much coveted for canes, and every young man hunts a few hours for a good specimen ; but though the bush is over-abundant, straight sticks are so rare that they are sold for five dollars on the spot.

After spending a winter in treeless Southern California, the sight of the dense and stately Sierra forests is as agreeable as that of the rare mountain shrubs and flowers. As we ascend higher and higher, the change in the forest trees is similar to that which we encounter in going northward towards Oregon and Washington. At a place where the oaks are still abundant, we notice two isolated pine-trees on a hill-side; these become more and more abundant, till, in the higher regions, they become replaced by firs, often prettily draped with yellow moss (which completely hides the branches, and makes the whole tree yellow), many of them dotted with innumerable holes in which woodpeckers insert their acorns,— so tightly that neither squirrel nor bluejay can get them out. The resemblance to Oregon scenery is heightened by the numerous burnt stumps, the mosses, and the ferns. Higher and higher we creep, and more and more magnificent becomes the scenic outlook over the mountain crests rising behind each other in endless succession like the waves of a stormy sea, with an occasional glimpse far down into the yellow, sunburnt San Joaquin Valley, and the Coast Range, one hundred and fifty miles away, like a faint silhouette. In this howling wilderness of desolate forests and mountains, which it takes the stage almost two days to traverse on a smooth road, the thought occurs again and again how in the world any one ever discovered this Yosemite Valley, hidden away in the heart of the Sierras, to which no arteries led them. Had it not been for the pursuit of that band of Indians by Captain Boling, in 1851, under the guidance of two Indian chiefs, it is possible that this

gigantic gorge of the Merced River might still answer
to the description given of it at that time by one of
the friendly chiefs: "In this deep valley one Indian is
more than ten white men. The hiding-places are many.
They will throw rocks down on the white men if any
should come near them. The other tribes dare not make
war upon them; for they are lawless like the grizzlies,
and as strong. We are afraid to go to this valley, for
there are many witches there."

Once discovered by white men, the Valley was sure to
become world-famed ere long, though the soldiers and
gold-hunters who first saw it did not realize that they
had come across the most wonderful collection of water-
falls, precipitous cliffs, fantastic peaks, and other scenic
features, to be found in a similar compass anywhere in
the world. In approaching a spot which, although discovered less than forty years ago, is already as well
known the world over as Niagara or Mont Blanc, expec-
tation is of course at fever heat. What adds to the
excitement, is the knowledge that the first bird's-eye-
view of the whole Valley which we get on this route
is also the finest. It is at Inspiration Point, where the
driver gave us just two minutes to take in the most
famous scene in California. But these stage-drivers
have sad experiences. Ours told me how some time
previously he had stopped his stage at this point, and
how every one was seemingly wrapped in admiration
too deep for speech, when a lady on the back seat suddenly broke the silence by exclaiming, "Oh, my! I
wonder why they have no lace curtains at the Wawona
Hotel!"

It is of the Valley as a whole only that one gets the
finest impression from this point; the individual features,

the giant precipitous wall of smooth granite, known as
El Capitan, and especially the water-falls, do not reveal
their full grandeur till we are directly beneath them.
As the stage winds down into the Valley, such a bewildering variety of scenic surprises crowd each other that
one should have as many eyes as an insect to take them
all in; and it is amusing to see all the passengers point-
ing at once in different directions to call attention to
something that particularly strikes their fancy, while
each one is too busy to heed the others. The stage traverses almost the whole Valley, which is over six miles
in length, landing the majority of the tourists at the
State-built Stoneman House, although some stop at Bar-
nard's, a mile less distant, directly opposite the triple
Yosemite Falls, which are what a reporter would call
a "three-decker." These falls, as well as the Bridal
Veil, and others less famous, are seen from the stage as
it traverses the Valley; but of course they want a whole
afternoon at the very least for proper inspection; so,
after washing off the abundant Yosemite dust, and par-
taking of lunch, we hire a carriage or saddle-horse, and
retrace our steps through the Valley, making our first
stop at the Yosemite Falls. In coming up the Valley
the driver had asked us how wide we thought the
Yosemite creek was at the height where it falls over
the edge. It looks about a foot wide, and the guesses
ranged from two to ten feet. "Sixty feet wide," he
replied. Our new driver made it forty feet, and on consulting Professor Whitney's "Yosemite Guide-Book"
(which still remains by far the most graphic and reliable
account of the Valley ever written, but of which it is
absolutely impossible to find a copy in the book-market,
though for years there has been a great demand for it —

a rare instance of publishers' stupidity) we found that he makes it only twenty feet in width and two deep, but still sufficient to furnish from half a million to a million and a half cubic feet of water in an hour to form the falls. Yet it is not so much by its volume that the Yosemite Falls imposes as by its unequalled height. The upper fall has a descent of fifteen hundred feet; the middle, of six hundred and twenty-six; and the lower, of four hundred; making together a water-fall (for they are almost in a vertical line) of over twenty-six hundred feet, or more than half a mile — sixteen times as high as Niagara.

With an umbrella or rubber coat one can get quite near the foot of the lower falls, and enjoy the spectacle of the spray, and of the rainbow which forever hovers over it, like a circle of humming-birds. To the left of the falls is a sort of Cave of the Winds, whence a strong blast is forced on the upper part of the descending water, swaying it to and fro several feet, and producing the occasional effect of a lateral curve. Indeed, the aspect of the falls changes as constantly as the expression on a human face, and one might visit it scores of times without seeing it exactly as it was before.

Having given as much time as possible to these falls, we continue our trip down the same side of the Valley, to the right of the clear and rapid Merced River, till we come under the shadow of El Capitan, the summit of which is thirty-three hundred feet straight overhead — almost seven times as high as the highest European cathedral. A single perpendicular wall of this height would make this rock one of the wonders of the world; but here are two such walls, half a mile in length, smooth as marble, meeting at a right angle, which makes "The Captain" an absolutely unique sight: "Sublimity materialized in granite," as Hutchinson puts it. Vast as this rock seemed from Inspiration Point, one must walk or drive along its base fully to realize its grandeur and sublimity. "The whole of New York," exclaimed an enthusiastic companion, "might have been quarried out of that rock without making a damaging impression on it!" The smooth surface is in one place darkened by what seems a young fir-tree a few feet high, but which is said to be an old tree over a hundred feet high. How it ever got a foothold and nourishment half-way up this naked rock, is a mystery. Even a tree, one would think, should become dizzy and lose its balance in such a situation.

Below El Capitan the Valley gradually contracts into a cañon, "not having the U shape of the Yosemite, but the usual V shape of California valleys." The descent is extraordinarily abrupt, and the Merced River rushes and tumbles along in a continuous headlong current almost as wild and impetuous as the Niagara Rapids. High up on the steep right wall of the cañon we see the Milton road winding upwards like a white thread. Our downward road continues as far as the Cascade Falls, which, though they would elsewhere be regarded as stupendous, here seem something of an anticlimax after the Yosemite Falls.

Not so with the Bridal Veil Fall, which we next visit, after returning as far as El Capitan and crossing the river to the other side of the valley. Although only about one-third as high as the Yosemite Falls, the Bridal Veil has features which make it fully their equal in charm. The proper time to visit it is at five o'clock in the afternoon, on account of the beautiful rainbows which then form in it; and it should be approached from the lower part of the Valley to see them to the best advantage. At first the rainbow hovers over the fall about two-thirds up towards its top; but as we draw near, it gradually sinks down, till at last it seems to be dashed to pieces on the cascades at the foot of the falls, where it covers everything with a mass of irridescent spray, including the neighboring rocks and grass and bushes, to which it is wafted by the wind. Like the Yosemite, this fall is constantly swayed to and fro by the wind, as much as twenty feet from its perpendicular course, and to this fluttering in the wind of its spray-like mass it owes its name. The wind constantly changes, so that at one moment the inverted water-rockets descend on the right, and the loose spray on the left, and the next moment *vice versa*. Sometimes there are *two* water-falls, — one upward and one downward; for when the wind blows towards the fall, a dense spray rises up to the very top of the fall, where it is blown over the ledge like a cloud. And what still more heightens the beauty of the scene is, that beyond the ledge nothing is visible, so that the water seems to tumble right out of the blue sky into the deep Valley.

More than any rivals, the falls of the Yosemite Valley are constantly altered by changes in the wind, moon, and sunlight; and it is this great variety of aspect, together with the unparalleled height, that constitutes their unique fascination and makes them superior to all other water-falls, except of course Niagara, which is so utterly different in character as to be incomparable. Over the magnificent fall of the Yellowstone they have the advantage that they can be seen from below as well as from above.

On the other hand, there is more charm of color in the Yellowstone cañon, the few spots and stains on the Yosemite walls being insignificant in comparison with the brilliant mosaic which covers the sides of the other cañon. Nor are the peaks and pinnacles which tower over the lower walls of the Yosemite quite as fantastic and architecturally suggestive as those of the Yellowstone, or those that may be seen on approaching the Engadine from Chur, or leaving it for Como. And yet they are so superb that the Yosemite would be hardly less frequented were all its water-falls blotted out of existence — as they practically are late in summer, when there are no more snows to melt and replenish them. When Horace Greeley visited the Valley, the Yosemite Falls were momentarily so insignificant that he pronounced them "a humbug"; yet his admiration of the Valley was none the less superlative. Cathedral Rock, the Three Brothers, The Sentinel, Sentinel Dome, Cloud's Rest, El Capitan, and North and South Domes form an assemblage of peaks sufficiently imposing to compensate the late summer tourist for the disappointment caused by the fickle water. Yet, if possible, Yosemite should be visited in May, not only because the water-falls are then at their best and the surrounding peaks still snow-capped, but because there may be, and often is, a belated snow-storm of a few days' duration, which gives an opportunity of seeing the Valley both in its summer and its winter aspects, in rapid succession.

On the way back to the hotel a dispute arose in our carriage as to the origin of the Valley. Clarence King states in his "Mountaineering in the Sierra Nevada" that various markings which he noted had convinced him that at one time a glacier no less than a thousand feet deep had flowed through the Valley, occupying its entire bottom. The eminent Californian geologist, Mr. Muir, also has advocated the theory that the Valley was eroded by glaciers; whereas, Professor Whitney emphatically declares that a more absurd theory was never advanced, and gives his reasons why he believes neither in the erosive action of ice, nor of aqueous erosion, as being the cause of the formation of the Valley, nor in its origin through a mountain fissure. He advances the startling theory that Yosemite Valley was formed by the sinking down of its bottom to an unknown depth during a convulsive moment of the surrounding mountains. We tried to find reasons for or against these various theories in the aspect of the opposing walls, to see if they would fit into each other, or show signs of erosion; but of course where doctors differ it was not to be supposed that amateurs could come to an agreement, so the question remains an open one. But there is a certain fascination in Professor Whitney's theory, with the corollary that at one time the cavity thus formed " was, undoubtedly, occupied by water, forming a lake of unsurpassed beauty and grandeur, until quite a recent epoch." Beautiful as the present floor of the Valley is, with its great variety of grasses, flowers, shrubs, and trees, one cannot help fancying that a *Lake Yosemite*, on which one might approach the foot of the water-falls in a boat by moonlight, would be more romantic still; and such a lake could be made by damming the Merced River below El Capitan. But it would cost many millions.

Too much for one afternoon are all these scenes and speculations, and we reach the hotel thoroughly exhausted and hungry. The bill of fare at the Stoneman

House is a considerable improvement on that of the original inhabitants of the Yosemite, who used to live on acorns, scorched wild oats and grass seeds, dried caterpillars, roasted grasshoppers, and similar delicacies; but in other respects the arrangements are somewhat primitive, and the lady who missed the lace curtains at the Wawona Hotel probably was equally disappointed at the Stoneman House, where the guests have to sleep with blue spectacles on unless they wish the sun to wake them at six, by shining straight into their faces through the bare windows. However, there is good reason for getting up early; for Mirror Lake must be visited before the breeze, which is apt to blow soon after sunrise, has had time to disturb the surface of the "Sleeping Water," as the Indians used to call this shallow little lake situated a few miles up the Tenaya cañon.

Mirror Lake deserves attention, not only because in it are reflected some of the finest mountain forms in America, but because it indirectly helped to give the Valley its present name. The Indian name for it was Ahwahnee. One morning, according to the Indian legend, a chief went to the Sleeping Water, where he ran across a monstrous grizzly bear. After a terrific combat, in which his only weapon was the limb of a tree, he despatched him, and henceforth his followers called him Yo Semite, or Big Grizzly, which name was handed down to his children, and ultimately to the whole tribe; and at the first white men's camp-fire in the Valley it was thus named. at the suggestion of Dr. L. H. Bunnell.

Mirror Lake is small, and not especially impressive as a body of water, but its grand surroundings and the absolute stillness of its surface make it perhaps the most perfect aqueous mirror in the world. The bunches of grass in the middle of the lake, the trees lining its borders, and the bold mountains in the background are reflected so clearly and so vividly that in a photograph it is difficult to tell which is the real picture or which the image, the water itself appearing like a thin sheet separating the two antipodal views. It is under the guidance of Mr. Galen Clark, the superintendent of the Valley, that the lake is seen to best advantage, as he knows all the best points of view, and is armed with a slightly concave looking-glass which makes the scene doubly a mirror-lake. No painting could equal in beauty the miniature views of subaquatic landscape shown in this glass, in all the natural colors — the blue sky resting on the gray and white rocks, and the dark green trees showing every branch and every needle with perfect distinctness. The climax comes when the sun begins to peep from behind the mountain summits, which here hide it an hour longer than in the lower Valley. In Mr. Clark's mirror it looks like a large electric light whose dazzle throws the mirrored views of sky, mountain, and forest into a gloomy shade, making the scene like a dream of the lower world. We had to keep on the move constantly to keep the sun in view, yet not too high, and I never before realized how quickly the sun does travel, or how the conformation of the mountain ridges can make it seemingly go now to the left, and now to the right. When it had climbed too high to be looked at comfortably even in a mirror, a breeze suddenly arose and obliterated the scenery painted on the lake's surface. Just at that moment two wagon-loads of tourists arrived from the hotel. They had known as well as we that Mirror Lake after sunrise is nothing but an ordinary pond, but had lingered too long over their breakfast or between their sheets. Such is the average tourist — travelling hundreds of miles, and enduring the fatigues of staging to see a world-famous scene, and then missing all for the sake of a few more bites of tough beefsteak!

The whole day still lies before us, and it is part of the regular programme to spend it in seeing the Vernal and Nevada Falls. The carriage takes us across a bridge, where saddle-horses are in waiting for those who dread the climb. Make the driver stop a few minutes on the middle of the bridge, because thence you get one of the finest views of one of those unique mountain formations of the Sierra Nevada, — the North Dome, as true to its name and as absolutely symmetrical and regular as any capitol or religious edifice ever constructed. The falls we have seen so far are formed by creeks which fall over the Yosemite walls and then join the river below; but those we are to see now are formed by the Merced itself, and therefore promise to be more imposing in volume, even if inferior in height. A wide bridle-path leads up the steep gorge, perfectly safe for the most nervous, though much blasting was necessary to make it so. Superb views of the Valley beneath, of the precipitous cliffs on all sides, and from them a water-fall or two which would make the reputation of any ordinary mountain region, but which here are hardly noticed amid the abundance of first-class cataracts. A deserted log cabin near the foot of the Vernal Fall marks the place where we can either follow the horses up to the top of the fall or climb up by a steep footpath by the side of the fall. By all means this path should be taken, either going or descending, the latter being preferable not only as being much easier, but because our descending from the top to the base of the fall makes it seem higher, grander, and louder every moment.

The Vernal Fall is about four hundred feet high and eighty feet wide — considerably lower than those in the Valley, but much wider and more voluminous, and therefore stands midway between the kind of falls which impose through their massiveness, of which Niagara is the type, and those whose principal charm lies in their height and eternal variation of aspect, as is the case with the Yellowstone, Bridal Veil, and Yosemite Falls. Few hear of the Vernal Fall before coming to the Yosemite; yet if it were situated amid the mountains of Switzerland, it would be surrounded by a dozen hotels and seen by a hundred thousand visitors every summer. Approaching it by the footpath, we are soon enveloped in a drenching spray, the haunt of a superb rainbow, which at first forms a complete circle, but as we get up higher is gradually reduced to the semi-circular form of ordinary rainbows (another reason for taking this path on returning, since a scenic *crescendo* is preferable to a *decrescendo*). The last part of the ascent is made on a series of stairs, dizzy but safe, built through a sort of cavern in the rock, where we can get a peep right into the home of rare ferns and mosses, kept green by the spray, and fortunately just out of reach of amateur botanists. At the summit, the guide steps out on the smooth granite to the edge of the fall, and holds out his hand for those who wish to approach and see its foot. The upper part can be seen by leaning over a curious

NORTH DOME, YOSEMITE VALLEY.

granite parapet, about three feet high, looking, as Professor Whitney remarks, "as if made on purpose to afford the visitor a secure position from which to enjoy the scene." It is only a foot or two wide, and looks as if it were rent off the rest of the rock to some distance below, and as if it might be easily kicked over; but this feeling of insecurity, where you know you are perfectly safe, only adds to the grandeur of the scene.

It would be impossible to find a more romantic and commanding spot than this. At your feet is the Vernal Fall and the turbulent Merced tumbling down the mammoth gorge; in the other direction, less than a mile upwards, is another water-fall, world famed, — the Nevada, — and between these two falls are endless combinations of wild rocks and shooting waters. Only a few yards above the Vernal is an eddying hollow known as the Emerald Pool; and immediately above this is "the flume, where the stream glides noiselessly but with lightning speed over its polished granite bed, making a preparatory run for its plunge over the Vernal Fall," as the first white man who ever saw this spot, J. H. Lawrence, happily described it. The guide here tells the story of an Englishman who wanted to "take a bawth, don't you know," in this flume, and who was carried down by the swift and powerful current into the Emerald Pool, where he caught on to a bush just in time to avoid being swept over the falls.

In low water the thin layer of swiftly moving water gives the flume a silvery appearance, whence it has received the name of Silver Apron; but if the Indians had any name for it, it must have been the more poetic designation of Arrow Water, or something similar. It is not safe to go near its edge; for it is sometimes suddenly widened by one of those curious irregular pulsations and reinforcements noticed in many cascades. We now cross a bridge over the raging torrent, and stop at the Casa Nevada, where Mr. Snow and his wife always are ready to provide a bountiful lunch at short notice. I believe that the principal reason why this lunch is so bountiful is because Mrs. Snow wants to get off her favorite joke at least once a day. Some one is sure to ask where she gets all these victuals, whereupon she replies, "We raise them," adding, after a pause and a look at the incredulous faces, "on mules." Mr. Snow is known as Perpetual Snow, from having lived here almost twenty years, and he sometimes facetiously offers to show summer visitors "six feet of Snow" right in his house. He has albums for sale containing fine collections of Yosemite ferns — thirty-six different kinds; and shows with pride his old registers in which many famous visitors have signed their names.

Only a few steps from the house, the Nevada Fall comes thundering down its six hundred feet or more, according to the season. To the left is Liberty Cap, almost as precipitous as El Capitan, yet often ascended. A path leads up to the summit of the Nevada Fall, which, however, cannot be approached near enough to get a downward glimpse; but this is compensated for by the fine side views one gets of it coming up. Further on is the mountain called Cloud's Rest, from which superb views of the valley and surroundings, as well as the high Sierras, are obtainable, but which can rarely be visited with comfort before the middle of May, on account of the deep snow-patches under which the path is buried. There is also a trail leading from the Casa Nevada over to one of the most famous parts of the

Yosemite walls, — Glacier Point; but there is so much to see there that one ought to devote a whole day to it. Therefore we return to the Valley the same way we came, and the next morning are again in the saddle, bound for Glacier Point, directly over the hotel. Everybody has seen pictures of Glacier Point, and the huge boulder which projects at one place several feet over the edge of the wall. On this boulder many persons have had their photographs taken, with nothing between them and the bottom of the Valley, more than half a mile beneath, than a bit of projecting rock, and nothing to hold on by. On the ledge to the right, however, an iron railing has been securely fastened, so that the most timorous can now look down with perfect safety.

At this point a flag is floating, and in the evening it is customary to build a fire, and afterwards throw the brands and coals over the brink. To the hotel guests directly below, who have been watching for them, these brands present the appearance of a golden water-fall, thus adding one more to the Yosemite's incomparable collection.

Looking up from this Valley, shut in on all sides by perpendicular walls, and lofty peaks from twenty-five hundred to seven thousand feet in height, it seems impossible that a way to the summit should have been found except by climbing up the cañon as we did yesterday; but there is a more direct path straight up the wall, to which the guide conducts us, after passing the village and the seldom-used, solitary chapel. The ascent is very steep in some places, and hard on man and beast; but so well planned as to be without risk or danger, even though the horse does occasionally poke his nose over a yawning abyss. Fortunately for the nervous, the most " ticklish " places are concealed by the dense brush clinging to the rocks, else the stubborn habit of the animals, of always walking as near the brink of the precipice as possible, would cause many a heart to stop beating momentarily. The air is wonderfully exhilarating and clear, and nothing could be finer than the aspect of the receding Valley, and the triple Yosemite Falls directly opposite, which are almost always in sight.

Half-way up, on our side, is the Agassiz Rock, — a huge boulder, in a state, apparently, of dangerously unstable equilibrium, and looking like some of the fantastic pinnacles of the Yellowstone cañon, as if it might be kicked over with one foot; but appearances are deceptive. There is a good hotel at the summit, where the horses are left with the guide, while we proceed a few hundred yards farther, to Glacier Point. Imagine how the Valley would look from a balloon, and you have some conception of the gruesome charms of Glacier Point, whence the outlook or downward look into the Valley is more perpendicular and awe-inspiring than from Inspiration Point, which affords the more picturesque view of the whole length of the Valley, its depth being a subordinate feature. But the advantage of Glacier Point lies in this, that by walking a few steps to the right, an entirely different scene is commanded, — a scene which includes both the Vernal and Nevada Falls, and beyond them an imposing array of snow-clad Sierra summits. It is here that every visitor must feel the impotence and barrenness of words to paint the images treasured in his memory; and were every word a photograph, a description would convey but a faint impression of the original. But we are to go up higher yet, where a still wider circle of mountains, cliffs, domes, cañons, and snow-fields will come within the field of vis, ion. The Sentinel Dome is our goal now, although the guide is not quite certain whether the path is sufficiently free from snow for the horses: we do come upon many large snow-patches, a foot or two deep, but we always manage to get through or around them. Fresh snow of this depth sometimes falls as late as the end of May, even in the Valley below.

At last we emerge from the forest, tie our horses to the last trees, and clamber up the bald pate of the Dome. Hence the billowy crests of the Sierra Nevada, including peaks of thirteen thousand feet and over, show themselves in something approaching their real height and sublime grandeur. The scene is not unlike that of the Spanish Sierra Nevada, as seen from Granada, thus presenting one of the numerous resemblances between Spain and California. The surface of the Sentinel Dome is full of curious small holes, probably the product of innumerable expansions and contractions of the rock under the influence of alternating heat and cold. The very top is occupied by a stunted, gnarled, and broken pine, presenting the appearance of a veteran warrior and storm wrestler, covered with wounds, upon which it exudes the soothing balm of a remarkably fragrant kind of pitch. Beware of touching it ! a second's contact will ruin a suit. Had Heine ever been in California, we might feel certain that this tree must have suggested to him that fine poem of the pine-tree dreaming amidst its winter snows of the palm-tree bathed in sunshine, — say in the Mojave Desert, but a hundred miles away.

Returning toward the Valley, we soon come to a

place known as Washburn Point, where the view of the falls and mountains is similar to that obtained from the Sentinel Dome, and perhaps even more impressive because of its being nearer. From here the scenery of the high Sierras can be seen even by those who are unable to walk or ride on such arduous paths; for there is a good wagon road leading hence to the Wawona Hotel, and striking the road to the Valley some miles above. For pedestrians, by far the best way to see the Valley would be to take this road from the Wawona, spending the night at the Glacier Point Hotel, devoting the next day to this place and the Sentinel Dome, and descending to the Valley on the day following by way of the Nevada and Vernal Falls. Thus the Valley may be visited without any uphill work at all.

It is well to make all one's plans in advance, so as to be able to reserve a good return seat on the stage as soon as you arrive at the Stoneman. The stage leaves early in the morning, and returns as far as the Wawona Hotel, where we arrive in time for lunch. After lunch uncovered stages drive up to the hotel, and everybody gets aboard for a visit to the Big Trees in the Mariposa Grove. The round trip covers seventeen miles only, thus leaving plenty of time to see the arboreal giants at leisure. The road takes us more deeply into the virgin forest than we have penetrated yet, and there are many superb trees which attract the attention long before the Mariposa Grove is reached. Some of the passengers begin to comment on a few big sugar pines, and even express a desire to stop and measure them; but the driver scornfully refuses to waste any time on such pigmies. So on and up we go, and at last come to a few scattered specimens which the driver admits belong to the real Big Tree family; but he does not stop till we reach the world-renowned Grizzly Giant, the thickest, though not the highest, of all the Sequoias. With the exception of some specimens of the African Baobab, this is the thickest tree in the world, so far as known, though by no means the highest. In one of the other nine Big Tree groves found in California (and only in California) — the Calaveras — there is a tree fifty-three feet higher than any one in the Mariposa Grove, and Professor Whitney refers to an Australian eucalyptus four hundred and eighty feet in height, overtopping the tallest Sequoia by one hundred and fifty-five feet. But for height and thickness combined, the Sequoia excels all other trees; and as the Mariposa Grove contains the thickest trees, it is the most impressive of all, since in the height of a three-hundred-foot tree a difference of ten or twenty feet is hardly noticeable, while in the circumference every foot tells.

Ten of our party clasped hands to encircle the Grizzly Giant, but the endmen could not begin to even see each other on the other side. I walked around it and counted fifty-three steps. The exact measurement is ninety-three feet seven inches, without allowing for that portion of the bark which has been destroyed by fire. The best idea of its enormous girth is conveyed by one of Taber's excellent photographs, in which a horse stands alongside of the tree, at full length, while a dozen men are scattered at intervals along the bark, without nearly filling up so much of the tree as is included in the view. Though blackened and cruelly hollowed out by fire, the Grizzly Giant is still alive, but its upper part is as dilapidated and time-worn as the lower; and no wonder, for it must have first stuck its roots into Sierra soil perhaps three or four centuries after the advent of Christ, by the most conservative estimate. The lowest branch of this tree is fully six feet in diameter — large enough to set up as a Big Tree by itself, — "as large as the trunks of the largest elms of the Connecticut valley."

Most of the tourists cut off little slices of the bark, which in this case is hardly a reprehensible practice, for it would take decades of such petty vandalism to make any impression on this monster. Yet there are other mementos that might as well be taken, such as the mosses clinging to it and the cones found under it. These cones are surprisingly small, — only about two inches in length, — especially when compared with other cones found in this region and offered for sale at the hotels, put up in wooden frames and covered with moss — some of them a foot and a half or more in length. But the Grizzly Giant must not detain us too long; for there are several hundred more Sequoias to be seen, and, as a punster suggested, a Big-treatise might be written on the Mariposa Grove alone.

As we pass from the Lower to the Upper Grove, these trees become more and more numerous among the pines and firs, until at last we come to a genuine grove of *Sequoia giganteas*, — a real forest cathedral. There is a flutter of excitement as we approach the Tunnel Tree, or Wawona (which is Indian for big tree), through which the stage drives as it stands, with horses, passengers, and all. The diameter of this tree at the ground is twenty-seven feet, or three feet less than the Grizzly Giant; the "tunnel" by which we go through it is ten feet high and from six to ten feet wide. Just as we drive into it, a poetic youth exclaims to his fair companion, "Now look out for spiders!" and others of the

BIG TREE—YOSEMITE VALLEY.

same class must nave passed through before, for names are written on the inside, and even visiting-cards tacked on. The wood chopped out here was of course made into relics and sold years ago, yet paper knives and other things made of it are still to be had in the grove in quantities to suit.

At a little log cabin, occupied by the guardians of the grove, the stage stops again, and the venturesome climb up the prostrate trunk of a fallen monarch, on a rickety ladder. The upper part of the trunk is rotten, and resembles the hull of a wrecked ocean steamer. It once took five men three weeks to fell one of these giants; and even after the connection of the trunk with the stump had been severed, it took three days of wedge-driving before the tree could be made to fall. Imagine, therefore, the force of wind required to throw over such a tree, and the nerve of Andrew Jackson Smith, who once remained in the hollow of one of them, known as Smith's Cabin (in the South Grove), during a Sierra storm which threw down "Old Goliath"!

The guardians of the grove have for sale packages of seeds of the Big Trees, though they frankly tell purchasers that not one in a hundred will grow. They have a nursery near the cabin, and often send young trees away. The *Sequoia gigantea*, although found nowhere except in the Sierra Nevada of California, grows readily elsewhere, and vast numbers have been planted in this country and abroad. The climate of England is said to be specially favorable to it, and from seeds planted there in 1853 have grown trees which are already over sixty feet in height and ten in girth. A thousand years hence England will have her Big Tree Groves, and they will be more beautiful than those of California, because better guarded against forest fires. But they will lack the majestic mountain surroundings.

It would almost seem as if the existence of these giant trees in the Sierra Nevadà were intended by nature as a striking artistic contrast and compensation for the utter absence of forests in Southern California,—a contrast heightened by the numerous other fine species of evergreen trees, especially the famous redwood groves, which Professor Whitney has described so poetically. Outside of Ceylon and other tropical countries there is, perhaps, no region which has so fine and varied an assortment of valuable woods as the Yosemite neighborhood. No visitor should fail to see the admirable collection of ornamental objects prepared by J. Starke, some of them inlaid with several dozen kinds of Sierra woods, making a mosaic as elegant as mother-of-pearl. And I must once more refer to another thing in which the Yosemite region is unexcelled,—the flowers.

After seeing the unrivalled Valley, in which Nature, as in a final operatic chorus, has grouped in an overwhelming *ensemble* all her motives—snow-peaks, domes, spires, precipices, lakes, rivers, and water-falls—all in the small compass of six or seven miles, the scenery on the way back to the San Joaquin Valley, fine as it is, and seemed on coming, cannot but have the effect of an anticlimax. Not so with the flowers, which have only gained in beauty, variety, and abundance during our week's stay in the Valley. Once I got off the stage, while it was climbing a hill, and in the space of half a mile gathered twenty-two kinds, which excited many " ohs " and "ahs" from the other passengers. California poppy patches, nestling under trees, formed such indescribably

lovely groups that sometimes every hand in the stage
was pointed at them by a unanimous impulse. In
some places the flowers stand so dense that a botanist, in measuring off a square yard, found over three
thousand plants on it. Here a flower-painter might
spend his life making perfect pictures which he need
only copy from nature; and he could not fail of at least
one of the attributes of genius, — he need never repeat
himself.

VIII.

SAN FRANCISCO AND CHINATOWN.

MOUNTAINOUS CHARACTER OF THE PACIFIC COAST — THE
HILLS OF SAN FRANCISCO — CABLE-CAR TOBOGGANING —
THE GOLDEN GATE AND CLIFF HOUSE — SCENES IN THE
CHINESE QUARTER — JOHN'S TABLE DELICACIES — LUNCH
IN A CHINESE RESTAURANT — AN HONEST BOOKSELLER
— CHINESE WOMEN — OPIUM DENS — BEHIND THE SCENES
IN A CHINESE THEATRE — THE ASIATIC TRADE — CAL-
IFORNIA HOTELS, RESTAURANTS, AND WINES — BERKELEY
AND THE UNIVERSITY — THE CLIMATE OF SAN FRAN-
CISCO.

A GLANCE at a relief map of the United States shows
a most striking contrast between the Atlantic and the
Pacific slopes, especially within a few hundred miles of
the coast. In the east, the mountains are few and low ;
whereas in the whole of California, Oregon, and Washington there is hardly a spot whence the view does not
include a mountain range with a few snow-peaks. And
this hilly structure characterizes also the three leading
cities of the coast, and many of the smaller ones. Los
Angeles, near one end, has recently built cable-cars to
climb the hills which shut it in; Portland, near the
other end, is beginning to build hers; and San Francisco, in the centre, has long had the most complete
cable-car system in the world. Rome may have been

built on seven hills, but San Francisco, as its inhabitants love to claim, is a city of a hundred hills. There is Californian exaggeration in this; for the greater part of the present city stands on about a dozen hills, with the intervening valleys and the level lots created by digging twenty million cubic yards of earth out of the hill-sides, and filling up the hollows; but beyond these there are scores of suburban hills, so to speak, waiting to be annexed; and when the city shall have grown to the size of London, — which, of course, is only a question of time, — it will probably cover a hundred hills: *q. e. d.*

For purposes of drainage and other sanitary reasons, this hilly structure of the city is a decided advantage, and that it adds greatly to the picturesqueness of the impression which it makes on visitors is obvious. Approaching it at night on an Oakland or Saucelito ferry-boat, or viewing it from an elevated point, it does not present to the eye such a limitless area of countless lights as does New York seen from Union Hill, Hoboken; but the grouping of the lights is more fascinating, some of them leading in straight, double lines up the hills; while others are arranged in semicircles along the amphitheatric valleys. To get a bird's-eye view of San Francisco in the daytime, one need not climb arduous towers, as in Eastern and European cities; but has only to take a front seat on a cable-car, — with an outlook unimpeded by driver or horses, — to see the city from half-a-dozen high hills, and as many different points of view. No city in the world can be seen so easily, so quickly, and so delightfully, as San Francisco, from these cable-cars, which, in the long run, make perhaps as good time as the New York elevated trains. It is a constant up and down, and the sensation of rapidly ascending a hill through rows of handsome residences and flower-gardens, without having to pity the poor, puffing horses, is as agreeable as the sudden plunges downward, so fast, and often so precipitous, that by shutting the eyes one can easily imagine himself to be out tobogganing. The feeling is similar to that experienced at Mauch Chunk, Pennsylvania, on decending the hill for twenty minutes on a car whose only motor is gravitation.

The most enjoyable of the cable-car excursions is the one in the direction of the Golden Gate and Cliff House, connecting in the suburbs with a new steam-dummy road only completed a short time ago, and not yet mentioned in the guide-books. This excursion is really one of the finest in California, and should be missed by no tourist; for it gives him superb views of the city from several hills, and of the bay studded with pretty islands, and finally takes him to the very edge of the Golden Gate, where he can see the ships and steamers entering or departing for China, Japan, Australia, and every port of Europe and America. The road continuously skirts the shore, being dug or blasted out of the precipitous hill-sides; and directly below us are the Pacific breakers blindly dashing themselves into foam and spray on the rocks. The terminus is the Cliff House, with its "seal rocks," densely inhabited by the sea-lions, which have been too often described to call for more than mention. There are countless seal rocks between San Diego and Sitka, but none so near a large city as these, which may be looked on as a free aquarium and an addition to the Golden Gate Park. They would have long since been depopulated were they not protected by law. The fishermen clamor for a repeal of this law, because

SEAL ROCKS, SAN FRANCISCO.

the seals kill so many salmon bound for the Sacramento River at the other end of the bay; but the gain of a few hundred fishermen would be the loss of three hundred and fifty thousand San Franciscans. As well let the city fathers turn over the Golden Gate Park to the vegetable gardeners. It takes up many acres which might be planted with useful cabbages and onions, — enough to enrich quite a number of gardeners; for it is three miles long and half a mile wide, containing one hundred and fifty acres more than the Central Park in New York. Besides, it contains poison-oak, and is so "unimproved" in part, that only a few years ago a wildcat was killed in it. Therefore, down with the Park! let it be exterminated, together with the useless, harshly barking, salmon-eating seals!

No doubt more people have had their first glimpse of the illimitable Pacific at the Cliff House than from all other places on the Californian Coast; and it is a most delightful spot to spend a few hours, although at any time of the year a light overcoat is desirable. When we are ready to return we have the choice of several roads, none of which, however, is as attractive as the one we came on. So we once more connect with the cable-cars and have another five cents' worth of tobogganing — without snow or danger of broken limbs. I should think that cable-car tobogganing parties ought to be among the most popular amusements in San Francisco. I am sure if I lived there I should ride to the Cliff House every day in the year. The return trip takes us through different streets from those we saw before, and on arriving at the corner of Jones and Washington Streets, a most magnificent prospect opens before us. We have risen to the crest of a hill, which seems to be the end of the world, when suddenly the whole city lies far down below us, and the car makes an almost perpendicular plunge a few hundred yards, as if determined to lose no time in getting there. You must hold on tightly, but there is no cause for alarm, as the frequent accidents on these roads do not happen in such places, but in the crowded streets below. Presently a still greater surprise awaits us. The car turns a corner, and without a moment's warning we are in China, which we had imagined five thousand miles away. In other parts of the city we see an occasional Chinese laundry and a few Chinamen mingled with the throng of Americans; but here the proportions are more than reversed, — Chinese men, women, and children, Chinese shops and signs, Chinese conversation, and Chinese smells monopolize the attention.

San Francisco has more than twenty thousand Chinese, hence it may be imagined that Chinatown is not a village. Anti-Mongolians like to compare it to a cancer which is eating its way through the vitals of the city, constantly enlarging at the edges. Blocks upon blocks in some of the best streets are given over to the Asiatic invaders; and while the large buildings formerly occupied by Americans have been left standing, they have undergone such a thorough metamorphosis that if the Chinese should ever be driven from the city (as they were from Tacoma), the simplest way to Americanize these streets again, would be to blow them up with dynamite and rebuild them — which would also perhaps be the best way for sanitary reasons. But while the main buildings and streets have been left as originally laid out, a number of side streets and narrow alleys — exact copies of those in China — have been created to connect them, and fill up every vacant yard and corner; for a Chinaman is not happy unless crowded as closely as salmon in an Alaskan creek. What adds to this effect of crowding is that all life and activity seems to be concentrated on the ground floor, no business being apparently carried on in the upper floors, which look uninhabited and empty, without window curtains, or shutters, or signboards, or other signs of habitation, excepting in the restaurants, whose outsides, from base to roof, are gayly and gaudily decorated, and illuminated at night with Chinese paper lanterns. The old stores with their large rooms have been subdivided into many smaller ones — some of them only fifteen to twenty feet wide or even less. The place of signboards is taken by the well-known wide scrolls of red paper with Chinese characters printed on them, and pasted vertically on the street side, while smaller ones are pasted on the windows. Some of the narrowest alleys have no stores, but only cheap eating-houses, gambling-places, and rows of barred windows, behind which wretched female slaves solicit passers-by. Among them are some rather pretty faces, but others are hideously marked by disease. In the gambling-dens domino-playing seems to be the favorite game. It is different from ours, though the blocks are similar, and some of the players are as expert in mixing and placing them, and as excited and flushed as the poker-players who monopolize the smoking-room on transatlantic steamers.

The principal impression given by Chinatown is that these Mongolians chiefly live to eat, though on looking at their provisions, one often wonders that they can eat and live. About two-thirds of all the stores are meat, fruit, or grocery stalls. The fruits and vegetables exposed for sale are mainly American varieties, though among them are some strange to our eyes. The bundles of long sticks tied together, seen everywhere, are sugar-cane from the Sandwich Islands, of which the Johns —and demijohns, as the boys are called—seem to be especially fond. Of watermelons, John seems to be as inordinately enamored as a negro. The butcher-shops have the largest collections of curiosities. Pork and poultry are the favorite meats of Chinamen, but they must of course do everything differently from our way. We smoke our pork and eat our poultry fresh; they eat their pork fresh and smoke their poultry. Smoked ducks, chickens, and geese are suspended everywhere as a bait to passing epicures. Dried and smoked fish, some from China, fill up large barrels, and some are eaten fresh. Poultry also is sometimes eaten fresh— at least certain parts, for in one heap on the counter you will see the entrails of chickens; in another, the combs and beards of roosters; and in a third, the heads and claws! Nothing is wasted. A frequent sight is a large tub filled to the brim with cold boiled rice. I bought a cake in a baker's shop, below the pavement, marked with neat Chinese letters. When I opened it, subsequently, I found that behind the inoffensive-look-ing crust it harbored rice and another finer grain, watermelon seeds, little pieces of bacon, several hazel-nuts, and some other mysterious ingredients. Obviously I had come across a sort of Chinese mince-pie. I didn't eat it. In another store I bought an album containing a collection of Japanese girls, some of them real beau-ties (the Chinese, I was informed, do not allow their women to be photographed), some very cheap silk hand-kerchiefs embroidered on both sides; and for seventy

cents an elegantly carved bamboo, shaped like a large
dude's cane and containing inside a telescoped fishing-
rod, which I subsequently found useful in trouting in
the brooks near Lake Tahoe.

An old man with a bookstall on the street, of whom
I bought an illustrated volume, altogether upset my
notions of Chinese morality. I asked him how much it
was, and understood him to say "four bits"; so I gave
him fifty cents and walked off with the book. But he
ran after me, and saying "*two* bits," gave me back a
quarter. His countrymen seemed to be pleased to see
me walking along with a Chinese book under my arm,
and several of them smiled and greeted me, which they
had not done before. The majority of the Chinese in
San Francisco belong, of course, to the lowest classes of
their race; but there are among them some of refined
and educated appearance, though I could not make out
whether those wearing goggles as large as butter-plates
thereby intended to convey the impression that their
eyes had been greatly injured by excessive study.
Women are frequently seen wobbling along the street,
dressed in blue or black blouses and baggy trousers,
almost like those of the men, though much wider.
Their deformed feet are placed on solid wooden soles
with embroidered silk above, and their faces are almost
as greatly deformed as their feet by the hideous Chinese
custom of combing the hair tightly back from the fore-
head. More numerous than the women are children of
both sexes, dressed in the most gaudy green, blue, and
other costumes and caps. Their round cherubic faces,
sparkling eyes, and fresh, healthy complexion present
a cheerful contrast to the sallow complexion, sunken
cheeks, and hollow eyes of the adults, victims of opium-
smoking and other forms of dissipation.

Chinatown in the daytime may be freely visited by the
" Melican " man and woman.   At night it is advisable
to take a policeman or a guide, and leave the women
at home, unless their nerves are shock-proof.   The
scene at night differs from that in the daytime; for
whereas in the morning Chinatown seems little more
than a big market-place, at night it is one vast barber-
shop in which half the population seems to be engaged
in shaving and mutilating the other half.   There are no
curtains; and if you stop a minute and look into one of
the tiny shops on the ground floor or in the cellar, you
will see a tonsorial artist deftly shaving his victim's
head, chin, eyebrows, lashes, nose, clean his ears, etc.
Perhaps you are standing this moment over a Chinese
dormitory; for space is expensive in so large a city, and
John utilizes every inch of it by making his bed under
the sidewalks.   We follow the guide into subterranean
haunts, down several flights of rickety stairs, to get a
peep at the opium-dens.   It is estimated that there is
only one Chinaman out of every five in San Francisco
who does not revel in his daily opium debauch, and
even that fifth man uses it occasionally as a sedative.
Some manage to get drunk on ten cents' worth a day,
while others need as much as a dollar's worth, of a
superior quality.   It was the ten-cent variety we saw
on this tour.   The guide occasionally drops a quarter
in certain places, and is in return allowed free access
with his protégés.   In dingy little rooms, not much
larger than a state-room in a steamer, there are several
bunks, in each of which lies or sits a Chinaman, in
varying stages of stupid intoxication.   Some are already
asleep, others are just lighting their pipes, and not one
of them pays the slightest attention to the intruders,

unless spoken to. One helpless old wreck lies on a
bundle of rags, which, the guide said, he has not left
for five years. His hands and face are mere bones
covered with yellow parchment, but he still has strength
and brains enough left to obey the guide when commanded to show us the process of opium-smoking by
holding a little lump of the drug in the flame of a small
lamp, where it burns and is turned round like sealing-
wax, and then stuffed into the small pipe and smoked,
the fumes being inhaled through the lungs and puffed
out through the nose. It is not a pleasant odor, but it
doubtless serves to disguise other odors infinitely worse.
The only ventilation in these rat-holes is a little slit,
six inches by two, above the door: yet here these
Asiatics spend the whole night, the lodging being included in the price of the opium. In one place we
passed through a kitchen with a closet in the middle of
it, but as a general thing we did not find subterranean
Chinatown as filthy as it has often been described; certainly not so bad as some of the places visited in New
York and London on "slumming" excursions. The
fear that Chinatown might become a breeding-place of
bacterial epidemics leads the sanitary authorities to
look well to their duties; and besides, San Francisco
never has any "hot waves," and its climate is in other
respects unfavorable to pestilential diseases, so that
Chinatown has not proved such a plague spot as it
might become under less favorable conditions.

Many tourists who are anxious to see the opium-dens
feel inclined to draw the line at the restaurants, at least
so far as eating there is concerned. But there are
Chinese restaurants in San Francisco which vie in elegance of furnishing and fine gilded carvings with the

most famous Parisian cafés. A good cup of tea can here be obtained, and there can be no harm in tasting the half-dozen kinds of preserves and cake served with it — all for twenty-five cents. There is preserved ginger, and small oranges, and pickled melon, China nuts and other delicacies, and a sort of oyster-fork to eat them with. In one of the rooms you will probably see several Chinamen eating a sort of ragout out of a large bowl, with chopsticks — every mouthful being first dipped into a kind of sauce. The bowl is held close to the mouth, to make the chopsticks less elusive substitutes for spoons. Eating with chopsticks is exciting and somewhat like fishing: you never know when you will get the next bite.

The thing to visit next is one of the temples, or Joss Houses, of which there are dozens in the city, some belonging to trade associations. Visitors are allowed to go behind the altars as close to the hideous idols as they please, the keepers themselves seeming to look upon their charge as a sort of dime museum; and as the admission is free, they try to earn an honest penny by selling little bundles of incense tapers to visitors.

It is getting late, and they are ready to lock the door after we are out; but the theatre is still a-going, and to that we now repair. As the floor is crowded, we walk right on to the stage, through a side gate, and sit down near the actors. Our presence does not jar with the scenery, as there is none of that commodity visible, unless it be the band, which occupies the centre of the stage and fills the air with Mongolian noise and dissonance. The instruments may be described as a gong or cymbals, a stick struck rapidly on a noisy board, and an embryonic banjo and violin which sounds like a hysterical oboe. Yet there is melody and harmony occasionally in these last two instruments, which almost incessantly accompany the actors' words, as in a modern music-drama, leaving their noisy neighbors to emphasize the murders and other striking episodes. The actors sometimes stand on the stage floor, sometimes on a chair or table. Their declamation is a sing-song in a high falsetto voice. There are no women, but the best actor is an impersonator of female rôles, and has his face painted and his hair combed back in the most "stylish" way. The faces of these actors are utterly void of expression. Having heard enough of their play, we went into the green-room, where one of the actors explained to us his costumes and their prices in China. In a corner there was tea on tap, to which every one seemed to resort at intervals of five minutes. We went out by the other stage door, and stood in the very centre of the stage, watching the musicians; yet our presence there did not seem in the least to disconcert the spectators, who, with hats on, were attending to the play with open-mouthed interest, though they never applauded or laughed or gave any other signs of approval or disapproval. Sometimes, however, they do throw cigar-ends and other objects at actors who offend them by their art or sentiments.

Dime museums, shooting-galleries, dirty little restaurants, cheap drug and clothing stores, and similar places generally mark the transition from Chinatown to San Francisco proper. In one or two streets the transition is of a different sort, leading gradually through more elegant Chinese stores and wholesale houses to the American quarters. San Francisco has many fine streets, in strolling through which one can easily believe the statements that the city has one-third of all the wealth on the Pacific Coast, harbors fifty millionnaires, and has exports including treasure to the value of more than a hundred million dollars a year. Such streets as Market, Kearney, Montgomery, and Post would attract attention even in Paris or London, and there is evidence of general prosperity in the numerous elegant residences as well as in the thronged business streets. Of late, an uneasy feeling has betrayed itself over the rivalry of the Canadian Pacific Railway and its harbor town, Vancouver, in attempting to secure the trade with Japan and China, the distance being somewhat in favor of Vancouver. But there is plenty of room for several large cities on the Pacific Coast; and San Francisco, having the only good harbor between San Diego and Puget Sound, need not be afraid of retrograding if the Canadians get some of the tea trade. Even if they should get the whole of the Asiatic trade, which is impossible, the handling and shipping of California wine, fruit, and agricultural products would suffice always to make San Francisco one of the three or four largest cities in America; and the opening of the Nicaragua Canal will give its trade a new and great impetus.

Market Street is the Broadway of San Francisco, but it differs from Broadway in New York in being as crowded in the evening as in the daytime. Yet the evening crowd is not the same as the day crowd, being bent on pleasure merely, like the multitudes which promenade in the alamedas of Spanish cities, late in the afternoon. San Franciscans are too busy to give up the afternoon hours to pleasure, so they have their daily street review and reception between eight and ten o'clock in the evening, during which hours Market Street is as crowded as Fifth Avenue on Sunday afternoons. The throng comes to an abrupt end a block or two above the Palace Hotel, and visitors stepping thence into a comparatively deserted street are apt to be surprised on suddenly finding that they have to elbow their way through a dense, moving mass of men and women. It seems strange that the crowd should not include the Palace Hotel in its promenading line, so as to give the guests in the large bay-windows, which make up the entire front of this immense structure, a chance to review it. San Franciscans are fond of boasting of this as being the largest hotel in the world, and one of the most sumptuously furnished, having cost about seven million dollars. Few cities, indeed, are so well supplied with good hotels as San Francisco, which has four of the first rank besides the Palace. There are accommodations and prices to suit all purses, but I do not believe there is another city in the world where one can get such an elegantly furnished, spacious room, with board, for three dollars a day, as on the upper floors of the Palace, where the air, light, and view are better than on the more expensive lower stories. The fare is generally good in these hotels, as it ought to be in the metropolis of a State which furnishes all the staples and delicacies of the table in abundance and always in season. Butcher's meat, however, as elsewhere on the coast, is frequently tough, and poultry seems to be exceedingly scarce or expensive, for it is seldom seen on the bill of fare. There are some restaurants, too, where good meals can be obtained; but it makes one indignant to find that even here in the chief city of California, some of the restaurateurs are too idiotic, or dishonest, or both, to furnish California wines under California labels at sensible prices. The California wines are there, of course, but under French labels and at fancy prices, varying from two to five dollars; whereas, if the wine (which is really much better and purer than nine-tenths of all imported French clarets) were honestly labelled, it could be sold at a quarter of those prices. The same humbug flourishes in most Eastern restaurants, but here one would think the mob would rise in its patriotic indignation and State pride, and summarily ·expel these short-sighted, swindling restaurateurs. Claret is so cheap by the gallon that it ought to be served free with meals, as in Spain, instead of that deadly American drink, ice-water.

There are cheap eating-houses in San Francisco where a poor man can get soup, meat, a dish of vegetables, and a glass of claret or beer,—all for ten cents. There is no exaggeration in Mr. J. S. Hittell's statement that " the wages of labor are still fifteen to thirty per cent higher than on the other side of the continent, and fifty to one hundred per cent higher than in Europe, while the cost of living is lower than in either." Notwithstanding Chinese competition (about which a great deal too much fuss is made in California, since the Chinamen are absolutely needed, especially in harvest-time), it is doubtless true that there are few places in the world where the laboring-man fares so well as here, owing to the cheapness of provisions and the ease with which a cheap suburban residence on the back hills or across the bay may be reached.

In the matter of picturesque suburbs, San Francisco is admirably supplied. Cross the bay in any direction, and you will find no end of fine sites for villas or towns, and the suburban capabilities of the islands which beautify the bay have hardly begun to be exploited. Every half-hour a large and comfortable ferry crosses the bay directly east to Oakland, noted as a city of elegant homes. A few miles beyond lies Berkeley, the Cambridge of California, being the site of the University of California. But neither Cambridge in New England nor in Old England has a view to compare with that obtainable from Berkeley University and the hills rising up behind it, — a view which includes San Francisco, the bay, looking like a large lake, and some fine mountain groups. Here is some of the best society to be found in the West, and connected with the University is a gallery and good library for the use of the students, whose ranks generally include seventy or eighty young women.

Another ferry runs from the city northward to the charming suburb of Saucelito, which, although but a few miles away, has a climate eight degrees warmer in winter than San Francisco, being sheltered by a high hill from the violent trade winds and the fogs which find free access through the Golden Gate, where they enter in order to take the place of the vacant spaces left by the rising of the air in the heated Sacramento Valley of the interior. Saucelito is the favorite picnic ground of San Franciscans, and it commands superb views of the bay and its islands, the city, and the Golden Gate. but its building-ground is limited, since the parts unsheltered by the wall of the hill are exposed, more even than the city opposite, to wind and weather. These trade winds and fogs constitute the greatest drawback of the climate of San Francisco, and make it unsuited for invalids, even in summer. For owing to the trade winds and the effect of the Japan current, arriving via Alaska, there are only seven days in a year when the thermometer rises to 80°; and the mean temperature of July is 60°, or 17° lower than in New York. Hence sea-bathing is a pleasure rarely indulged in near San Francisco, the temperature of the water being only 53° in July, — 10° or 12° lower than at Santa Barbara.

Eastern people, and especially Europeans, coming to California for climatic reasons are too apt to forget the immense size of this State and its infinite variety of climates. California, if transferred to the Atlantic Coast, would extend from Boston to Charleston, having as much coast line as in the East is divided between ten States. A year ago I crossed the ocean with an Englishman who was apparently in the last stages of bronchitis, and we agreed to meet in January at San Diego. He had not appeared in April, and I concluded he had died on the way across the Continent. But he had gone to San Francisco, where his trouble at once increased so much that he found himself in a worse condition than ever, and cursed the climate and the London physician who had sent him to California. Fortunately, a friend enlightened him on the diversity of climate in California, and he went to Santa Barbara, where I accidentally came across him, looking hale and vigorous, gaining weight, climbing hills, and eating like a bear. For persons with weak lungs, therefore, San Francisco is not a desirable residence; but for healthy folk it is an ideal climate, because the temperature is hardly ever oppressively warm or uncomfortably cold for those who are well supplied with flannels. If there are only seven days a year when the thermometer rises above 79°, there are, on the other hand, only five days in a year when it falls to the freezing-point. Such a climate breeds no numbness, lassitude, sultriness, *dolce far niente;* hence the San Franciscan is energetic, quick in his movements, but not morbidly nervous. The pale-faced fragile clerks and dudes of New York and Philadelphia would either die here of lung disease, or if "fit to survive" would soon assume the healthy, robust appearance of San Franciscans, to whose strong lungs the trade winds, which sweep the city and ever renew its atmosphere, are a tonic and a luxury.

IX.

LAKE TAHOE AND VIRGINIA CITY.

THE climatic conditions of San Francisco are anomalous and curious; shade trees, for instance, which are the greatest desideratum and blessing in Los Angeles, are not desired by San Franciscans, because the air is cool enough in summer without artificial shade. On the other hand, it is never so cold but that many semi-tropical plants will survive a whole winter in a sheltered situation outdoors; and San Francisco has in its public places some palm-trees high enough to attract attention even in San Diego. The avoidance of extremes is what constitutes the charm and value of the climate of San Francisco. But if the natives tire of this "golden mean," and desire to experience the extremes for the sake of variety, they can gratify their wish by a few

126

hours' ride on the Central Pacific Railroad. At Sacramento they may find the thermometer above ninety in May, and just beyond it a place where oranges ripen six weeks sooner than at Los Angeles ; while the station of Summit, a few hours further on, may be buried under four or five feet of snow, — an article almost unknown in San Francisco. Californians, however, are not greatly addicted to the habit of seeing the wonderful sights of their State, and such places as the Yosemite Valley, the Big Tree Groves, and Lake Tahoe owe their fame and vogue chiefly to Eastern and foreign tourists. There are now half-a-dozen transcontinental routes to choose between, so that it does not necessarily follow that every one crosses by the Central Pacific; but those who prefer the Northern or the Canadian Pacific should not neglect at least to patronize the Central Pacific to the extent of twenty dollars for a round-trip ticket, which includes the finest scenery along the whole road, — the semi-tropical Sacramento Valley, the sudden transition to the snow-crowned summit of the Sierra Nevada, the snow-sheds, Donner Lake, with a side excursion to Lake Tahoe, and the silver mines in Virginia County, Nevada. Lake Tahoe has been as often described as San Francisco ; but as every pair of eyes looks at the world from its own point of view, perhaps I may be allowed to tell briefly what I saw. Lake Tahoe has only been known a few decades, while the sights of Greece and Egypt were described two thousand years ago, and are still "written up" in newspapers and periodicals.

Until two years ago the time-tables of the Central Pacific were so arranged that the passengers lost all the fine mountain scenery between Sacramento and Reno in the darkness of the night, unless they took an emigrant train. Now, however, Donner Lake and the snow at Summit and Cape Horn, where the train rounds a mass of precipitious rock over an abyss two thousand feet below, and the thirty-four miles of snow-sheds, which cost the company three hundred and fifty thousand dollars, can be seen by getting up at five o'clock. Previous to this we come upon one of the curiosities of California, — a ferry-boat four hundred and twenty-four feet long and one hundred and sixteen wide, which carries the whole train across a branch of the San Francisco Bay, thirty miles from the city. It is dark, and the motion is imperceptible. "What are we stopping here for so long?" asks a lady of the porter. "We are on a ferry." "But why don't they start?" "Why, we are half-way over!" It must be admitted that although the change in the time-table is an improvement, much of the Sierra scenery still remains unseen, being hidden by the snow-sheds in which the train moves along mile after mile, as in an interminable tunnel. There are a few gaps and window-holes here and there, but not nearly enough to give the passengers a satisfactory view of either the mountains, or of the lovely Donner Lake. This lake is otherwise unfortunate in having the attention drawn from its fine elongated outlines and mountainous surroundings by the eternal tale which some one in every seat is sure to tell of the unfortunate Donner party of emigrants who were snowed in here, and lost thirty-four of their eighty-one members through cold and starvation; or else some one will begin to tell of big hauls of trout recently made, for Donner Lake is as full of trout as Tahoe, and more convenient to the city markets.

At Truckee we leave the train to connect with the

Tahoe stage. This is only a rough, lumbering town, but the laws of etiquette are enforced all the same; for in the hotel office a notice is posted, that "Gents are Requested to wear their Coats in the Dining-room." We comply with this rule the more readily as the temperature at this early morning hour, and at this height, offers no inducement for sitting in our shirt-sleeves. We find that although our train was on time, the stage with which we were to connect had left without us. The stage company is in an evil predicament. It has fifteen miles to cover between Truckee and Tahoe; and if it waits for the train, the boat at Tahoe City probably will not wait for it. However, an extra stage was provided for our party, and the driver informed us that if we had come a day sooner we should have been caught in a first-class snow-storm (this was about the middle of May). To-day, however, the sun was out bright and warm, melting the snow rapidly, without thereby improving the road. The trees still had on a snow-costume, fitting as snugly as if tailor-made, so that while there was not a speck in the blue sky, every gust of wind sprinkled us with a shower of loose snow and solid crystals. The extraordinary difference in California between shade and sunshine was prettily demonstrated by the fact that although the sun had already melted the snow on and near the small shrubs, little patches of it remained wherever a tiny isolated plant of six inches cast its little streak of shade.

The road keeps alongside of the rapid Truckee River, which forms the outlet of Lake Tahoe and connects it with the great Pyramid Lake in Nevada, — being, therefore, like the Niagara, not a river in the ordinary acceptation of the term, having its source directly in the springs or melting snows and its mouth in the ocean, but a mere connecting link between two fresh-water lakes entirely isolated from the ocean. As both these lakes are alive with trout, — Pyramid even more than Tahoe, owing to its greater size and difficulty of access, — it may be imagined that the Truckee is good fishing-ground. Not so good, however, as it used to be; for whereas formerly the trout used to come up the Truckee from Pyramid Lake in great numbers to spawn in Tahoe, a dozen dams are now in the way, impeding their progress; and the difference this makes is already so perceptible that last year the fish commissioners had to place half a million young trout in Tahoe, and this year a still larger number was to be put in, since in a lake twenty-two miles long and ten wide, half a million is after all a mere handful. Besides trout, there are many whitefish, suckers, chubs, and other fish in this river, and the driver showed us a deep pool in which some law-breaking Chinamen once killed over three thousand pounds of fish by a dynamite explosion.

The Truckee River is also utilized by the lumbermen to float their logs to market. We saw many of the loggers rolling in the timber and wading in the snow-water with their big rubber boots. They get five dollars a day and board, which is not too much, considering that their amphibious life in ice-water exposes them to rheumatism and pneumonia; while at the same time they are sure to earn their wages, since they have to keep at work briskly all the time in order to keep warm. Slides are to be seen on the mountain sides, on which the timber is shot down into the water, and the driver had a story of an Indian who once for a bottle of whis-key tobogganed down on one of these logs, saving himself by a plunge in the pool at the end.   It sounded like a "California story," but was told with so much circumstantial detail that we were forced to believe it. Near its outlet at the lake the river is dammed, and whenever desirable the floodgates are opened, and the rush of liberated waters carries the timber down to the station.

By and by, when the population of San Francisco has reached over half a million, this dam will doubtless be raised a few feet and the Truckee outlet converted into an aqueduct.   It will cost a neat little sum, for it takes the train eleven hours to come from San Francisco to Truckee; but the city needs the water, as its present supply is of poor quality and inadequate.   With Tahoe on tap, the San Franciscans will have the best water of all the cities in the world; for Tahoe has no equal in purity and clearness, its bottom being pure gravel, without a trace of slime or mud, so that stirring it with a cane does not cloud it the least shade.   But before the San Franciscans can get permission to swallow the Truckee River they will have to reckon with the Nevadans, who utilize it extensively for milling and irrigating purposes, and who, moreover, own the eastern half of Lake Tahoe.

Tahoe City is situated on the shore of the lake, not far from where it finds an outlet in the Truckee River. It consists of a dozen houses, including a "Grand Central Hotel" and a boarding-house, the latter being open all winter, while the hotel was closed when I was there. The boat which makes a round trip of the lake every day had left an hour before we arrived, so we were obliged to stay here till next morning.   But this was far from being a misfortune, for Tahoe City commands one of the finest views on the whole lake shore. Those who arrive in the morning are apt to feel that the lake does not quite come up to its reputation. It seems, indeed, a large, majestic body of water, and the knowledge that it lies as high above the level of the ocean as the summit of Mount Washington adds to its apparent grandeur; but the sun is on the wrong side, and the profiles of the mountains opposite do not stand out clearly enough. But in the afternoon, and especially towards sunset, when Tahoe City is in the shade, and all the light withdrawn from it seems to be concentrated on those mountain ridges, intensified by reflections from the glowing surface of the lake, then the snow-peaks do stand out superbly against the blue sky and the golden clouds; and the scene becomes truly sublime as we watch the faint, rosy sunset glimmer gradually climbing one summit after another, and fading away till only one tip retains its tinge, thereby proving that it is the highest of the peaks, though seemingly it is not. Knowing the rate of the sun's motion, why should it not be possible to measure the height of inaccessible mountains by thus watching the fading sunset glow on them? An old fisherman, to whom I described the Swiss *Alpglühen,* declared that he had never seen anything just like it at Tahoe, but the scene I had just witnessed was a very fair substitute for it.

Strolling along the shores of Tahoe one can enjoy a solitude as profound as if no human eye has ever before gazed on this liquid mountain mirror in a Sierra frame. A few logs here and there, in the water or washed ashore, are the only visible signs that man has ever been there. The faint, distant roar of a torrent, or the mocking of that sound by the melancholy voices of pines,

only intensifies the feeling of isolation. Two weeks previously I had been at the Yosemite, where the flowers and bushes were in full bloom; but Tahoe lies two thousand feet higher, and some distance farther north than that Valley, hence the season is later. The first flowers were just budding out here, and the smooth, alligator-skinned manzanita bush was only in flower, while at Yosemite it had already formed its "little apples" a fortnight sooner. There, too, the hotels were open in the middle of April, while of those on the shores of Tahoe only one had opened its doors for the season, and the fire was burning all day long in our little inn at Tahoe City. At the supper-table Nevada beef was neglected for the more succulent lake-trout. They are delicious, especially the silver trout: yet I saw a man at the next table commit the gastronomic atrocity of putting Worcestershire sauce on Tahoe silver trout. Then he called to the waiter-girl, a buxom, rosy-cheeked country maiden, for a tea-spoon — probably to eat it with. "Great Cæsar!" exclaimed the maiden. "Haven't you got a spoon? Why didn't you sing out?"

Next morning, as the little steamer starts with us on its round trip, a pleasant surprise is in store for us. As seen from Tahoe City the lake had seemed so perfect as to make us fancy we had seen about all there was of it. But hardly have we left the pier when new groups of snow-capped mountains, grander even than those we had been gazing upon, arise where before nothing had been visible but a dense, gloomy forest. And when we get far enough towards the middle of the lake to take it all in at a glance, we find that it is indeed a mountain lake, being shut in on all sides by giant peaks rising from nine to eleven thousand feet above sea-level. There is reason to believe that the site of the present lake was once a monstrous volcanic crater. It is now a reservoir in which is stored the outflow of more than fifty brooks and creeks, which drain an area of about five hundred square miles of mountains, and its depth is from fifteen hundred to eighteen hundred feet — water enough to extinguish a crater of even such vast size. It is a curious fact that this lake, though lying more than a mile above sea-level and surrounded by snow-fields, never freezes, even in the coldest Sierra midwinter. Perhaps this is due to the frequent squalls which agitate its surface and prevent the ice from gaining a foothold. These squalls, blowing down the cañons, make sailing on the lake somewhat risky at any time in the year, and tourists desiring a Christian burial for their mortal remains will do well to avoid sail-boats, because the bodies of those who are drowned here are never recovered, the coldness of the water preventing decomposition and the formation of gases which would bring them to the surface.

The steamboat, however, does not fear these squalls, which seem to strike only certain limited portions of the lake at a time. It makes half-a-dozen or more stops at points where there are summer hotels, which are open from about the middle of May to the end of October. Tallac's opens a few weeks earlier, and I made that my headquarters for a few days. The superb view from here includes Mt. Tallac, highest of the Tahoe peaks, bearing on its hollow sides dazzling Alpine snow-fields, so large that one looks instinctively for solid ice-rivers at its lower end; but the California summer sun does not tolerate perennial glaciers even at these Sierra heights, and the straggling pine-trees sticking up like stubbles here and there through the lower névés indicate that not even these snow-fields are eternal like those of Switzerland or Alaska. But in early May the scene is still quite Alpine, especially the immense snow-ridge with perpendicular sides, which resembles the snow-wall that connects the Mönch with the Jungfrau as seen from Mürren.

Tallac's is the largest of the hotels on Tahoe, but not large enough to indicate that San Franciscans come here in vast crowds during the season. The reason is obvious. Though scenically incomparable, Tahoe is not in midsummer as cool a place as San Francisco, which, during July and August, is the coolest place on the Pacific Coast. Were Tahoe within eleven hours' ride of sultry New York, there would be a score or two of hotels on its bank in place of half-a-dozen. Residents say it was Eastern tourists who made Tahoe the resort it is now. Tallac's is situated in the midst of a primitive mountain wilderness, and tourists anxious to see a wild animal in its native haunts will have no great difficulty in gratifying their curiosity. One day I set out to climb part way up the mountain which begins to rise about a mile or so behind the hotel. I followed a cow-path, but it soon was lost in a swamp which is fed by snow-water brooks, and which I had some difficulty in crossing. Beyond the swamp, on beginning to climb the mountain, I soon found myself in the midst of thousands of manzanita bushes, which presented a curious spectacle. The branches were bowed down by heavy snow, which formed a continuous layer over them thick enough apparently to walk on. But appearances were deceptive; for as soon as I came into contact with the bushes, the snow slipped off, the liberated branches flapped against my face, and I was surprised to find them covered with blossoms. To add to the contrast, several butterflies were flitting about in the warm sunlight. It takes California for such odd mixtures of the seasons, — snow-fed swamps haunted by mosquitoes, flowering bushes bowed down by snow, under a blue sky, and visited by butterflies.

The finishing touch was given by a large cinnamon bear, who suddenly hove in sight only a few hundred yards below me. As these bears are considered quite as vicious and aggressive, at certain times, as grizzlies, and having no means of defence except an olive walking-stick, I concluded not to molest the poor beast, but edged off quietly to the left, unseen, and made my way back through the trackless jungle of the swamp. In the evening I met two ladies who had been out alone in the afternoon for a walk, and had seen "a large yellowish animal with a slender body and a long tail." They changed color on hearing that it was undoubtedly a California lion, and made a vow never again to go into the woods alone. A small boy who is attached to the hotel as a guide for brook-trouting parties told us his bear story, which had a somewhat more dramatic climax than mine. He went fishing alone one day, and having found a good place, he tied his horse to a tree, and started up the creek. Suddenly he heard a crackling and whining noise near him, and at the same moment a cinnamon bear thrust her head through the brush. A small tree being close at hand, the boy climbed out of reach just as the bear arrived at its foot. She was in a dangerous mood because she had her two cubs with her; but it was to the cubs that the boy owed his release; for after a moment they became impatient and moved away, and the old bear followed them. As soon as they were out of sight, he slid down the tree, ran for his horse, and thus survived to tell the tale.

The same boy assured me that he had seen trout caught in the lake weighing twenty-two, twenty-four, and twenty-nine and three-quarters pounds respectively. This being both a fish story and a California story, seemed a tough combination; but in the morning he took me out in a boat to fish, and as luck would have it, we were followed for a time by a monstrous trout which must have weighed fully twenty-five or thirty pounds. He would not take the bait, however, and such monsters are not often caught, the average catch being from one to three pounds. I caught three in a couple of hours, weighing together about four pounds, and that seemed to be considered a good catch at the hotel for that season. Fishing luck at Tahoe varies greatly with the season, the time of day, and the knowledge and skill of the fisherman. The best place to throw the line is just where the water becomes so deep that the bottom is no longer visible. Row slowly all the time, and let out a very long line, with a very bright silver spoon, to attract the game. The bright spoon seemed to be of prime importance; for I had one and caught three fish, while the boy, who had a dull spoon, did not get a bite. Whole minnows are used as bait, and the catching of these in a brook, or in the lake with bread crumbs and a net, gives employment to a thin, mummified old Indian who haunts the premises.

Another local character is old Yank, who formerly owned Tallac's and now has built a rival hotel on a smaller scale near by. Yank is eighty-two years of age, and he presents a unique sight, standing upright in his boat, propelling it with one oar and jerking his fish-line with the other hand. His clothes are greasy rags and tatters, and he himself boasts that his baths are about as frequent as the blossoming of the century plant. Yet his cheeks are rosy, his frame vigorous, his voice firm, and eyes sparkling, bearing eloquent testimony to the tonic value of the combined lake and mountain air of Tahoe. He has lived here more than a quarter of a century. With pride he showed me some boats lying in the yard which he had constructed and painted with his own hands, and the use of which was to be free to the guests (this was aimed at the other hotel). He seemed to feel somewhat conscious of his tramplike appearance, and explained that those were only his winter clothes, and that as the season opened he would have to dress up "on account of the ladies." An enormously fat and large dog is his companion. "Fat?" he exclaimed, echoing my exclamation, — "fat? You ought to see my wife!"

The salubrious Tahoe air is responsible for an appetite which would fatten a consumptive. But if the dinner-bell coincides with sunset and its concomitant celestial fireworks, it would be an exhibition of the purest animality to go and eat. The end of the long pier is a good place to see the colored sunset clouds, but better still is it to take a boat and row a mile or two from shore. About sunset the wind usually subsides, and Tahoe becomes as placid and perfect a mirror as the famous Mirror Lake in the Yosemite, but on an infinitely larger scale. Here are not only mountain peaks and pine-wooded shores reflected in the water, but the whole sky, with its sunset clouds, more brilliantly colored and more fantastically shaped than anywhere in the world, is mirrored below. The earth no longer seems a hemisphere, but a perfect symmetrical globe with the spectator in the centre, floating on the invisible water like a disembodied spirit. I have never been up in a balloon, but I do not believe that even ballooning can make one so vividly realize what must be the sensations of an eagle soaring with outspread, motionless wings through the azure ether. However, Tahoe does not need these colored cloud reflections as borrowed plumes to adorn itself with. Its own varied and ever-changing surface-colors are equally enchanting, though more sombre and melancholy. There are several zones of color. The shore is lined with sand, coarse as bird-shot and clean as the water itself, and for a distance of several hundred yards this sand is visible as we row into the lake, corrugated by the waves like the tiny furrows in the palms of our hands, and giving the water a yellowish tint. Farther in, it becomes blue, gradually shading into so deep a hue that we are ready to believe that a ship with a cargo of indigo must have gone down here, and feel tempted to dip a pen into it to see if it will do to write with; but dip up a glassful, and it is as clear and colorless as if it had just spouted from an artesian well, and as cold.

An artist endowed with the courage to reproduce these colors realistically would surely be denounced by the critics as a visionary idealist. But no artist could ever paint them as they appear to the eye, because no palette has ever held colors so rich and deep and at the same time so delicate and transparent. And still less than the sombre brilliancy of these colors could a painter reproduce an idea of their movements, in which lies half their charm. Cloud shadows climbing up a mountain side are a fascinating sight, but not to be compared with the spectacle of the irregular patches of color that are chased by the wind across the crests of the Tahoe wavelets, like semi-liquid purple, green and violet mists, vanishing in the distance into air, and followed by other color-waves in rapid succession. The best place to enjoy this unique spectacle is not in front of the hotel, where the trees act as a wind-break, but to the left, near the first bridge. As I stood here the first morning, a brisk breeze was blowing, with a clear blue sky overhead. Looking leewards, the water nearest the shore appeared gray, bordered by a light violet, with yellowish and purple patches; then came a deep green streak, followed by a broader indigo band, and finally a deep violet field, bounded by a faint mist raised a little above the surface of the water and slightly veiling the mountains. Every morning the details were new, and would have been so, no doubt, had I remained four hundred instead of four days. Tourists go into raptures over the waving motions of the Western wheat-fields, but what are these monochromes to the polychromatic waves that chase one another across Tahoe?

In making the circuit of the lake, we had passed a place where a railway was seen climbing up the steep lake-side, not far from the little town of Glenbrook. This railroad is a connecting link between Lake Tahoe and the distant silver mines at Virginia City. At first sight the connection between an inclined railway on the shore of Lake Tahoe and the Virginia City silver mines seems as enigmatic as that pointed out by Darwin as existing between old maids and clover-fields. But the mystery is easily explained. Nevada is as treeless as the greater part of Spain; wherefore the miners have to come to California for fuel, and for planks to build their shafts.   Lake Tahoe is surrounded by densely wooded hills which are gradually being denuded to supply the demands of the Nevadan miners.   The logs are floated across the lake, hauled up the hill on the railway, and cut up into boards and planks, which are thence floated down in a V-shaped flume to Carson, whence they are taken by another mountain railroad to Virginia City. No visitor to Tahoe should fail to follow these planks to Carson and beyond — not necessarily in the flume, but by taking the stage at Glenbrook.   The stage road to Carson is dusty, but most interesting.   The first half of it is all up hill, the second half of it is all down hill, and the distance fourteen miles.   Just before we reach the summit, Tahoe once more shows its face and casts a parting glance at us.   Then we get a splendid view of the Carson Valley, deep down below us, and walled in on the other side by chain upon chain of bare, desolate, lofty mountain ridges.   Unprotected by tree or stump, the snow has melted from even the highest peaks, and the snow-peaks which we see later (and which seem to justify the name of Nevada or "snowy") are in California.   We stop at a wayside inn for a moment, and a comely young girl asks the driver if there is "room for one more."   But a stage is not a street car, and the driver had to confess that he was "afraid not, Nellie, unless one of the men will hold you on his lap."   Nellie looked non-committal; and if none of the passengers spoke and offered to take her, this was surely owing to bashfulness, and not to a lack of gallantry.

Once or twice the driver stopped to collect a letter that had been placed in a box fixed on a post by the the roadside.   To prevent useless stoppages and delay, these letter-boxes are uncovered, and the depositor has to take his chances of rain, which, however, are hardly worth considering in summer. Frequently we cross the flume, or drive alongside of it, but of course it makes a shorter cut to Carson than the stage-road, and in some places descends at such a steep angle that the timber in it is said to be carried along at railroad express speed. Half a million feet of timber can be thus floated down in a day, provided there are none of those jams which sometimes extend for half a mile along the flume and cause much trouble. Just before entering Carson we come to the end of the flume, where the timber is dropped, and piled up in rows of interminable length. The Carson Valley, through which we had been passing, is dry, dusty, and entirely devoid of trees, and the town, therefore, with its surrounding green meadows and fine rows of shade trees lining the streets, seemed like an oasis in the desert.

Carson, the capital of Nevada, has some good public buildings, and about four thousand inhabitants, but is not likely ever to have many more. It was crowded on this occasion with visitors from the country, and Piute Indians with their squaws and pappooses were loitering at every street corner. The monstrous, startling circus posters pasted everywhere explained this influx from the country and neighboring towns. It was nothing more nor less than Sells Brothers' "Enormous United Shows"; "A Grand Olympian Festival"; "The Eureka of Canvas Entertainments"; "Prodigious, Overshadowing, and Enormous"; "Gigantic, Sweeping, and Brilliant Centralization of Sterling and World-Endorsed Entertainments"; "Fully a Century in Advance of all Contemporaries." I bowed my head in awe on reading these announcements.

The appearance of the women and girls in this circus crowd did not seem to indicate that the climate of Carson Valley is invigorating, or its resources fattening. Though they wore white dresses, they looked so thin and sharp that it seemed a wonder the strong wind did not carry them off bodily. On account of the circus there were extra trains, but not enough cars, so that half the passengers had to stand. 'Twas always so, said a local privileged jester; " You never can get enough of Carson." This train, en route for Virginia City, took home those who had attended the matinée. For the evening performance another extra train was to be sent down all the way from Virginia City, which appears not to have held out sufficient inducements to the circus company to come up, so that " it served them right if they got left and had to come down to Carson," as one of the passengers remarked, with much feeling. This railroad from Carson to Virginia affords one of the most marvellous and entertaining rides in the world. The puffing of the engine would tell a blind man how steep is the grade all the way up; and how crooked and winding the road is, may be inferred from the printed notice to employees that fifteen miles an hour is the highest speed allowed. Sometimes the engineer might almost shake hands with a man on the last platform; and there is a story of an engineer who jumped off the locomotive on seeing a red light straight ahead, which proved to be the lantern on his last car. Some one has added these curves together and found that between Carson and Virginia passengers travel seventeen times round the circle. Several miserable shanty villages are passed, half buried in empty tin cans, and as we get up higher the outlooks become more and more desolate and rugged.   Even Arizona has nothing more bleak and naked than these endless vistas of Nevadan mountains.   No tree or other vegetation, except coarse sage bush.   Yet the soil is said to be fertile, and to need only water to make it valuable.   Deep down in the cañon below us, where the Carson River winds along, this statement is verified by the green fields and orchards which border it.   Interminable wooden steps lead down from the railroad stations to these oases. "With water," says a Nevadan, "all the mountain sides may be made veritable hanging gardens"; and all that is needed for this metamorphosis is to store the winter water in artificial cañon-reservoirs for summer tapping.

We are also told that between these forbidding bare mountain ranges lie valleys from one to thirty miles in width, but hidden by the intervening ridges, so that the State as a whole is really not so forbidding as it looks.   Little, however, has been done so far in agricultural development, and Nevada is still almost exclusively a mining State.   Were it not for the mines and the mineral deposit in dry lake-beds, there would be no railway except the Central Pacific; and as the mines now worked are much less productive than formerly, it is not surprising that Nevada should be the only Western State whose population is decreasing.

It cost about three million dollars to build the Virginia and Truckee Railroad, from Reno, on the Central Pacific, to Virginia City — a distance of fifty-two miles, although a bee-line would make it only about seventeen miles.   Three millions may seem a big sum for so short a road, but it led to a region whence more than three hundred and fifty million dollars in gold and silver have been taken by mule, ox-team, stage, and rail, since the discovery of the Comstock Lode, thirty years ago. Should the mines ever become exhausted, it would be worth while, though it might not pay, to keep up the road as a scenic route. As we near the mining regions, the mountain scenery becomes more and more stupendous. We pass through a few tunnels, and suddenly a most unique view is spread out before us : a series of immense wooden buildings scattered picturesquely along the mountain sides, like mediæval castles, though without towers or other architectural features. Smoke is belched forth from the high chimneys, and by the side of every such building is a huge gray mound of waste ore, —the accumulation of years. Other mounds are seen where there are no buildings, but only holes into the mountain side, looking as if some gigantic animal had been burrowing and thrown out the soil. These mounds are graves in which some miners' dreams of millions are buried.

As the train winds along and up the hill-side, these sights disappear and reappear repeatedly, in different groupings, till at last we come to Silver City, the first of the three towns which perch closely together on the side of the silver mountain, Mt. Davidson, about seventeen hundred feet above the river, and as far from the summit. Mining is not as profitable here as it was formerly, and as it is now a few miles beyond; but there are many small gold veins. "Nearly every head of a family in the town," says the guide-book, "has his own mine; and when he wants money, he shoulders his pick, goes out to his mine, and digs it, as a farmer in the East digs a 'mess' of potatoes."

Two miles beyond Silver City is Gold Hill, which

once had as many inhabitants as Virginia City has now,
— eight thousand, — but has only about three thousand
at present. At Virginia City, many pleasant surprises
are in store for us. In this aërial town, built like an
eagle's nest on the side of a rocky mountain, surrounded
in all directions by similar bleak mountains without a
sign of civilization or habitation on them, you naturally
expect to take up lodging in a one-story shanty, eat
canned beef, and sleep on a cot; but nothing of the
sort. Crawling up the hill—everything is up and
down hill here — a few hundred steps, you come to
the International Hotel, six stories high, with elegantly
furnished rooms, and fare good enough for the very
reasonable charges. It stands in the principal business street, which is lined on both sides with not
only such indispensable places as drug stores, grocers'
and butchers' shops, but with fine jewelry and fancy
stores, and even book and music stores. Elegantly
dressed women, many of refined appearance, promenade
the streets, bent on shopping; and, by way of contrast,
there are groups of squaws sitting on the rubbish on
corner lots, or following their lords and masters.

Every block, of course, has its saloon; for aside from
the naturally bibulous propensities of miners, the great
dryness of the air at this elevation creates an irresistible
thirst every hour, so that the bar-keepers must do a
thriving business. Excepting this elevation of over six
thousand feet, there is little here to mitigate the action
of the sun's rays, which in summer must be intolerable.
The trees are not high enough to afford much shade,
having been destroyed, like everything else, in the great
fire of 1875. But that fire, which annihilated the town,
as usual taught a good lesson, and now there is a hydrant

at every corner whence water can be forced high above the highest building by its own pressure, no engine being needed. The waterworks of Virginia are perhaps the most interesting in the world — both above and below ground. The pipe which bridges the Washoe Valley is seven miles long and has a capacity of over two million gallons a day. This water had to be brought over to Mt. Davidson from the main range of the Sierra Nevada, because there was not enough on the surface of Davidson. Below the surface, on the other hand, there was an ocean of unwelcome water, hot and cold, which constantly filled up the shafts and had to be pumped out at an enormous expense. To overcome this trouble, the Sutro tunnel was built 1650 feet below the surface, and almost four miles in length. Ten million gallons of water have passed through this tunnel in twenty-four hours. A day or two can be profitably spent in seeing these hydraulic wonders, besides the reducing mills, with their ingenious machinery, in which electricity is yearly playing a more important part, economizing power by transmitting it at different points from the Sutro tunnel, and preventing waste by superior processes of amalgamation. Of course no tourist must fail to don a miner's suit in order to experience a sensation like that of falling from a balloon in descending a shaft, and to feel a heat more stifling than a desert blast. It is the strangest thing about this strange mountain city that you need only walk a block or two from any given point to find a place where you can descend from two to three thousand feet into the bowels of the earth, till the six-foot opening at the top appears no bigger than a hand.

The miners only work a few hours every day, and

you understand why when you come back to daylight bathed in perspiration. After waiting long enough to cool off, climb to the top of Davidson. Contrasts are always pleasant; and none more so than this transition from half a mile in the dark interior of this planet to the summit of a mountain which rises a mile and a half above sea-level. Davidson is isolated, like the Rigi, and the view is therefore very extensive, embracing a large portion of Nevada. On one side is a fine circle of Sierra snow-peaks; on another, Washoe Lake, and the green meadows along the Truckee River; all of which, however, — snow, meadow, and lake, — form mere oases amid the barren wastes of illimitable gray mountain ranges. A flag-pole has been erected on the summit of Davidson, and the way in which it is fastened by means of granite blocks piled on high and iron chains on every side, indicates the strength of the winter storms at this altitude.

X.

MT. SHASTA AND CRATER LAKE.

THE OREGON AND CALIFORNIA RAILROAD — CALIFORNIA'S GRANDEST MOUNTAIN — ISOLATED PEAKS OF THE CASCADE RANGE — VOLCANIC REMNANTS — SISSON'S — INDIANS AT HOME — SOURCES OF THE SACRAMENTO — EFFECTS OF RAIN — OREGON'S NUMEROUS RIVERS — FISH AND CRAW-FISH — SOUTHERN OREGON — A MYSTERIOUS MOUNTAIN LAKE — THE OREGON NATIONAL PARK — THE WILLAMETTE VALLEY — OREGON WHEAT AND FRUIT.

WITH the exception of the Canadian Pacific and the Rio Grande, there is no railway on this continent which offers to tourists such a unique and imposing variety of mountain and forest scenery as the Oregon and California, or Shasta Route, which connects San Francisco with Portland. For many hours after leaving Sacramento, the train follows the banks of the Sacramento River, whose water in this upper part of its course is as clear as the Rhine in Switzerland. No fewer than eighteen times does the train cross the winding river, which at every turn offers a new picturesque view. But it is not till Mt. Shasta comes into view that the real grandeur of this route is made evident. Mr. Bryce, in his "American Commonwealth," insinuates that there is little fine scenery in this country; but if there is another railroad in the world which skirts the base of an isolated snow mountain over fourteen thousand feet in height,

and so vast in circumference that it takes the train five
or six hours to get around it, I have not seen it or heard
of it; and Shasta is only one of half-a-dozen snow-peaks
which may be admired on this route and its continu-
ation north to Tacoma and Seattle. There is something
absolutely unique about what may be called the Oregon
System of mountain peaks (since Oregon once embraced
all this region), beginning with Shasta (14,440 feet), in
Northern California, and including the Three Sisters
(8,500), Mts. Jefferson (9,000) and Hood (11,200)
in Oregon, and Mts. St. Helen's (9,750), Adams (9,570),
and Tacoma (14,444) in Washington. Elsewhere, as in
Switzerland, or along the Canadian Pacific Railway,
snow-peaks are always adjacent or jumbled together in
irregular groups; and this is the case even in the Sierra
Nevada of Central California. But the 'Oregon' earth-
giants, from Shasta to Tacoma, are all isolated peaks,
separated by many miles from other peaks, with only a
low range of mountains to connect them; and this gives
them a grandeur and individuality which is lacking in
peaks that simply form one of an irregular group. As
Mr. Joaquin Miller poetically puts it: " Here, the
shining pyramids of white, starting sudden and solitary
from the great black sea of firs, standing as supporting
pillars to the dome of intense blue sky, startle, thrill,
and delight you, though you have stood unmoved before
the sublimest scenes on earth."

It is owing to this isolation that Shasta is the grandest mountain in California. Mt. Whitney is several
hundred feet higher, but it stands in a region where
there are a hundred peaks each over thirteen thousand
feet in height, and therefore is not able to assert itself
properly. Moreover, Whitney is several hundred miles

further south, where the solar heat disposes of the snow-fields every summer, and does not compel them to seek the valley in the shape of glaciers; whereas Shasta has five glaciers, one of which is more than three miles long. Jefferson, Hood, and Tacoma also have fine glaciers, easily accessible.

As compared with the mountains of Switzerland, Shasta has this advantage: that whereas the former rarely, even in summer, have the advantage of standing out against a clear blue sky, which adds so very much to the sublimity of the scene, Shasta rears its snowy head day after day and month after month into the cloudless azure. Late in summer, however, it loses some of its grandeur through the melting of most of its snow-fields; and in this respect Mt. Hood is superior to Shasta, as it keeps its snow-mantle throughout the usual Oregon summer. Besides the California sun, the snows of Shasta have another enemy in the internal volcanic heat which has not yet subsided. Shasta has its big craters, and there are a score of smaller ones in the lower neighboring cones. A few hundred feet below the summit there is a hot sulphur spring, to whose heat John Muir and Jerome Fay, being caught in a snow-storm in 1875, owed the preservation of their lives.

One of the best ways to realize the great height of Shasta, is by noting the very long time the sun lingers on the mountain side after it has set at Sisson's, in Strawberry Valley, — fully half an hour. After it has gone down, on dark nights in May, a solitary star will arise immediately over the summit, looking at first as if some venturesome climber had started a fire, dwarfed by the distance. One does not realize how jagged are the ridges of Shasta until the evening sun casts their gray silhouettes on the adjacent white snow-fields.

All this can be seen from the porch of Mr. Sisson's hotel — the same hotel that used to feed the passengers and the horses of the stages so many years before the Oregon and California Railroad was built; and the same Mr. Sisson who, twenty years ago, served as Clarence King's guide up the mountain. Mr. Sisson now has the satisfaction of seeing quite a respectable village which has grown up in the picturesque spot selected by him a quarter of a century ago; but he no longer has the strength to act as guide; nor does he need to, as he is well-to-do. Accordingly, I had to content myself with one of the Indians in his employ, as guide up the mountain side. May is too early to make the complete ascent, but we thought we could get above the timber line at any rate. But even this proved impossible, owing to the deep masses of snow which carpeted the sombre forest at a height of eight thousand feet. Yet the trip proved worth taking without the final climb. The path led through the densest imaginable forest, and was impeded every five minutes by a fallen tree. In looking at the millions of dead trees which rot on the ground in these California and Oregon forests, one cannot suppress the thought, "What a blessing this wood would be to the starving, freezing thousands in our large cities, during the winter months!"

It is this superabundance and natural waste of wood everywhere that breeds indifference in the people of this coast and the natives to the devastating forest fires which occur every summer. My Indian guide amused himself by setting trees on fire in several places, and to

MOUNT SHASTA.

the question why he did this, I could get no satisfactory answer. He also very kindly tried to amuse me by rolling huge rocks down a tremendous precipice. I should have been less surprised than hurt had he thrown me down too, in retaliation for the injury inflicted on him and his race by the intruding white man, who has reduced the former lords of this region, where they could hunt and fish to their heart's content, to the condition of day-laborers earning their bread by the sweat of their brow. How galling it must be to the noble savage to have to dig stumps and level roads while his squaws look on, because, forsooth, the perverse white man will not permit the squaws to do the grubbing, and him to look on!

Mr. Sisson took me to a small Indian camp near his house, where he wanted to engage a man for a job. The young buck was gorgeously arrayed in a pair of old trousers and a new linen shirt, evidently just arrived from San Francisco, with its bosom starched stiffly enough for a city dude. He was obviously conscious of this ornament, and, probably in consequence of it, wanted more money for the job than Mr. Sisson had previously paid him. *Noblesse oblige!* The squaws, young and old, and the children, were all very fat, dirty, and stupid-looking, and were crowding around a fire, eating fried meat and flat, round cakes of dough baked in a pan, looking as if it would give chronic dyspepsia to an ostrich or a goat. I was also shown an Indian hut where there had been a dance on the preceding Fourth of July, white visitors being charged twenty-five cents admission.

One of the most interesting places Mr. Sisson has to show his guests is the source of the Sacramento River.

About a mile from his house, at a place to which steps lead down from the railway track, the water rushes out from several springs in a great volume, forming immediately a trout-brook of respectable size, which hurries away in the new daylight, as if glad to have escaped its subterranean source. These springs issue from under Mt. Shasta, and doubtless owe their being to the melting of snow and glacier ice by the internal volcanic heat — a worthy origin of so romantic a river as the Sacramento. Near these springs is a valuable iron-water spring, which also belongs to Mr. Sisson, and is one of his most important possessions, now that the town founded by him is getting to be a regular resort for San Franciscans, Portlanders, and Eastern tourists, not only on account of the view of Shasta, but because of the beautiful forest scenery, and the excellent trout-fishing in the neighboring McCloud River. Six large rivers and many smaller ones are born of Shasta and neighboring peaks, and it is these icy streams that the trout and the salmon delight in. The Sacramento itself, however, does not afford any sport in this vicinity.

After leaving Sisson's, Shasta still remains in sight for some time; for it takes some time even for a railway to get away from a mountain, of which it has been remarked that "if it could be sawed off at the four-thousand-foot level, or five hundred feet above the valley, the oval plain thus made would be eighty miles in circumference." Some of the views of Shasta after leaving Sisson's are even grander than at the station, and in certain atmospheric conditions the snow-cone may be seen floating, as it were, on a mystic haze resembling water. The aspect of the mountain gradually changes, and what had seemed smooth, gradual slopes are now seen to be rugged precipices rising one above the other.

We now approach that mammoth fragrant forest between the Pacific Ocean and the Cascade Mountains which is known as Oregon, and it becomes obvious at once that the chief difference between Oregon and California is comprised in the word RAIN. Shortly after crossing the Oregon line evidence begins to multiply that we have entered the rain belt. There are more deciduous trees, more ferns and mosses, more underbrush in the pine forests, and, most significant of all, more rivers. California has in its whole coast line of seven hundred miles only one navigable river, while Oregon, with a coast line of only three hundred and fifty miles, has four fine navigable rivers, — the Rogue, the Umqua, the Willamette, and the Columbia, — with many smaller ones. All of these run from east to west, except the Willamette, which divides the State by flowing northward into the Columbia near Portland, thus creating the fertile Willamette Valley, to which Portland chiefly owes its wealth.

The Willamette has some tributaries which alone would make the fortune of several counties in Southern California, where nothing can be done without irrigation; whereas in Oregon no one but vegetable gardeners ever thinks of such a thing. One of these tributaries is the Pudding River, along the banks of which many charming scenes may be enjoyed, and which is full of fish, which, however, have the peculiarity that they never take a bait. In the Santiam and some of the other rivers the fishing is excellent, and the creeks are full of trout and of crawfish, which are delicious, and of which I have caught as many as a hundred in an hour, with three strings and three pieces of beef. A favorite form of picnicking in Oregon is to take a sauce-pan and salt, catch a few hundred of these tender and juicy crawfish, boil them, and enjoy a feast fit for prelates.

The rain, to which Oregon owes its numerous rivers and creeks, is not as abundant in the southern as in the northern part of the State. There is a gradual transition from thirty-two inches at Jacksonville to thirty-eight at Salem, fifty-three at Portland, and seventy-two at Astoria. The Rogue River Valley climate has been described as "a compromise between the droughts of California and the great rain of the Willamette Valley." Grapes are raised here equal to the best in California, and the peaches have been known to fetch higher prices in the San Francisco market than the California varieties. Melons also are raised here in great abundance for the Portland market, Northern Oregon (where the thermometer sometimes does not register above 85° during a whole summer) being too cold for their successful cultivation. Southern Oregon is at present but thinly settled; but if its climatic, scenic, and agricultural advantages were generally known to immigrants, it would fill up rapidly.

Two large lakes, the Upper and Lower Klamath, will in course of time become popular resorts of Oregonians, and some miles north of the Upper Klamath is Crater Lake, which, although much smaller, is by the Oregonians considered the greatest curiosity on the Pacific Coast, and which used to be, and still is, regarded as holy ground by the Indians of the neighborhood. Local authorities tells us that "in the past none but medicine men visited it; and when one of the tribe felt called to become a teacher, he spent several weeks at the lake, in prayer to the Shahulah Tyee."

Crater Lake lies in the heart of the Cascade Mountains, and at so great an elevation — 6,257 feet — as to be rendered inaccessible, except in summer, by the depth of the snow in the surrounding forests. It is about one hundred and twenty miles from Ashland, and may be reached from that city, or from Medford, by stage. The road follows the banks of the tumultuous Klamath River, and passes through the Klamath Indian Reservation, near Fort Klamath, which was abandoned in 1889, as being no longer necessary. A narrow defile known as Mystic Cañon is also of interest, and it is well to bear in mind that in the older guide-books Crater Lake is put down as Mystic Lake. Mystic it certainly is, but its present name is preferable because more definite; for Crater Lake is really a body of water which, like Lake Tahoe, fills up a volcanic orifice. And a most gigantic crater it was, for the circumference of the lake is more than twenty miles. There is only one place where one can climb down to the water; the rest of the shore consists of precipitous walls from fifteen hundred feet to three thousand feet in height, which are less slanting than they appear in photographs. These high walls, which are mirrored in the water with their fringe of trees, effectually shut out the mountain breezes, so that the water is placid, and rarely ruffled. There is something mysterious about this water; for it has no visible or discoverable inlet or outlet, and yet it is always clear and sweet. Fish, however, do not inhabit it, probably because none ever succeeded in getting there; and even water-fowl, it is said, avoid this solitary, silent mountain lake. In the middle of the lake stands an island, about three miles long, of volcanic origin, rising to a point eight hundred and forty-five feet high, and ending in a crater four hundred and seventy-five feet in diameter. There are caves along the shores which may have some connection with the water-supply, as a current is observable near them. The depth of the lake has never been ascertained, but it has been sounded for two thousand feet without reaching bottom.

A few years ago an effort was made to have the Crater Lake region reserved as the Oregon National Park, and in 1888 a bill to this effect passed the United States Senate. As there is much valuable timber on the neighboring mountain ranges, and much fine grazing land, there is reason to believe that a branch road will ere long connect Crater Lake with the Oregon and California Railroad; and when that has been built, every visitor to the Pacific Coast will feel that he can no more afford to miss this lake than the other two scenic wonders of Oregon — the Columbia River and Mt. Hood.

Going southward towards Portland, the wonderful fertility of the Willamette Valley is what chiefly arrests the attention of tourists. Wood being cheaper than coal in this region, the train frequently stops to get a fresh load of fuel from the huge piles of timber which at intervals extend along the road, sometimes a quarter of a mile without a break. During these stops, some young man may be seen running to a neighboring wheat or oat field to compare height with the stalks, sometimes to his disadvantage. But these rich agricultural lands were all taken up long ago, and the emigrant with a slender purse and a desire for government land has to seek a region more remote from the railway. The towns along this route, including Roseburg, Eugene, Albany, Salem, and Oregon City, have not grown so fast

CRATER LAKE.

during the last ten years as Portland, or as the towns of
Washington and California; but the inhabitants confi-
dently believe that their day will come when the more
sensational California and Washington towns have
passed through their boom period, and they modestly
claim that they prefer steady and slow growth to a
boom which too often becomes a retrograde boomerang.
At Oregon City, tourists should be on the lookout for
the falls of the Willamette, below which the Indians
formerly used to spear salmon, but which now serve the
more prosaic purpose of furnishing water-power to the
woollen mills on the spot, and electric power to Portland twelve miles away.

The Willamette Valley, through which our train has
passed on the way from Roseburg to Portland, is the
garden of Oregon. Twenty years ago wheat and apples
were almost exclusively cultivated in this region. Then
the discovery was made that the soil and climate are
remarkably well adapted to hop culture, and most of
the farmers at once gave up their grain fields and
orchards and raised hops. Farmers have their fashions
as well as city folks, and they are just as apt to go to
extremes. The hop-raising business was overdone;
prices fell; and now many of these farmers are returning to their grain and fruit, in which no other
State surpasses Oregon, in quality as well as in quantity.

Concerning Oregon fruit I can speak from personal
experience, as I was brought up near an orchard num-
bering two thousand apple, pear, and plum trees. For
peaches and grapes the climate of Northern Oregon is
hardly warm enough, and the apples and pears, too, are
perhaps a little *smaller* than they are in California, but
in flavor they are vastly superior. Indeed, neither in

the East nor in any part of Europe have I ever tasted apples to compare with those of Oregon. They have a richness and delicacy of flavor which must persuade any one that, if apples were less abundant, they would be considered superior in taste and fragrance to those tropical and semi-tropical fruits which are more highly valued because of their scarcity in our latitude. In most parts of the East an apple is an apple, and few people know or care about the names of the different kinds; but an Oregonian would no more eat certain kinds of apples than he would a raw pumpkin. An epicure is no more particular in regard to his brands of wine than an Oregonian is in the choice of his favorite variety of apples; and there are half-a-dozen kinds which I have never seen at the East, and the systematic introduction of which in the New York market would make any dealer's fortune.

For some reason or other the Oregonians seem less enterprising than their California neighbors, and instead of sending their fruit East, they often allow it to rot on the trees — including superb plums, and Bartlett pears that would fetch eight to ten cents apiece in New York. Eastern capital is wanted to start transportation enterprises ; and a still more important desideratum in Oregon is a larger population. The growth of the State has been remarkably slow, considering its agricultural advantages and its fine climate. In the census of 1880, the population numbered only 174,767. But there were already "16,217 farms, and their products are tabled at a cash value of $13,234,548," — a curious commentary on the exclamation of a member of Congress forty-five years ago, that he would not "give a pinch of snuff for the whole Territory."

Eastern notions regarding the climate of Western Oregon are almost as widely astray as they are regarding Alaska. Barrows points out that, although the mouth of the Willamette is two hundred miles further north than Boston, no ice has been formed on it thicker than window-glass since 1862; and that in some of the counties snow has not covered the ground for three consecutive days for a score of years. The rainy season, which takes the place of the Eastern winter, is trying to the patience of some; yet this rain is very different from our muggy, foggy, sultry winter rains in New York. It is known as a "dry" rain, because however it may drizzle, it does not seem to saturate the air and depress the spirits by impeding the natural evaporation and healthy action of the skin. Doubtless this peculiarity of climate is largely responsible for the remarkably beautiful complexions of Oregon and Washington women, though something may be due to the fact that, as children, they live almost entirely on fruit. The heat of Oregon summer days is not often oppressive, being generally mitigated by a gentle breeze, and the nights are always cool enough for refreshing sleep.

XI.

PORTLAND AND ITS SEA-BEACHES.

IF the greatest commercial advantage which a city can enjoy is to be situated on a large river, it is equally true that of all possible æsthetic advantages no other is equal to that of having a scenic background of snow mountains. It is to this that so many cities of France, Spain, Switzerland, and Italy owe their principal charm. To find anything similar in the United States we have to go far West, and especially Northwest. Portland, Tacoma, and Seattle are the three most picturesquely situated cities in the United States, and of these three I would assign the palm to Portland, from a purely scenic point of view. For although Mt. Hood does not seem quite so near and imposing at Portland as Mt. Tacoma does as seen from Seattle or Tacoma, it must be remembered that the Portlanders have full-size views from their streets, not only of Hood but also of St. Helens, while the summits of Tacoma, Adams, and Jefferson are seen from the hills which encircle the city. And while Portland has no Puget Sound, it is only twelve miles from the Columbia River, which is scenically superior even to the "American Mediterranean," as Puget Sound has been aptly called.

Architectural monuments of importance there are none as yet in Portland, but the trees and gardens which frame in all the houses are equally attractive in their way, and, from a sanitary point of view, more desirable. Garden City or Forest City would seem an appropriate name for Portland, as seen from the Portland Heights, which every tourist should visit; and the Cascade Range to the east, with the Willamette River separating the city from East Portland and Albina, gives the ensemble a slight resemblance to Stuttgart, if not to Florence, though neither of those cities can boast of a line of five volcanic snow-peaks like Portland.

Of Mt. Hood in particular the Portlanders have a magnificent view from their house-tops or from the heights west of the city. Though it is about fifty miles away, there is not a hill between to impede the view; and, as the particular Cascade ridge with which Mt. Hood connects is of insignificant height, the peak stands revealed from head to foot in solitary grandeur, with snow reaching down two-thirds of the way even in August. As previously stated, it is a peculiarity of all the Oregon and Washington peaks that they thus rise abruptly from the ground, without any clustering neighbors to lean upon; and this isolation, combined with the lowness of the snow-line, adds much to their grandeur and apparent height. With such fine scenery constantly in view, and with trees and flowers around every house, it is perhaps not surprising that the wealthy Portlanders have hitherto shown a remarkable indifference to the condition of their parks and streets. The large piles of wood in front of every other house appear more useful than ornamental, and give parts of the city a semi-rural aspect. They make excellent and cheap fuel, however, and the large quantities of pitch they contain give them a delightful fragrance. Another peculiarity of Portland streets is that the blocks are uncommonly small. Fewer streets and wider ones would have been much more acceptable. The waste of space involved in the present arrangement is beginning to be felt now that real estate is rapidly rising in value.

Portland owes its growth and its commercial importance to the fact that the Willamette River is navigable up to its wharves by the largest ocean steamers; so that the rich farm products of the Willamette Valley can be at once shipped to all parts of the world without a long and expensive railway transportation.

In a book dated 1855 — Thornton's "Oregon and California" — we read that "ships drawing twelve or fourteen feet of water ascend the Willamette to the pleasant and flourishing village of Portland, twelve miles below Oregon City." This "pleasant and flourishing village" is now a city of at least sixty thousand, which hotly disputes with Los Angeles the honor of being the second largest city on the Pacific Coast. The Los Angeles papers claim seventy thousand for their city and speak encouragingly of Portland as a promising city of forty thousand; while the Portland papers reverse these figures, claiming seventy thousand for their city and generously conceding to Los Angeles forty thousand. One thing is certain : that Portland is growing very rapidly, as is proved by official statistics, showing that the grand total of receipts and payments of money order and postal funds increased more than a million dollars from June 30, 1888, to June 30, 1889. Portland, however, has never had a real "boom" like her southern rival, or like Tacoma and Seattle. Oregon, indeed, has been somewhat unjustly neglected, being thrown into the shade by her more brilliant neighbors, California and Washington. Her growth has been gradual, and not by spurts, but it has been as steady as it has been quiet, and the total result is surprising. Salem, the State capital, has not, indeed, greatly out-grown the condition in which it was found a number of years ago by Mr. Joaquin Miller, who referred to it as "rather thickly settled for the country, yet far too thinly settled for a city"; but Portland has always gone on ahead, thanks to the fact that it has been, and still is, the headquarters for wholesale supplies not only in Oregon, but in Washington and Idaho. This, com-bined with the fact that it is the outlet for one of the richest grain and fruit States in the Union, ac-counts for the metropolitan aspect of Portland. Front Street, where the large wholesale houses are, might be easily taken for a street in New York or Chicago. Farther away from the river, elegant rows of residences occupy the ground where a few years ago ferns and mosses grew, and the festive stump asserted its omni-presence. A large and magnificent hotel has just been completed, the Portland, one of the finest and most sensibly constructed in the country, every room being practically a front room, with plenty of light and air. This hotel was much needed. I have known tourists

to leave Portland disgusted because they could not get
comfortable quarters in the overcrowded small hotels.
Cable and electric roads have also been introduced
recently, and besides all these things, there is evidence
of Portland's prosperity in the appearance of the daily
Oregonian, which is at present compelled to add four
pages almost every issue to its usual eight pages, just
as were the Los Angeles papers during the "boom" in
Southern California. The *Oregonian* is one of the best
edited papers in the United States, liberal in its views,
and generally on the right side of important questions.
It has obtained such a firm hold in Oregon soil that
rival papers find it almost impossible to make headway
against it; and Portland is perhaps the only city of its
size in this country which has only one first-class daily
paper.

Some Portlanders are distressed at the fact that Second Street, one of the three principal business streets
of the city, has fallen almost entirely into the hands of
the Chinese; but in her general treatment of Chinamen,
Portland differs widely from her rival cities in Washington. From Tacoma the Mongolians were driven
formally, a few years ago, by a mob, headed by the
mayor and a brass band. Seattle tried the same game,
but there the mob was foiled by the interference of the
sheriff. Portland, on the other hand, deals gently with
its two thousand Chinamen, because they are found useful, and sometimes indispensable. A Portlander has
explained this matter as follows: "In a city where
white help cannot be got at the rate of thirty dollars a
month for plain cooks and twenty dollars for chamber-
maids, Chinamen at those prices, either in the kitchen
or overhead, are a blessing. Indeed, the amicable rela-

tions between the Chinese and the whites here is due largely to a tacit agreement on a division of labor. All over the city you see that the men employed on street-mending and other public works are white. Wherever you see a pile of cordwood and a man sawing, splitting, and carrying it in, you will find him a Chinaman. When a well-to-do Chinaman wants a drive in a hack, a white man sits before him on the box. The Chinese have not intruded into any of the skilled trades to the exclusion of the whites. Their barbers shave only their own countrymen. Their cobblers confine their mending to Chinese shoes. Their compositors set only Chinese type. Their carpenters are employed on Chinese buildings and cabinet work exclusively. You will often see a drayman delivering freight with a Chinese helper, or a white gardener directing his Chinese assistant in the use of the hoe and the rake. The absurd notion, so prevalent in some parts of the East, that the Chinaman works for almost nothing, is quickly dispelled when you come to strike a bargain with one. If he is to dig in your garden as a common laborer, he stands for his dollar a day as firmly as the white man. He will saw your wood gladly, but he must have a dollar a cord for it, or a dollar and seventy-five cents if he also splits it, carries it in, and piles it up in your cellar."

In the country, the Chinamen are even more indispensable than in the city; and the demand for them during harvesting and hop-picking time is always greater than the supply. They are hired through the agency of Chinese bosses, who send them wherever they are wanted, with cooks and a general outfit, and pay them a small sum a day, keeping the lion's share for themselves. At other times of the year the Chinese are employed in making "clearings" for agricultural purposes. Oregon has about fifteen million acres of timber land, with a soil that is excellent for grain or fruit, provided the timber can be removed. To do this with white labor is so expensive as to take away the possible margin of profit. But the Chinaman does it for a smaller sum, and thus, instead of being the farm-laborer's enemy, he enables him to earn a living on the ground cleared by the heathen. The cost of clearing an acre varies from twenty-five to one hundred dollars.

Market-gardening in Oregon, as in California, is almost entirely in the hands of the Chinese, and where-ever in the neighborhood of Portland you see a brook large enough to irrigate a garden, you will usually find a Chinaman in possession of the ground. Even where the gardens or orchards belong to Americans, Chinamen are hired to do most of the work. And they do it well, with rare exceptions. Usually they have a separate hut, where they do their own cooking; or else they occupy a portion of the barn, in which case, if the chickens lay their eggs therein, it is sometimes found that the number of cackling chickens exceeds the num-ber of eggs found in the trough in the evening.

To judge by the articles found in their provision stores, the wealthier among the Chinese appear to be as great epicures as their countrymen at home; while of the poorer ones, if you ask one what he had for dinner, he will invariably reply, "I eatee licee" (rice). Yet they are always glad to get what is left over at the table, and this makes it the more remarkable that they are so contented with their insipid boiled rice, without con-diment of any sort.

Heathen John is, of course, quite as willing to work

on Sunday as on any other day; but once in a while a day comes along which is marked sacred in his calendar, and then it is difficult to persuade him to do anything. I once witnessed a curious scene on a farm near East Portland. Strawberries being over-ripe, the four Chinese laborers had been persuaded to pick all day, though they had expressed a great desire to have a holiday. In the evening they had a grand performance in front of their barn. A whole roast chicken was brought out in a plate and placed on the grass, surrounded by half-a-dozen bowls of rice-wine, and a number of burning candles, though it was still daylight. The oldest of the men went through a series of bows and genuflections, and then poured out libations of the wine, after offering some to the spectators, who politely declined it. Then a few dozen perforated papers with Chinese characters on them were thrown into the flame, one after another, the chicken was carried back into the barn, and the ceremony was over. One of the younger Chinamen explained to us that what we had witnessed had been done to conciliate the gods. " We workee to-day, long (wrong). 'Ligious holiday. Now allee lightee " (right). He added that he and the other two young men would not have done it, but that the old man was very strict in his religious observances and had induced them to join him.

Afterwards we asked this same young man to sing for us, which he did after much coaxing, and a solemn and repeated promise that we would not laugh. He sang three verses in a shrill falsetto voice, each time a few notes higher, the effect being similar to that of the Edison phonographic speaking-dolls. He accompanied his song with dance and pantomime, but when one of his companions tried to accompany him on a peculiar instrument which sounded like a cross between a violin and oboe, he did not encourage him, and explained to us " he no play."

John sometimes manages to pick up a fair knowledge of English, but one word he cannot get into his brain, and that is the word "get." Tell him to "go and get the milk" and he will have no idea what you want. "Catchee" is the word for him; and if you say "John, go catchee him milk," he will go at once and get it. His logic also is sometimes peculiar; and if you make a bargain with him at so much a month, he will work exactly one Chinese month, or four times seven days, and then refuse to do anything on the two or three remaining days of the month unless he gets extra pay. Nash, in his " Two Years in Oregon," relates a funny story of a Chinaman who accompanied him on a trip through the country. On arriving at a steep hill, he got off the wagon and made John get off too, much against his will, apparently; for presently, on looking around, he noticed that John had crawled up again from behind. On being remonstrated with, John exclaimed, " Never mind; horsee no see me get in; they know no better."

The same writer tells of a Chinaman who stole the picture of a pretty girl from an album and concealed it in his room. And an Oregon lady related to me an incident which gives further proof that John has a sense of beauty. She has two daughters, one a very pretty brunette of eleven, the other a blonde with irregular features and freckles. Lee had one day promised a handkerchief to the blonde, but on looking at the two he decided to give it to the other one. He often spoke of her beautiful black eyes, "just like a China girl's,"

and said he would take her along to China. "How
much will you give me for her?" asked the mother.
"Hundred dollars," was the answer. "And how much
for the other one?" "Two bits" (twenty-five cents).
Lee used to tease these children by running away towards his cabin with their favorite cat, pretending that
he was going to cook her for dinner. One day he was
left alone in the house, and when the family returned
late in the evening, they found he had attended to
everything, even to winding up the clock. But at one
o'clock they were awakened by a most infernal noise;
Lee, with the thoroughness of his race, had wound up
everything he could find — alarm clock and all!

Lee always gave the children Christmas presents of
preserved ginger, candy, or silk handkerchiefs, and occasionally ten cents "to go to the theatre"; but after a
time he became lazy and unmanageable, and was finally
chased away because he impudently gave notice that he
would not work the next day: "To-mollow I'll be sick."

One of the greatest advantages of Portland as a place
of residence is that one can stay here all the year
round, as there are very few days in summer when the
thermometer rises high enough to make one uncomfortable; while the winter climate is similar to that of Virginia. When a few successive warm days do come,
however, the Portlanders have an unusual variety of
excursions to choose from. Picnic boats go up the
Columbia River every day, to visit the Cascades or the
Multuomah or Latourelle Falls. Others go down the
river to Astoria and the sea. Mt. Hood can be reached
in a few hours, and a hotel has been built near the great
glacier, where fans are never in demand. Portland
is a hundred miles from the sea, yet it has three sea-

side resorts, accessible by rail or boat, which are much frequented in July and August, less because the city is considered uncomfortable, than because all residents on the Pacific Coast seem to have a passion for camping out a few weeks each year.

In selecting a seaside resort on the North Pacific Coast, the most important consideration, next to a good beach, is protection from the cold winds which often make even the summer months chilly. In this respect the most southerly of Portland's summer resorts, at Yaquina Bay, is well favored. It is situated about a hundred miles south of the Columbia River bar; and expects to be some day an important commercial place, owing to the facilities for transportation of wheat and fruit to San Francisco, the distance being two hundred miles less than from Portland. At present a steamer leaves every two weeks for the Golden Gate. Newport, on this bay, is a place of about five hundred inhabitants, who claim that their town will never need a fire company because the salt spray from the ocean renders the houses fire-proof — an assertion which they probably expect to be taken *cum grano salis.* Yaquina Bay formed part of a large Indian reservation until 1865, and up to that time the San Franciscans who found it profitable to fish for oysters in their bay had to pay the Indians a shilling a bushel for this privilege.

The other two seaside resorts of Portlanders are due west, — Clatsop being a few miles south of the Columbia River bar, and Ilwaco, or Long Beach, a few miles north of it. Of these two, by far the most frequented to-day is Long Beach, because it is accessible by boat and rail, while Clatsop has hitherto involved a dusty stage ride of eighteen miles from Tansy Point. Ilwaco is opposite

Astoria, on the Washington side of the Columbia estuary, and lies at the southern extremity of the long, sandy peninsula which separates Shoalwater Bay from the Pacific. A few years ago a primitive sort of railway was built on this peninsula for the accommodation of visitors to the seaside, and now hotels and camps are scattered along its whole length. There are two hotels, but they are expensive and not very good, and most of the Portlanders prefer to bring their tents along and rough it. A site for the tent may be purchased for two dollars and a half a season, and hay for the beds is supplied by the neighboring farmers to those who are too fastidious to use the fragrant fern which is an omnipresent and irrepressible weed in Washington and Oregon. Fern has its advantages, not only because it costs nothing, but because it offers no temptation to the cows which have the freedom of the camp in the early morning hours. It is hardly conducive to comfortable rest to know that at any moment after daylight a cow may poke her head under your tent and chew up the substratum of your bedding. The owners of these cows provide for a plentiful supply of milk and vegetables, while meat is daily brought from Portland or Astoria, and is offered for sale, together with canned goods, at booths which are more numerous than they need to be. One can hardly blame these venders for asking somewhat high prices for their supplies, but the person to guard against is the thrifty farmer's wife who buys "store" butter and eggs at Ilwaco and then peddles them around as "fresh farm products" at double prices.

Shoalwater Bay is a famous oyster-ground, and the bivalves, together with mud-clams and razor-clams, are daily brought over to the camp. These oysters are small and inferior in flavor to Eastern oysters. Crabs and fish in great variety are also to be had for a trifle, but the popular way at Long Beach is to catch them yourself. When the tide recedes, some crabs (occasionally weighing four or five pounds) are always left in the hollows on the beach, where they can be easily caught. But once every month there are several mornings when the tide recedes about half a mile, and then the sport becomes lively. Everybody is out with poles and large sacks, in which the crabs are packed and afterwards gathered in by wagons. Another kind of sport peculiar to this region is gathering in the large hake (two to five pounders), which in their eager pursuit of sardines are occasionally caught by the breakers and cast ashore, where they can be gathered in by the hundred. Larger fish, too, are often cast ashore, among them ten-foot sturgeon, and large salmon with a big hole in the side. The seals which abound in this region have a destructive and abominable habit of taking some favorite tidbit out of the salmon and then leaving them to die. These dead fish on the beach have to be carefully covered with sand, or else they become a malodorous nuisance.

In the evening the scene along the beach is rendered brilliant by numerous bonfires, fed with the logs that are scattered along the beach in countless numbers. These logs are brought down the Columbia during the high-water season, and deposited along the beach for miles each way. Some of them, in fact, have been carried to distant islands in the Pacific. They supply the campers with plentiful fuel, and no one objects to the wasteful bonfires, because the stock is replenished every year. During storms this driftwood adds a unique element of grandeur to the scene, the huge logs being tossed about like straws by the angry waves, now lifted up straight as trees, and again dashed against each other with a thud which is heard above the roar of the breakers.

Long Beach is a place where even a victim of insomnia will sleep ten hours every night, and still yawn all day. But as a bathing-place it has its disadvantages. Bathing on the North Pacific is a different thing from bathing on the New Jersey coast. The waves are so rough — positively rude, one might say —and the undertow so strong, that there is only one hour each day when bathing becomes safe and enjoyable. This hour varies of course daily with the tide, and a bell is rung to announce it. Immediately hundreds of campers, who have put on their bathing-suits in their tents, rush into the waves; but few of them stay in more than twenty minutes, as the water, even on summer afternoons, is rarely warm enough to invite a longer stay. That it is perilous to go into the water at any other than the official hour announced by the bell is proved by the sad case of a young lady, a well-known heiress, who lost her life here a few years ago. She was engaged to a young man, whom she asked one day to accompany her into the water when the tide was going out. Of course he flatly refused, whereupon she was piqued and invited another young man, who foolishly complied with her request. They entered the breakers, when suddenly the young lady disappeared under the waves and was never seen again. Although a large sum was offered for the recovery of her body, it was never found, and it is possible that it was devoured by sharks; for these fish are occasionally seen here, though there is no danger near shore, and the noise made by the bathers is said to frighten them away.

The greatest objection to Long Beach is the cold winds which almost constantly sweep along the coast, very often accompanied by dense fogs. During three weeks in July and August, 1889, that I spent there, the sun shone only on five days. On account of these disadvantages it is probable that before long Clatsop Beach will become the favorite summer resort of Portlanders, because it is protected against wind and fogs by Tillamook Head on one side, and forests on another. A railroad has just been built to Clatsop, and it is probable that this summer the Portlanders will desert their favorite Long Beach and establish their summer quarters at Clatsop, which has the additional merit, from their own patriotic point of view, of being in Oregon, while Long Beach is in Washington.

From Clatsop a very interesting excursion can be made on foot to Tillamook Head, where a much-needed lighthouse was built ten years ago in a most exposed and romantic situation. It stands on an isolated rock, about a mile from the shore, and twenty miles south of the Columbia River bar. The foreman of the party that built the lighthouse was swept away by the waves and drowned, when he first put foot on the rock, and the workmen were repeatedly in great danger while building the lighthouse, being once cut off from all supplies for over two weeks by a storm. The almost incredible fury of the "Pacific" Ocean when it gets roused may be inferred from the fact that during a recent winter storm the wild waves broke over this tower, the summit of which is one hundred and thirty-six feet above sea-level, leaving fish and rocks scattered on the roof. One of these rocks weighed sixty-two pounds, and is now on exhibition in Portland.

Sea-lions are abundant in this neighborhood, and it is interesting to watch them fishing for salmon, or quietly basking in the sunshine on the rugged rocks, regardless of the cacophonous roaring of the monstrous sentinels. The Indians have a tradition that pearl-oysters used to be obtained a few miles off shore; but at present the less ornamental but more useful rock-oyster only is to be found, together with mussels and razor-clams, which have their habitat on the sandy shore, and on being disturbed dig their way down so rapidly, that it requires some skill to catch them with a little spade. In some places along the beach the curious phenomenon of "singing sands" is encountered, the sand on being trod on giving out a peculiar sound.

The Elk Creek region, through which this part of the coast is approached, is a veritable hunter's and botanist's paradise. Here bears and deer abound, and more dangerous game, like timber wolves and cougars, may be encountered, as well as otter and beaver. In the south fork of Elk Creek there is good trout-fishing. But it requires a decided talent for "roughing it" to enjoy all these things; for here we are in a forest truly primeval, where paths are few and far between, and where the sunlight rarely penetrates through the dense groups of firs and spruce to impede the growth of the moisture-loving ferns and mosses which carpet the ground everywhere. Trees of over two hundred feet in height and straight as masts abound, some of them up to ten feet in diameter, and therefore too large to tempt the lumbermen to destroy them.

As for these Oregon mosses and ferns, one would have to seek in moist tropical regions for anything to match them in variety, beauty, and verdant luxuriance,

Not only is the ground covered so deeply that one could walk noiselessly, were it not for the dead twigs, but every tree, standing or prostrate, has its green mossy cover. Rotten logs are adorned with ferns waving gracefully over the lovely mosses amidst which they have gained foothold; and even the rocks, which are so bare and bleak in California, are here covered with a mosaic of mosses and lichens — green, gray, red, and yellow. Of the ferns the loveliest is, of course, the black-stemmed maiden-hair, which attains a height of several feet along the banks of shaded brooks, and looks so graceful as it waves about in the gentle breezes that it seems fully to deserve its poetic name. Less graceful and poetic is the common Oregon fern, which sometimes grows as high as California wild mustard, so that hunters may lose their way in it, and which is, from an æsthetic point of view, one of the most charming features of Oregon, since it covers up the unattractive gray of the soil everywhere with a delicate pale green garb which contrasts delightfully with the darker green of the fir-trees. But the farmers look on this species of fern as a dreadful nuisance, because it is the most irrepressible of all weeds, whose roots have more lives than cats. Oregon, it must be admitted, is almost as weed-ridden as California. Besides the fern, the most troublesome weeds are sorrel, dog-fennel, wild carrots, and oats, thistles, and the beautiful corn-flowers in every imaginable color. The most curious thing about these Oregon weeds is the tendency they have to supplant each other every three years, as if there were fashions among weeds. But whereas thistles and wild carrots and corn-flowers may come and go, the fern always remains, unless it is ploughed down persistently, and a *harrowing* war is waged against the last inch of root remaining in the soil.

It goes without saying that a soil which is so favorable to the growth of weeds also extends a generous welcome to flowers. This is most strikingly shown on deserted farms where *annual* garden flowers continue to seed themselves year after year, without any care. I have seen half-a-dozen garden species of flowers growing wild in a place where they had received no attention for twenty years. Wild flowers do not grow here in such profusion or variety as in California, but there are few flowers in California that equal in beauty the pendent red clusters of the wild Oregon currant, or the trifolium, whose petals are at first snow-white, and subsequently change to purple. Lilies of the valley, tiger-lilies, bleeding hearts, lady's-slippers, iris, columbines, larkspur, and many other flowers that are carefully reared in Eastern gardens, grow wild here in great profusion.

In the matter of berries, Oregon is greatly ahead of California. The delicious wild strawberries on long stems are so abundant in May and June that they perfume the air along country roads like clover-fields. Blackberries are even more numerous, and a single county of Oregon would supply enough for all our Eastern cities. Wild currants and gooseberries are also abundant, as well as black and red raspberries and huckleberries. Then there are berries peculiar to Oregon and Washington, including the yellow salmon-berries, the scarlet thimble-berries, and the odd salal, a bush which grows everywhere and is quite ornamental with its glossy leaves and bell-shaped white flowers which turn into bluish black berries of a rather agreeable flavor. Usually these berries are small and dry, but in the swampy regions along the seacoast they grow as large as gooseberries, and are very sweet, although care has to be used in eating them, as they are apt to be inhabited. Bears are very fond of these salal-berries. But perhaps the most curious berry in the State is the so-called Oregon "grape," a small blue berry which makes good wine, but requires plenty of sugar, as it is perhaps the sourest thing that grows, unless it be the Oregon crab-apple, a small berry-like fruit growing in clusters, and of which a jam is made that would give European or Eastern epicures a new sensation of delight. Speaking of epicures, I claim to be an amateur in that line myself, and I must acknowledge that I have never tasted any French château wine with a more agreeable bouquet than that of Oregon cider made exclusively of the finest apple that grows — white winter pearmain — and kept in bottles, unfermented.

The wild oranges which grow in Mexico indicate that oranges, lemons, and limes must be among the most profitable crops grown there; and in the same way the wild crab-apples, cherries, various sorts of berries, and wild oats prophetically indicated that the wealth of Oregon lay in the systematic cultivation of fruit, berries, and grain.

I have apparently wandered away from my topic, which, I believe, was Portland and its summer resorts; but these things may as well be referred to here as elsewhere, since all of rural Oregon is practically a summer resort. I can only briefly refer to other attractions, such as the numerous wild canaries and other song-birds which fill the Oregon air with glad music; or the game-birds which may still be hunted but a few miles from Portland, — the stoical, hooting grouse on the tree-tops,

undaunted by the repeated shots of the amateur rifle-
man; the partridges, which do not allow a passing train
to disturb them at their breakfast in a wheat-field; or
the wild pigeons, which save you the trouble of hunting
them by giving you a few shots at them every morning
on your cherry-trees; or the deer, which still abound in
the mountains; etc. But in conclusion I must once more
refer to what after all constitutes the greatest charm
and attraction of Oregon, next to the snow-peaks;
namely, the omnipresent fir-trees, tall, stately, dark
green, and shady. Artists and others who have grown
up in firless countries can have no idea of the true grandeur and beauty of a real forest, of the cathedral-like
gloom and silence in its midst, of the exquisite serrated
lines formed by the branching tree-tops standing against
a deep blue sky, and of the infinite variety of tints and
shadows produced by the play of clouds and of sunlight
at different hours of the day. More beautiful still, if
less imposing, than the full-grown trees, are the young
fir-trees of ten to thirty feet in height which are rapidly
filling up the regions destroyed by forest fires. They
look like so many square miles of Christmas-trees, but
no Christmas-trees adorned by Santa Claus with colored
wax candles ever present so brilliant an appearance as
those young fir groves when the morning or evening sun
shines horizontally on them. Such lights and shades are
to be seen nowhere else in the world, and the tints seem
so warm and glowing that on a cold morning one invol-
untarily edges up to them to get warm.

XII.

UP AND DOWN THE COLUMBIA RIVER.

AN UNGRATEFUL REPUBLIC — THE COLUMBIA COMPARED WITH OTHER RIVERS — SNOW-PEAKS — SALMON-CANNERIES — ASTORIA AND THE MOUTH OF THE RIVER — CAPE HORN AND ROOSTER ROCK — WATER-FALLS — THE CASCADES — SALMON-WHEELS — IN THE HIGHLANDS — THE LAST OF THE MOHICANS — LOW AND HIGH WATER — THE SCENERY AND THE RAILROAD — THE "PLACE OF THE WINDS" — "SWIFT WATER" — A RIVER TURNED ON EDGE.

THE proverbial ingratitude of republics has never been better illustrated than by the fact that not one of our forty-two States is named after the discoverer of America. True, there are more than fifty Columbia counties, townships, cities, and villages in the United States, and thirty more have adopted the name Columbus, while the capital of the country lies in the District of Columbia; but this district comprises an area of only sixty-four square miles, and in a country where so much is thought of big things, Columbus surely ought to have been sponsor of one of our largest States. An excellent opportunity was missed, on the occasion of the recent admission of Washington Territory to statehood, of changing its name to Columbia. This would not only have prevented much confusion in the mails, but would

182

have been singularly appropriate, for the reason that Washington is bounded on the south by the Columbia River, and on the north by British Columbia.[1]

However, even if it failed to use its opportunity for adopting the name of Columbia for one of its States, the Northwest has done more to honor the name of Columbus than any other part of the country; for here is British Columbia with its magnificent mountain scenery, more than eight times as large as the State of New York; and, better still, the Columbia River, three thousand miles in length, with the grandest river scenery in the world. I have repeatedly seen the Hudson, the St. Lawrence, Mississippi, Missouri, Sacramento, the Rhine, Elbe, and Danube, and none of these rivers impressed me as deeply as the Columbia, which, with the exception of the castles on the Rhine, combines the best features of all of them, and adds to them what they all lack — a background of lofty mountains covered with eternal snow. Grandeur is the watchword of the Columbia, which, with this mountainous background and the stupendous sculpture of its banks, towers above other famous rivers as the high Alps of Switzerland do above our Adirondacks and Catskills.

In entitling this chapter "Up and down the Columbia" I do not wish to frighten the reader into the belief that I intend to take him over the same ground — or water — twice, but merely to indicate that Portland is to be our starting-place. From that city steamers leave daily to make the trip of one hundred miles down to Astoria and the ocean, while others go up the river about one hundred and ten miles, to the

---

[1] When Washington Territory was separated from Oregon, an effort was made to have it named Columbia, but it was defeated in Congress.

Falls. The former trip should be taken first, to avoid an anticlimax.

Portland, Oregon, — which, although founded two centuries later than its namesake in almost the same latitude in Maine, has already almost double the population of the latter (sixty thousand), — is, as I remarked in the last chapter, doubtless the most picturesquely situated city in the United States. From the densely wooded green hills which enclose it on the west, the city is seen spreading itself comfortably and without unsanitary crowding along both sides of the Willamette River, which is about a mile wide at this place. East Portland and Albina are on the east side of the river, and beyond them, at a distance of about fifty miles, this picture is framed in by the Cascade Range and half-a-dozen giant snow-peaks. Mt. Hood and Mt. St. Helens, both covered with eternal snow, are so vast that on clear days they seem to rise just beyond the outskirts of the city, and delightful glimpses of them are caught in the streets. Less conspicuous, because farther away, but still adding to the charm of the scene, are Mt. Tacoma and Mt. Adams on the left, while on the right, the snowy tops of Mt. Jefferson and the three sisters are visible. To the left of Mt. Hood the Columbia River can be seen in the distance, like a silver cord showing the way to the deep cañon which it has worn through the Cascade Mountains.

Portland is practically a seaport, although situated a hundred miles up the Columbia, and twelve miles more up its tributary, the Willamette, which, up to this point, is deep enough to receive the largest ocean steamers, although in dry summers the channel has to be carefully watched, and lighterage resorted to in some cases. For hours after the day boat to Astoria leaves the city, the snow-mountains above mentioned are visible on deck, in ever-new groupings as the boat follows the winding course of the river. This is by far. the most striking feature of the lower Columbia scenery; for the minor ridges of the coast range are insignificant compared with the cascade ridges of the "middle" Columbia, and the fir-fringed banks are usually low, and have none of the steep palisades and isolated rocks which give continuous grandeur to that part of the river. The banks of the Willamette River, below Portland, resemble those of the Columbia, and indeed this river, which is hardly known outside of Oregon, becomes so wide and majestic before it reaches the Columbia, that a careless passenger would not notice the transition from one river to the other. It would be difficult, however, to be inattentive here, for the place where the Columbia receives the Willamette is one of the most interesting spots in its course. The Willamette — which should be called the Oregon, since that name has been taken away from the Columbia ("where rolls the mighty Oregon," as Bryant still could write), or should at least receive back its old Indian name Wallámet — meets the Columbia almost at right angles in two currents, being divided here by one of those pretty little islands which abound along this part of the river and give it some resemblance to the St. Lawrence. They are submerged in spring, and but a few inches above the level of the water in summer, when they are covered with a luxuriant growth of grass and shrubbery — ideal grazing-grounds for thousands of head of cattle; yet Oregon still imports much of her meat and butter from the East.

As the river-banks become wider and wider, and the scenery somewhat monotonous, the salmon industry begins to attract attention. During the legal salmon season, from the first of April to the end of July — which is also the tourist season in Oregon, since in July the forest fires begin which shroud the whole State, with its fine mountain scenery, in a dense cloud of smoke, lasting till September — the river steamers are liable to be stopped at any moment in midstream by boats loaded to the edge with salmon, which are to be conveyed to one of the numerous canneries that line the last thirty miles of the stream. These canneries are buildings of the flimsiest construction, inhabited chiefly by Chinamen, and by young bears caught in the neighboring hills and chained to the front door. The salmon are thrown on the wharf, where they are seized by the Chinamen, who carry them in, throw them on long tables, chop off the heads, disembowel and clean them, and cut them up into small lumps for the cans — all in about as much time as it takes to write this sentence. In the larger canneries everything, from the making of the cans to putting on the labels, is done on the premises. Some of the canneries are built on the shore; but as the river, where the ocean comes in sight, widens out into a bay seven miles wide, the canneries are built in midstream, on piles, and it is an odd sight to behold horses — real land-horses, not hippopotami — dragging in the nets on these flimsy mid-river structures. The river view is disfigured on all sides by the ugly stakes driven in to hold the nets that constitute the salmon-traps. The meshes of these nets are large enough to allow the small salmon to escape, but not large enough for the seals, which occasionally get into one of these enclosures and work sad havoc with the fish and the nets. Several million dollars are said to be invested in the boats, nets, and canneries of the Columbia River: but the recklessness of the fishermen threatens to kill the goose that lays the golden eggs; for the Columbia River fisheries, which a few years ago were the largest in the world, have of late yielded less and less each year, and in 1889 they sank to third rank, with three hundred and thirty thousand cases, Alaska being at the head, with six hundred and eighty-eight thousand, and British Columbia second, with four hundred and thirteen thousand cases. The law is stringent enough, but it is not always obeyed; and it will have to be supplemented by extensive hatcheries if the Columbia River salmon, which is the best flavored on the Pacific Coast, is to regain its former supremacy.

The headquarters of the salmon-fisheries are located at the amphibious town of Astoria, the first civilized settlement in Oregon, but whose hoary age of eighty years does not seem to protect it against the gibes of irreverent tourists — probably because it is so small for its age. Mr. Joaquin Miller describes it as a town which "clings helplessly to a humid hill-side that seems to want to glide into the great bay-like river"; and Mr. Nordhoff unkindly insinuates that the most important building in the town is a large saw-mill, which is kept busy day and night in a wild struggle to curb and suppress the forest which is forever encroaching on the town, and threatens to crowd it into the river. However, just at present the Astorians are very busily engaged in digging away at the hill-side and filling up the bay. They expect to have a railway some day, which will bring the wheat and the apples of the Willamette Valley to their wharves, instead of to Portland; but it will require a good deal more digging and filling up before there will be room for all those products. At present the greater part of Astoria is still built on piles, washed by the tides; and as the pavements are not very well looked after, tourists should beware of walking about after dark. The occupants of many of the houses might easily take a salt-water bath before breakfast, by simply tying a rope round the waist and lowering themselves from the window.

Although Astoria is only about a hundred miles distant from Portland, it has nearly twenty inches more of rain per annum, and in summer its climate is considerably cooler; wherefore some Portlanders use it as a summer resort. A much larger number, however, go across the bay to Ilwaco, and camp on the fine beach which extends for over twenty miles northward. The boat which takes them across touches at Fort Canby, whence an interesting walk of a few miles through a dense forest takes one to the lighthouse on Cape Disappointment, just north of the notorious Columbia River bar, which in spite of all improvements continues at certain seasons, and in stormy weather, to detain ships for days at a time. The view from this lighthouse of the foaming breakers in the bar is splendid, and in low tide the scene is varied by long sand-banks on which thousands of seals bask in the fitful sunshine. These voracious animals do their fishing in the daytime, and at night their place is taken by the human fishermen, who show the same reckless spirit in regard to their own lives as they do in regard to the extermination of the salmon. In their eager rivalry, some of them approach too near the breakers, and many have thus shared the fate of the sailors lowered from the *Tonquin* in 1811, which is so graphically described by Washington Irving in his "Astoria." By the way, I could not help noting the difference between these Astorians and the Granadans in Spain, in their attitude towards Irving. Both have been celebrated by him in fine volumes of poetic prose; but whereas in Granada the principal hotel is named after Irving, whose name is thus heard whenever a train arrives, the Astorians seem to ignore entirely the author who has chosen the name of their town for one of his most readable books.

The trip back to Portland may as well be made on a night boat, as everything worth seeing can be seen on the down trip. Not so with the upper or "middle" Columbia, from Portland to the Dalles, which cannot be seen often enough, and which present on the down trip aspects of the scenery so different from those enjoyed on going up, that a return ticket should be taken by all means. Such a ticket, from Portland to the Dalles and back, costs five dollars, for which you can spend two whole days on the Columbia. I have seen a great part of three continents; but if I were asked what I considered the best investment of a five-dollar bill I had ever made for combined æsthetic enjoyment and hygienic exhilaration, I should name this return trip on the Columbia River. Tourists who have time for one trip only should go up the river, because in that direction the scenery is arranged most effectively, becoming ever grander and wilder till the climax is reached in the marvellous rapids above Dalles City.

The day boat leaves Portland at six o'clock in the morning, and on the way down the Willamette we once more can admire the imposing white forms of Hood, St. Helens, Adams, and the top of Tacoma, — now in full view, now peeping from between the firs which line the banks.   At the Columbia junction the boat turns to the right, and makes its first stop at Vancouver, noted for its fine site, with a superb view of Mt. Hood, and as being the military headquarters of the Department of the Columbia.   It lies on the northern or Washington side of the river, and, oddly enough, almost all the stations along the whole river, excepting Dalles City, are on that side, the Oregon side being generally wilder and less hospitable.   The scenic features are about equally divided between the two States.   Each has its low green islands at intervals along the banks; each its densely wooded shores, its bare rocks, precipitous palisades and water-falls; and each its snow-mountains — Hood and Jefferson being on the Oregon side, St. Helens, Adams, and Tacoma on the Washington side.   Generally the trees or shrubs grow right to the water's edge, but here and there is a strip of sandy beach.   On both sides there are innumerable charming home sites, on gently rising ground, with fertile soil, plenty of wood and water, excellent market facilities by rail and steamer, and the finest scenery in the United States for a background.   Yet these shores, which in the next century will hold hundreds of thousands of happy farmers, are now an absolute wilderness, and an hour may pass before a farmhouse or village is sighted from the steamer. Had the unreasoning multitudes who rushed to Oklahoma quietly taken up homesteads in this region, which is so favored by climate, soil, and scenery, they would have avoided their wholesale disappointment.   The steamship company is very accommodating to the few settlers along the river, and stops at frequent intervals to take on their lumber, shingles, salmon, farm products, and to land merchandise for them.   In low water much ingenuity is required to make a landing at these informal stations.

Two hours after leaving Portland, Mt. Hood, whose base has been previously concealed by the Cascade ridges, suddenly comes into view, life size, from top to base. Were the banks of the Columbia as flat and monotonous as those of the lower Mississippi, this sight alone would crown it king of rivers. For a full hour the steamer sails straight towards this mountain, as if intending to land at its base for a supply of ice from its glaciers; but all at once it moves to the left as the steamer provokingly changes its course. For two hours more, however, the mountain remains in sight till it is once more hidden behind the crests of the Cascades. Tourists who wish to ascend this mountain or to explore its glaciers and cañons, get off above the Cascades at the town of Hood River, near the mouth of the river of that name which carries the melting snows of the mountain to the Columbia. A hotel was opened last summer, just below the snow-line, so that the trip can now be made with great comfort. Mt. Hood is eleven thousand and two hundred feet high, and is ascended by numerous parties every summer, including ladies. Like all the Oregon chain of mountain peaks from Shasta to Tacoma, it is an extinct volcano, and still gives evidence of its past condition by the sulphurous fumes which in some places are encountered during the ascent.

Nothing could be more delightful than the ingenuity with which the Columbia panorama is arranged. For the first five hours, while the banks present nothing of thrilling interest, the giant snow-peaks lend grandeur to the scene. As soon as the last of these, Mt. Hood, disappears, the banks themselves begin to fascinate the attention by innumerable picturesque formations, and a few hours later, when the Highlands have been left behind and the banks become lower again, Mt. Hood once more comes into view, more and more prominently, till at the last station of our trip, the Dalles, it seems nearer and more magnificent than even at Vancouver or Portland. Thus there is not a dull moment between Portland and the Dalles.

The river itself is almost as awe-inspiring in its grandeur as the snow-peaks visible from it. No other river has ever given me such a vivid and overpowering sense of sublimity as the Columbia by its great expanse of watery surface, and its tranquil, deep, majestic movement. And whereas the Mississippi, at a corresponding point in its course, is so muddy that one almost hesitates to bathe in it, the Columbia is so clear and pure that in a glass it seems like well-water and tastes almost as good. The color varies with wind and weather, but is usually a yellowish green, as grateful to the eye as a new-mown lawn. Standing at the prow of the boat, surveying this vast expanse of placid or agitated water, it is a fascinating exercise of the imagination to think that almost every gallon of this mammoth stream came originally from some different creek, spring, melting glacier, or snowfield—some of them in the Cascade Mountains close by, some in the Rocky Mountains in distant Territories; for the Columbia's sources are in British Columbia and in seven States and Territories,—Oregon, Washington, Idaho, Montana, Wyoming, Utah, and Nevada. Think what romantic cañons, what vast, gloomy forests, these waters have passed through on their way from the crest of the continent to the ocean;

what numbers of speckled trout have darted through them in the mountains; what hordes of big salmon and sturgeon in the Columbia; and what exciting scenes they have noted of seals chasing these unfortunate fish! For even as far up the Columbia as this the seals make their excursions. A hundred and fifty miles from the ocean, they can be seen here basking on a sand-bank projecting from an island into the middle of the river. Some of them float about on logs, and others swim to within thirty feet of the steamer, looking, with their heads above the water, exactly like swimming dogs.

About eleven o'clock, as Mt. Hood disappears, Rooster Rock comes into sight, and the scenery begins to resemble that of the Hudson River Highlands. Rooster Rock is a large boulder which, from different points of view, looks like an uplifted thumb, or like a mammoth seal with head on high, just ready to plunge. It stands on a projection from the shore, which looks like an island, and it has a few small firs growing on its bare sides that subsist apparently on the food of air-plants. The interesting points now begin to crowd each other, and barely fifteen minutes elapse before another of the famous sights of the Columbia comes in view, — Cape Horn, which, at first sight, seems merely a precipitous rock projecting into the river; but as the boat draws nearer and begins to round it, all the passengers rush to the left side of the ship, and a chorus of rapturous admiration bursts from their lips. Cape Horn is a vertical wall of bare rock, rising abruptly out of the water, and standing on a pretty row of grooved stones, resembling little pillars sculptured in high relief. In the centre of the rock a miniature cascade runs down smoothly over a mossy bed. Presently, as the boat moves on in close proximity to the rock, another precipitous wall, even higher than the first, rises above it, adorned with several more miniature water-falls, whose moss-grown channels are the only green in the brown, rocky scene. Cape Horn deserves its name, not only because it is a promontory which the boat has to round, but because at times the wind blows so wildly that none but steam-vessels can pass, and canoes and sailing-vessels have been detained there for days. The Columbia River wind-current, by the way, is very accommodating to sailing-vessels; for it usually blows up stream, so that it is almost as easy for them to go up as down. In the future commercial development of this region this will be a factor of considerable importance.

The Master Landscape-Gardener who planned the Columbia River provided not only for a gradual dramatic *crescendo* to a climax, but for constant scenic variety. So, after the snow-mountains and Rooster Rock and Cape Horn, the tourist is treated to the sight of a few picturesque water-falls. The first of them is the Multnomah Fall, which is sighted only a few minutes after leaving Cape Horn. At first it is somewhat disappointing, since only the upper part can be seen; but as the boat approaches nearer, it is revealed in its true size, of eight hundred feet, in two divisions. It is the death plunge of a lively mountain stream which has worn a channel in the rock that looks as if a giant had scooped out a wide groove with a shovel. The trains of the Oregon Railway and Navigation Company pass very near the falls, and always stop a few minutes to enable the passengers to see them. But after all, the only way to see them properly is to visit them on a special picnic excursion, one of which leaves Portland

for this spot almost daily in summer. There is a bridge
spanning the chasm in front of the falls from which an
excellent view is obtained, and the adventurous climb
down and pass under the falls, through a delightful fern
grotto and "cave of the winds." The water in the pool
formed by the fall is cool as ice even in midsummer.
The picnic parties generally visit another fine fall, the
Latourelle, on the same day, noted for the beautiful
cave into which it seems to fall, directly from the blue
sky, and for the curious markings of its rocky surroundings. This fall, however, though close to the Columbia,
is not visible from the river; but only ten minutes above
the Multnomah Falls the boat passes the Oneonta Falls,
less high but more massive than the Multnomah. A
curious phenomenon is here seen sometimes — a *shadow-
fall*, reproducing the water-fall with all its movements
and its inverted water-rockets. Still another fall is seen
above the Oneonta, so close to the edge of the river that
in high water it probably plunges directly into the
Columbia.

After this water-fall episode the highland mountain
scenery again monopolizes the attention; for we are now
in the midst of the Cascade range, which is a continu-
ation of the Sierra Nevada of California. That the
Columbia should have ever been able to force a passage
through this lofty chain is a marvel. But then marvels
abound in this region. Here, for instance, on the
Washington side, is a monstrous basaltic rock, close by
the river, completely isolated, without a trace of connection with the neighboring ridges. It is called Cathedral Rock, is curiously marked and furrowed by wind
and weather, and covered in patches by the irrepressible
fir-trees, which are larger than they seem at their great

elevation. How did this rock get there? It looks like a mammoth glacier boulder; but, incalculable as is the force of glaciers, no ice-river could have ever borne this massive rock on its back. Perhaps Mt. Hood, in a volcanic fit, hurled it there. But impressive as this sight is, the passengers should not allow Cathedral Rock to distract their attention from the surrounding mountain scenery, which is really much more noteworthy than the rock itself. Near it, to the right, is a mountain about two thousand feet above the river, which is an exact copy of Mt. Hood, without its snow; and adjoining it is a unique mountain of about the same height, but with a summit at least half a mile long and absolutely level. But it would take volumes to describe all these imposing mountain formations. Opposite Castle Rock, and below, are miles of magnificently sculptured palisades, compared with which those on the Hudson River are of toy-like dimensions. They are beautifully mottled with green shrubs and mosses and yellow lichens, and fringed above and below by ribbons of young fir-trees. And to think that all this superb scenery has been known to civilized man only one century !

We now approach the famous Cascades of the Columbia, the place where, according to the Indian tradition, a natural bridge once existed, formed by the water digging a tunnel for itself through the mountain. The legend goes on to relate how the rival volcanic monarchs, Hood and Adams, which face each other on opposite sides of the river, once had a fight and hurled huge rocks at each other, some of which fell on this arch which spanned the Columbia, and demolished it. The fragments, filling the river-bed, created the rapids which

CASTLE ROCK—COLUMBIA RIVER.

now obstruct navigation. Day excursions from Portland do not go beyond this point; but tourists who wish
to get a glimpse of the Cascades themselves, and of
some of the finest scenery on the river, must leave the
boat here and take another one about five miles up the
river, for the Dalles. The Columbia River boats at
present depend for their existence on freight more than
on passengers, and the greatest drawback to the enjoyment of the Columbia River trip is the tedious delay of
an hour or two, necessitated by loading all the freight
on the train which takes us from the Lower Cascades to
the Upper Cascades, on the Washington side, and then
again loading it on the upper boat. However, the
mountain scenery is very fine at this place, and the air
so exhilarating that the offence is greatly mitigated
thereby.

The government has been at work for about twenty
years constructing a canal and locks for the boats ; but
a million dollars are still needed to complete the task,
and meanwhile the building of the railroad on the
Oregon side has rendered its completion a matter of
less urgency. The little six-mile railroad on the Washington side, which connects the two boats, is the first
ever built in the Northwest, and is a curiosity not
only on that account, but also because it affords a
good view of the rapids from the car windows. The
fact that the river is here narrowed to a quarter of its
regular width, assists the rocky débris in its bed in
creating a dizzy rush of tumultuous, roaring waters and
foaming waves o'erleaping each other. It contrasts
finely with the calm, majestic movement of the lower
Columbia. But it must be admitted that these rapids
are not so grand or exciting as those of the Niagara

or the St. Lawrence; nor do passengers ever get an opportunity to "shoot the rapids," as on the last-named river. Not that it is impossible to do so. One captain has taken down several steamers and smashed only one so far; but the risk can only be taken in very high water.

Usually the Columbia is very high in early summer, especially when there are a few hot days, with much snow in the mountains. The difference between high and low water is forty-two feet, and some care has to be used, therefore, in building houses near the bank. In 1889, however, there was no snow in the mountains to melt, as there had been no snow-storms and hardly any rain in Oregon during the whole of the preceding winter; consequently the Columbia was lower than it had been for almost a generation; not quite as low, however, as the rivers of Europe in 1132 and 1313, when the Rhine and the Danube could be crossed on foot without wetting the shoes. Fishermen do not like the low water in the Columbia, because in that State it is so clear that the salmon succeed in avoiding the traps laid for them, including the murderous "salmon-wheels," which are turned by the current and scoop in the fish, young and old, with the nets attached to them. These wheels are especially numerous about the Cascades, and do much to hasten the extermination of the salmon.

Before the advent of civilized man on the banks of the Columbia, the Cascades used to be the great fishing-place of the Indians, who congregated here in large numbers to catch and dry their winter supply of salmon. They were a lazy, cunning, treacherous crew, who gave the early explorers much trouble, and proved by their actions that although fish may possibly be good intellectual or brain food, it does not equally develop the moral faculties. For these tribes used to guard the narrowest parts of the river, and levy toll on all passersby, very much like the robber-barons on the Rhine. But that was in the good old times, a hundred years ago. At present only a handful of these Indians are left to haunt these regions and fish for their daily bread. The salmon-wheel has displaced the canoe and spear, and the Indian, who used to be so hardy that he went about unclothed the greater part of the year, has become so weakened by the clothing, whiskey, and vices of "civilization" that old and young are now dying out rapidly of consumption. In return for all the harm it has done them, the government allows the Indians the privilege of fishing with spears for their own sustenance during the " closed " season. Consequently it is easy in Portland during that season to get salmon "caught by Indians," or "in the Rogue River." It is well to have laws and law-abiding communities.

One of the most interesting features of the Cascades is that the upper steamer can be moored quite close to the head of the rapids, where there are some picturesque islands. This absence of a dangerous current is due to the great depth of the river. The débris which causes the rapids has blocked up the channel so effectually that the average depth of the Columbia is twenty feet greater from the Cascades to the Dalles than below, although the banks are almost as widely apart. A splendid view of a black forest scene is obtained from the deck of the upper steamer before it leaves for the Dalles. It is a sportsman's paradise, and a brakeman assured me he had seen two bears at once on one of the steep banks. For two hours after leaving the Cascades we are still in the midst of the Cascade Mountains, and the scenery is, if possible, more inspiring than below the rapids, and the air more exhilarating. It is interesting to note the way in which the railroad on the right bank overcomes the rocky obstacles in its path, seeking a winding pathway around them here, and time and again boldly plunging into a huge rock partly projecting into the river, forming a picturesque tunnel which looks like a natural cave. In some places there is so little room for the track, and the hill-sides are so steep, that, to intercept the constant shower of stones, a broad roadway had to be constructed a few hunded yards above the track. Railroads usually mar natural scenery, but this one only adds to the variety and charm of the Columbia trip, and Mr. Ruskin himself would hardly venture to object to it. The reason of this is that the scenery is on such a colossal scale that it cannot possibly be spoiled by such a tiny thing as a railroad. Indeed, one needs such a human toy as a railway and a train of cars to bring out by contrast the true grandeur of this scenery.

As we approach the end of the Highlands, the mountains to the left rise in gigantic terraces, one, two, and three stories high, resembling the curious formations in the Grand Cañon region in Arizona. The view of the highlands down the river must not be missed, as it is finer even than the view on entering. As already stated, Mt. Hood now emerges again, as imposing as ever, and the view of it at the Dalles is as fine as at Vancouver or Portland. But even without this snowy monarch to follow us up the river all day long, this part of the Columbia would be one of the most fascinating, which does not allow the attention to flag even after nine or ten hours of fatiguing sight-seeing. A few miles below Dalles City is a formation on the right bank (going up) which is perhaps the greatest curiosity along the whole river. It is a wonderfully illusive natural fortress, with battlements facing the river and the regulation watch-tower in the middle. If political exigencies should ever require a fortress on the middle Columbia, here it might be constructed, one would think, in one day, by utilizing nature's plans.

The river now becomes narrower, and is walled in on both sides by low but finely sculptured basalt palisades, beautifully carved and moss-covered in some places. A strong wind seems to blow here almost constantly, and the water is decked with white-caps, and as turbulent as the Rhine at the Lorcley Rock. We are only a few miles below Celilo, "the place of the winds," as the Indians called it. There is no swell, however, and the boat runs smoothly. Of course, ladies who become "seasick" in railway cars and stage coaches may find the Columbia in this place equally trying; but for such persons travelling was not invented. All, however, should look out for their hats and parasols. I have never passed up or down this part of the river when one or two of these commodities were not carried off by the gusts of intoxicated and intoxicating air. The palisades are marked by a white line showing the high-water mark of 1889. Twelve feet above is the high-water mark of 1888. Dalles City is not an interesting place in itself, but it is most delightfully situated, and seems doubly picturesque after a whole day's sail up the desolate Columbia, on which evidences of human habitation are hours apart.

Here ends the second or "middle" portion of the Columbia. As the word Dalles or "Swift Water" indicates, navigation is here again interrupted by rapids. Thirteen miles above the Dalles, at Celilo, it used to be resumed in former days, but since the completion of the railway the boats of the upper Columbia have been shot down the various rapids, and are now used in the middle and lower portions of the river. If a day can be spared, no tourist should fail to visit the Great Dalles, five miles above Dalles City, where the Columbia, which below and above is almost a mile wide, is confined in a basaltic channel only one hundred and seventy-four feet wide in its narrowest place. It is a river literally "turned on edge," and its depth at this place has not yet been determined, owing to the rapidity of the current. In that portion of the Columbia lying between Celilo and Walla-Walla there is little interesting scenery along the banks, but tourists returning East on the Canadian Pacific Pailroad once more come across this river, — the real upper Columbia, — where it again courses amidst snow-mountains, and where it still is navigable for one hundred and fifty miles. Truly the Columbia is a sublime river which some day will have its monograph, and will inspire as much immortal poetry as the Rhine.

THE GREAT DALLES—COLUMBIA RIVER.

XIII.

OREGON AND WASHINGTON SNOW PEAKS.

FROM PORTLAND TO TACOMA — VIEWS OF AND FROM MT. HOOD — AMERICAN SCENERY — ADVANTAGES OF ISOLATION — ASCENT OF MT. ST. HELENS — MASCULINE AND FEMININE PEAKS — TACOMA AND THE JUNGFRAU — AMERICAN NAMES FOR AMERICAN MOUNTAINS — INDIAN NAMES — A HOP VALLEY — CASCADE DIVISION OF THE NORTHERN PACIFIC RAILROAD — MT. TACOMA — ITS FOURTEEN GLACIERS AND FIVE RIVERS.

THERE is geological evidence that Washington's great inland sea, Puget Sound, the Pacific Mediterranean, once extended as far south as the Willamette Valley in Oregon. To-day, Portland and Tacoma are about one hundred and fifty miles apart, and the trip may be made either by boat down the Columbia and through the Straits of Juan de Fuca into the Sound, or by the branch road of the Northern Pacific Railroad overland. In either case, if the view is not impeded by smoke or clouds, a magnificent panorama of snow-peaks is unfolded as the boat or train moves along. Ruskin's assertion that "mountains are the beginning and the end of all natural scenery" is strikingly verified on this route. Oregon without Mt. Hood, Mt. Jefferson, and the Three Sisters, Washington without Mts. St. Helens, Adams, and Tacoma, would be robbed of half their scenic charms. All of these mountains, except Jefferson and the Three Sisters, are seen to best advantage on this trip, — Hood, Adams, and St. Helens before reaching the Columbia River (which the train crosses on a large ferry-boat), and Tacoma at the other end.

Although these peaks resemble each other in standing each in selfish, proud isolation, far from neighbors, and high above the general crests of the Cascades, which barely rise to their snow-line; and although they are all more or less regularly conical in shape, broad at the base and gradually tapering to a point, there is still quite enough difference in the details of their conformation to give them a distinct individuality of appearance. Mt. Hood, as seen from Portland, bears a striking resemblance to Mt. Hecla in Iceland. The south side, which slopes more gradually than the north side, is one vast snow-field, with hardly a dark spot of bare rock, till late in summer. In the forenoon the mountain often throws such deep shadows that it seems as if the snow had melted from its sides; but the noon sunlight reveals it all in its old place. During a long warm summer the snow-line recedes considerably, but the upper half of the mountain is crowned with everlasting snow; and it is for this reason that Hood seems larger and higher than Shasta in summer, though it is half a mile lower: for white makes every object seem larger or broader than black or gray. Over the peaks of Washington, Mt. Hood has at present this advantage, that it alone is accessible by a road; and more than this, a hotel was opened in 1889 above the snow-line, and only a few hundred yards from the great glacier; so that Portlanders can transfer themselves half-way up their favorite mountain in about eight hours by rail and stage.

Mountains are not only the beginning and end of all natural scenery, but they are the scenic feature of which one is least apt to tire.   A snow-mountain is a fresh object of interest every clear morning.   Unlike a leopard, it constantly changes its spots under the influence of the sun's rays; and when these dark patches have become too numerous and too large to be ornamental, a snow-storm comes along and covers it with a new white magnifying cloak.   Surely the man who has no love of mountains in his soul is fit for treason, stratagem, and crime.

Mr. James Bryce, who has given us the most just and discriminating work on this country ever written by an Englishman, but who, as noted in a previous chapter, speaks somewhat disparagingly of the mountain scenery of the United States as compared with that of Europe, was nevertheless compelled to pay his tribute of admiration to "the superb line of extinct volcanoes, bearing snow-fields and glaciers, which one sees rising out of vast and sombre forests, from the banks of the Columbia River and the shores of Puget Sound."   These are encouraging and kind words, coming from an English source, but they hardly do justice to the subject.   It is not only from the banks of the Columbia and the Puget Sound region that these giant peaks are visible, but there is hardly a place in Western Oregon or Washington, elevated above the level of the forests, whence one does not enjoy a superb view of from one to six isolated snow-mountains.   This isolation must be again and again emphasized, not only because to it these Oregon and Washington mountains owe their individuality and unique grandeur, but also because the view from any one of these isolated peaks is much more striking and comprehensive than a mountain view in ranges where the peaks are grouped closely together. Everybody knows that the Rigi owes its world-wide fame solely to the fact that its isolation enables tourists to get a comprehensive view of the Swiss Alps from its summit. Now our North Pacific peaks are even more isolated than the Rigi, which has the Pilatus for its immediate neighbor, and they are, moreover, twice as high as Rigi. Imagine, therefore, the grandeur of the view from their summits. I have made the ascent of some of the highest Swiss peaks, and of Mt. Hood; and although in the latter case I missed the bewildering view of closely grouped snow-peaks which meets the eye on a Swiss summit, there was something to compensate for this in the superior restfulness, individuality, and comprehensiveness of a Pacific scene which included only eight or nine isolated snow-peaks, but with an illimitable ocean of green forests between them. All the Oregon and Washington peaks were visible, and had the air been perfectly clear, even Mt. Shasta, two hundred and fifty miles away, might have been seen with a telescope. Add to this the mountains which encircle the Umpqua and Rogue River valleys, on the south, and Puget Sound with the snowy Olympic mountains on the north, and by way of contrast, the Columbia River and Willamette valleys on the west, and the vast plains of Eastern Oregon on the opposite side, and you get a faint idea of the grandeur of the view from the summit of Mt. Hood, provided there is no smoke or haze in the air.

I cannot stop to describe all the peaks in Oregon and Washington, but a few remarks on the two best known Washington peaks — St. Helens and Tacoma — may

not be unwelcome while our train is speeding on towards
Puget Sound, through a region which, except for these
glimpses of superb mountains, would be a monotonous
ride across a dreary, desolate forest wilderness.

Mt. St. Helens is so prominent an object as seen
from the streets of Portland, that tourists are apt to
fancy that it must be an Oregon mountain, like Hood.
But it must be remembered that the Columbia River,
which forms the boundary between Oregon and Washington, is only twelve miles distant from Portland, and
that East Portland is practically situated on a peninsula
formed by the approaching Willamette and Columbia
rivers.   Being farther north than Mt. Hood, Mt. St.
Helens retains somewhat more of its snowy whiteness
in summer; but there is a place near the summit which
is always kept bare by its internal volcanic heat.   The
slopes of St. Helens are steeper than those of Hood,
and its conical shape is beautifully symmetrical and
smoothly rounded, as compared with the more rugged
Hood, which gives it a feminine appearance.   The
Indians have a legend that when St. Helens, Hood, and
Adams were created, they were big women who had
one husband in common.   The result was jealousy, and
a fight in which St. Helens whipped Hood and the
other mountains, and made slaves of them.   In this
legend the Indians did not, I think, show their usual
poetic imagination.   The lovely, rounded, and regular
appearance of St. Helens should have suggested a legend
in which this mountain was made the wife of the more
irregular, muscular, and sinewy Hood.

St. Helens, although its slopes are steeper than those
of Hood, is considered quite as easy of ascent.   But the
attempt is very rarely made at present, because the

mountain is so inaccessible, — Woodland, the nearest place where supplies can be obtained, being nearly fifty miles away, and the path very indistinct. Two years ago the Oregon Alpine Club decided to put a copper box and a record book on the summit of every snow-peak on the Pacific Coast. In pursuance of this object, a party last summer made an ascent of Mt. St. Helens, of which Mr. W. G. Steele wrote an interesting account in the *Oregonian* (July 27, 1889). About twelve miles from the mountain they came across Trout Lake, in which two of the party caught one hundred and fifty pounds of trout in a day. The base of the mountain has an elevation of 4625 feet, and from this point St. Helens seems higher than Hood, because it rises more rapidly from the surrounding country. The main summit was found to be 11,150 feet high. "Judging the mountain as it appears from Portland," Mr. Steele says, "we had been led to suppose that the summit would be almost a perfect circle. Instead of that, however, it is slightly inclined to a square, and probably contains half a section of land, or rather snow." Magnificent rugged glaciers were found near the summit, and on the way up the party made the interesting discovery that beneath the confused masses of scoria which made up the mountain side, an immense glacier was concealed, "which day after day moves downward with its marvellous load, that is being ground into powder or hurled to the plain below."

One of the most interesting facts regarding St. Helens is that it has given more recent evidence of its volcanic origin than any other of the Pacific peaks ; namely, as late as 1853 and 1854, if Winthrop and Swan may be credited. Corroborative evidence is furnished by the

Indian name of the mountain, Lou-wala-clough, which means, " the Smoking Mountain."

About thirty miles south of the city of Tacoma, Mt. Tacoma suddenly emerges into sight from behind the trees which had previously hidden it from the passengers on the Northern Pacific train, and soon it stands before them in life size, and follows them up to the Sound, with that peculiar ease which mountains that are supposed to be firmly rooted in the soil have in keeping up with an express train, — frisking around it, now on oue side, now on another, like a gambolling white elephant. From this point of view the mountain bears some resemblance to the Jungfrau; but whereas that beautiful Swiss peak weakens the impression of her grandeur and power by putting her arms for support on the neighboring Mönch and Ebenefluh, almost equal to her in height, Tacoma stands in solitary grandeur, appearing more sublimely isolated even than Hood or Shasta ; for the range on which it rises seems merely a hill. And whereas the tourist who sees the Jungfrau at Mürren, or the Matterhorn at Zermatt, or Mont Blanc at Chamounix, is already five or six thousand feet high, and therefore gazes at a mountain whose summit is only eight or nine thousand feet above him, Tacoma, on the other hand, is seen from the very level of the sea, and therefore rears the whole of its three miles of sloping snow-fields and glaciers before the awed spectator. Its exact height is 14,444 feet, or just four feet higher than Shasta. But thanks to its magnifying snow-mantle, which never disappears, and the fact that it is seen from ocean level, it seems much higher and grander than California's finest peak. Tacoma, indeed, is the king of all our mountains, from the tourist's and artist's point of view; for although Fairweather and St. Elias in Alaska are higher still, they are beyond the range of excursion steamers, and are, moreover, generally buried behind clouds; while Mt. Whitney in Central California is almost equally inaccessible in the Sierra wilderness, and in beauty of outlines does not bear comparison with Tacoma for a moment, lacking as it does its fine conical shape and the advantage of isolation.

Such being the case, it is surely the height of absurdity to continue naming the grandest mountain in the United States after an obscure English lord. When Vancouver first discovered all these North Pacific mountains, in 1792, he had a perfect right to name them after anybody he pleased; but Washington now happens to belong to the United States, and every American with a spark of patriotic feeling in his constitution must feel that Anglo-mania could not show a more humiliating form than in the disposition still shown by many persons on the Pacific Coast, to use Lord Rainier's name in designating the king of all our mountains. The same objec- . tion might be urged against Hood, which bears the name of Lord Hood; but in this case it happens that the name is appropriate, for this peak is hood-shaped, and the uninformed always fancy that to this fact it owes its name; so it may be allowed to stand. Louwala, too, would be a more musical and acceptable name than St. Helens, and there is no reason on earth why a mountain in Washington should bear the name of a British ambassador in Madrid. But in this case also the matter may be overlooked, since the name St. Helens, like the shape of the mountain itself, has a vague feminine suggestiveness. But for Rainier there is no excuse whatever, as we have an infinitely more euphonious name for it in Tacoma, which, moreover, designates the mountain's character exactly; for in the Indian dialect it means "the mountain." The fact that the Northern Pacific Railroad, which really "created" the State of Washington, by first developing its resources, always has Mt. Tacoma on its maps, has already done much to popularize this musical name, and to oust the memory of the English lord; and if all tourists of taste will unite in tabooing Rainier, they will soon succeed in effacing that name from all the maps. Tacoma cannot fail to triumph in the long run, just as the attempt made some time ago to name Lake Tahoe after a governor of California failed, the original Indian name being instinctively and unanimously preferred by tourists to such an ugly word as Bigler. Even the Seattle people will find that they will gain more in the estimation of other Americans if they will allow a sentiment of national patriotism to override the local pride and jealousy of a neighboring town which now make them act in a very silly manner when you use the expression "Mount Tacoma."

To those Pacific Coast people who stubbornly cling to such words as Rainier and Bigler, I commend chapter twenty-three of Washington Irving's "Astoria," where he laments "the stupid, commonplace, and often ribald names entailed upon the rivers and other features of the Great West by traders and settlers. . . . Indeed, it is to be wished that the whole of our country could be rescued as much as possible from the wretched nomenclature inflicted upon it by ignorant and vulgar minds; and this might be done, in a great degree, by restoring the Indian names," which are "in general more sonorous and musical."

In insisting so strongly that the monarch of American mountains should have an American name, and not be called after an obscure English lord, I intend no offence to English sentiment, but merely wish to emphasize a patriotic right. No Englishman would fail to express his disgust and indignation if an attempt were made to name the grandest scenic feature in one of the British colonies after an American president or statesman. Finally, it must be remembered that along the line of the Canadian Pacific Railroad in British Columbia there are scores of superb peaks on which the English may without protest bestow the names of earls, lords, sirs, esquires, and ambassadors, if they choose. In my opinion, however, there is something equally ludicrous and presumptuous in naming a mountain after a puny mortal, however great he may seem to his generation. The mountainous map of the Pacific Coast is marred by too many of these blunders. To realize their full significance, read Tourgenieff's wonderful dialogue between the Jungfrau and the Finsteraarhorn, in his "Prose Poems." The futility of man's pretensions to immortality has never been more vividly portrayed than in this dialogue, resumed at intervals of hundreds of thousands of years, and commenting on the intervening changes, till finally the whole earth is covered with a sea of ice, amid which the Jungfrau and Finsteraarhorn still rear their now silent heads unchanged.

Thanks to its great height and complete isolation, Mt. Tacoma is visible as far as Portland to the south, one hundred and twenty miles in an air-line, and one hundred and fifty miles to the east. One of the most perfect views of it is obtained from the piazza of the large Tacoma Hotel. Though it is over forty miles away, it seems so near, when the air is clear, that tourists are apt to fancy they could stroll to its base after dinner.   To see it at its best, however, Mt. Tacoma should be viewed from the deck of a Sound steamer, or, better still, from the car windows on the Cascade Division of the Northern Pacific Railroad.   Tourists who do not use the Northern Pacific Railroad, either going or returning, should by no means fail to make an excursion on this Cascade Branch, in order to get a view of Mt. Tacoma from within fifteen miles of its base. To do this it is not necessary to go as far as Pasco Junction, in Eastern Washington, where the cactus blooms in the sandy plains in June, as in Arizona and Southern California; but one can get off at Clealum or thereabouts, and return to Tacoma next day.   Much of the land through which the Cascade Branch passes is disfigured by dead black trees and stumps.   Other portions are in full cultivation, and the crop most favored appears to be hops, especially in the Puyallup Valley, where these vines attain a most luxuriant and prolific growth.   Indians are still employed in considerable numbers during the hop-picking season, when they come in canoes from all parts of the coast.   Oddly enough, this valley is the most pronounced "temperance" region in the Northwest, and one of the largest hop-growers will not, under any circumstances, allow a saloon to be opened within his extensive domain; though he seems to see nothing sinful or inconsistent in accumulating wealth by selling his hops to wicked brewers.

This hop valley lies between Tacoma and the Cascade mountains, and — aside from the picturesque hop-vines and a mountain stream with waters so clear that the passengers can see the fish in it from the car windows, for half an hour, as the train speeds along — it is in these mountains that the scenic attractions centre. Unfortunately, one of the most fascinating and exciting features of this route — the Switchback — has ceased to exist. This was a part of the road where the train ascended the mountain range by a series of zigzag movements, like a sailing-vessel tacking at sea. There was one monstrous one-hundred-and-ten-ton engine in front of the train, and another one behind, and when the train had reached a certain point, it was switched off and started ahead in the opposite direction. This was done repeatedly, until a place was reached where as many as six parallel tracks could be seen, each a few hundred yards higher than its predecessor. Several times the train ran over trestle-works of a most giddy height, and looking so frail as to make timid passengers wish they were back in Tacoma. But this " elevated " railway was merely a temporary arrangement, con-structed at a cost of six hundred thousand dollars, in order that the Northern Pacific Railroad might not be dependent on the tender mercies of the Oregon Railway and Navigation Company for a Pacific Coast terminus, pending the completion of the Stampede Tunnel, which has now taken the place of the Switchback.

The chief attraction of the Cascade route is of course Mt. Tacoma, which can be seen from many points of view, as the train sweeps around it in a wide curve, somewhat similar to the way in which Mt. Shasta is circumvented. When Tacoma was ascended for the first time, about thirty years ago, by Lieutenants Kautz and Slaughter, the party required nine days from Steilacoom on Puget Sound and back. Since the completion of the railway, however, a trail has been made from the nearest point on the road, from which tourists can ascend the mountain on horseback to a height of about two miles, where the Puyallup and Carbon glaciers may be seen to advantage. The remaining mile offers difficulties and dangers sufficient to daunt any but the bravest and most expert Alpine climbers. Perhaps the summit of Tacoma will always remain as inaccessible to ordinary tourists as the Matterhorn; but so few parties have as yet made the ascent that a route may yet be found, by which the summit will be made as easy of access as that of Mt. Hood. But it must be borne in mind that even from the lower point now accessible to all, Tacoma is nearly as high as Hood; and those who are averse to endangering their life for the sake of seeing the craters at the summit, two hundred or three hundred yards in diameter, now filled with snow, but still having enough heat and sulphur vapor in their environs to save a party caught in a storm from freezing (see Hazard Stevens's article in *Atlantic Monthly*, November, 1876), will thus find infinite enjoyment in viewing the extensive scene, and in exploring the glaciers and the grand cañons leading from them, with the rivers of ice-water and their innumerable rapids, cascades, and falls. There are fourteen living glaciers on the sides of Tacoma. At the latitude of this mountain the vast snow-fields cannot disappear airwards by evaporation, and therefore they follow the law of gravitation downwards as glaciers, till the melting-line is reached, which becomes the birthplace of mighty rivers. Of these solidified snow-fields, or ice-rivers, some are from two to four miles wide, and the Nesqually, Wenass, and White River glaciers are respectively four, five, and ten miles long. Of the rivers which find their sources in Tacoma's glaciers, five are from seventy to a hundred miles long, and three — the White, Puyallup, and Cowlitz — are navigable.

Surely there is reason to believe that when tourists once begin to realize the grandeur and the still largely unexplored attractions of the mountain region of our Northwest, Switzerland will be neglected for a time, and the cities of Tacoma and Portland will become the Interlaken and the Zermatt of America.

XIV.

THE AMERICAN MEDITERRANEAN.

STUDENTS of American history, a few generations hence, will find it difficult to believe that the magnificent Puget Sound region in Washington, which offers such unequalled advantages for navigation, commerce, lumbering, agriculture, and mining, should have remained almost entirely undeveloped till the last quarter of the nineteenth century, almost a hundred years after the exploration of this fine and tortuous inland sea by Vancouver. Indeed, it seems probable that the end of this century might have been reached without a general appreciation of the manifold attractions of Western and Eastern Washington had it not been for the building of the Northern Pacific Railroad, which has been practically the creator of this State. In the few years since its completion it has been demonstrated that if the United States authorities had carried out the intention held at one time of ceding this territory to England, as an expression of good will, they would have given away a

State as rich in natural resources as New York or Pennsylvania, either of which it exceeds in dimensions by one-half.

No spot in Washington has been so literally created by the Northern Pacific Railroad as " the City of Destiny," Tacoma; for when the decision was announced in 1873 of making this spot the terminus of the new transcontinental railroad, the old village of Tacoma had only three hundred inhabitants, and on the site of New Tacoma there was nothing but a dilapidated log cabin. In 1886 the post-office business at Tacoma amounted to $9,040, and in 1889 to $32,446; and it is assumed that these dollars in each case represent an equal number of inhabitants.

The selection of Tacoma seems to have been determined by considerations similar to those which made Portland the "City of Destiny" in Oregon. As Portland was built at the highest point on the Willamette River where ocean vessels can go with ease and safety, so Tacoma has been located at the most convenient southern branch of Puget Sound which ocean vessels can reach at all times, independent of the tide. The State capital lies further south still, it is true, but its arm of the Sound is so much affected by the tide that a wharf had to be built projecting almost a mile into the bay. The Tacoma harbor, on the other hand, has forty to seventy-five fathoms of water, and shippers are inclined to growl that it is too deep, which makes anchoring at some places inconvenient. It is on this fine harbor, as much as on the fact of its being the terminus of the Northern Pacific Railroad, that Tacoma bases its hope of taking a large part of the exceedingly profitable Oriental trade from the British, and also from the San Franciscans. Tacoma is about three hundred miles nearer to Canton than San Francisco, which makes a day's difference in its favor each way. Among the chief articles imported by the Asiatics in return for their teas and silks, are flour, canned goods, and lumber, all of which, and especially the last, Tacoma is eminently qualified to provide. Seventeen years ago its site was a dense forest, and dense forests still cover the greater part of the Puget Sound region and Western Washington, and will for centuries to come, even at the present rate of wholesale destruction. It has been estimated that the forest district of the State includes 175,000,000,000 feet of lumber.

What threatens to exterminate the superb forests of Washington and Oregon is not so much the lumberman's axe as the forest fires, which, instead of diminishing year by year, seem to increase in frequency and extent. They are caused by camp-fires left burning by careless hunters or Indians, or by sparks from railway engines. But even when there are no extensive fires originating in this way, the summer air in Washington and Oregon is odorous, pungent to the eyes, and opaque from the innumerable clearings, or places where farmers burn down their dense timber to secure land for the plough. A volcano in full activity could hardly be a more brilliant and thrilling sight than the dazzling nocturnal splendor of these fires — the united brilliancy of scores or hundreds of blazing fir-trees, some lying prostrate in confused groups, others, several hundred feet high, standing in solemn array, like condemned criminals, until the flames rush up to their tops and bring them down too, or else leave them standing as blackened, ghastly trunks. These transitory fireworks, however, do not compensate settlers in the long run for the loss of so much valuable timber, or tourists for missing sight of the snow-mountains. I have often seen the sun here day after day looking like a full red moon, and the air is for weeks so densely filled with smoke that the eyes become inflamed. Indeed, unless there has been a shower, tourists have little chance of seeing Mts. Hood or Tacoma in July or August. Owing to Tacoma's destiny of becoming the American Interlaken, this is a matter of some importance; but little can be done to remedy the evil until the national government can be induced to spend some of the surplus in the treasury on measures for the protection of our Northern forests, — the envy of the whole civilized world.

The lumber business is still the most important industry in Tacoma, and will probably long remain so. In 1873 there was one saw-mill on the premises, and now there are seventeen, employing nearly fifteen hundred men, and with a combined capacity for turning out more than a million and a quarter feet a day. It is interesting to see these mills at work. There is one at which the steamers on the way to Olympia stop to take in water, so that passengers have time to watch the chain which, like a moving cable, carries down the débris of the timber in a flume-like trough, high in the air, and throws it down on a pile which is kept burning constantly. One cannot suppress the thought what a boon the fuel thus wasted would be to the poor in our Eastern cities. Vessels are always seen loading to carry the available part of the timber to all parts of the world.

But although lumber is the staple of Tacoma's trade, the city's prosperous growth would hardly be arrested by a decline in this business; for its importance as a centre for the exportation of wheat and coal will grow much more rapidly than the forests diminish. As the timber is cleared away, the farmers can take possession of the soil, which yields heavy crops of the best wheat. Puget Sound extends from north to south about one hundred and twenty miles, and has a shore-line of almost sixteen hundred miles, much of which is tide land; and on these tide lands grain yields the fabulous amount of over a hundred bushels to the acre. Eastern Washington, also, which differs so widely in soil and climate from the western half of the State, has been found excellently adapted for grain and fruit raising, with the help of irrigation, preparations for the use of which are now being made on a vast scale. All these products will of course seek a market *via* the Puget Sound cities.

I saw Tacoma in 1887, and again in 1889 and 1890, and the growth of the city in this short time was such that in both cases I hardly recognized the place. It seemed as if some fairy had visited the town and changed every black stump into a four-story brick building by touching it with her wand. The cause of this sudden "spurt" was the completion of the Cascade Division of the Northern Pacific Railroad, and the Stampede Tunnel, which opened up the vast coal-fields along this road, and made the Pacific Coast cities independent of Pennsylvania coal. The export of coal to California ports is already second in importance to Tacoma's lumber trade, and the business is as yet in its infancy. Bituminous or soft coal is at present chiefly mined, but it is said that "near the foot of Mt. Tacoma is the best anthracite mine in the world, the product running ninety-eight per cent of fixed carbon," the smallest vein being four feet through. "This will be opened up very shortly, as soon as a railway can be built through to tap it." Such a railway would also prove a great boon to tourists. The words just quoted are from the *Oregonian*, which by the way is still read by almost as many Washingtonians as Oregonians, — a reminiscence of the time when Portland was the metropolis of both the States which formed old Oregon.

As this chapter is intended to be devoted to the scenic rather than the commercial aspects of Puget Sound, I cannot give any more space to the latter. It is worthy of note that the Tacomans, however enthusiastic they may be in regard to their business prospects, never fail to appreciate also the æsthetic and climatic advantages of their location. Excessive summer heat is as unknown as excessive winter cold, the thermometer having been known to keep within the limits of 30° and 90° for six successive years; and though it rains a good deal in winter, the rain is not depressing through a sultry atmospheric condition. As for the site of Tacoma, it has the double advantage of being not only picturesque in itself, as seen from the bay, but of affording at the same time a superb bay and mountain view from the residences. The city is built on sloping ground and terraces rising one behind the other; and as in San Francisco, the business streets are on level ground, and the residence streets run up hill; but we read that "the engineer declared when he entered upon his work that the streets should have such easy grades that a horse with buggy and driver might go from one point to another in a lively trot, and he carried his point." The greater part of the city having been at first in the hands of the Northern Pacific Railroad, the directors were able to lay

out the town on principles of good taste, which was done
by putting the matter in the hands of an expert landscape gardener.   The streets in consequence are all from
eighty to one hundred feet wide, and nearly seventeen
hundred acres of land have been put aside for parks.
The future hundreds of thousands of Tacoma will ever
be grateful for these sanitary and far-seeing provisions.
For, however salubrious the climate may be, a large city
always needs breathing-spaces and wide streets.   Until
recently Tacoma was behind Seattle in the matter of
street-car facilities, but within a year cable cars have
been built, and almost twenty miles of electric street
railroads, which have solved the problem of going up
hill at a grade of fourteen feet to one hundred, and
enable the merchants, in rainy weather, to reach their
elevated residences in comfort.   Concerning these residences I may add that almost all of them command a
superb view of that compound octopus-like arm of the
Pacific known as Puget Sound, and of the incomparable
Mt. Tacoma.

To get a perfect impression of Mt. Tacoma, however,
we must board the steamer going either to Olympia
or to Seattle and Victoria.   Both these trips will be
taken by every tourist who is wise.   In certain hazy
conditions of the atmosphere Mt. Tacoma, as viewed
from the bay, presents a most unique and mysterious
appearance.   The haze completely conceals the broad
base and the wooded part of the mountain, leaving only
the vast cone in sight, like a floating island of snow on
an illimitable ocean of mist.   As the steamer leaves
the harbor for Olympia, we have this mountain on one
side, and on the other side rows of fine villas on the crest
of the steep hill-side, with their feet, as it were, dangling

over the precipice, and looking as if the slightest earthquake shock would make them tumble into the harbor.
But there are no earthquakes in Washington and Oregon, though their volcanoes are not quite cold yet;
nor are there any other violent disturbances, such as
cyclones and tornadoes. Hence the waters of Puget
Sound are always safe and usually unruffled, so that
sea-sickness need not be dreaded. That part of the
Sound which lies between Tacoma and Olympia is not
so straight and wide as the stretch between Tacoma
and Seattle, but winds about like a river and embraces
between its curves many large and small islands, bays,
promontories, and inlets where rivers and creeks add
their sweet water to the briny substance of the Sound.
The comparison to an octopus, which I ventured to use
a moment ago, bold and fantastic as it may seem, describes the shape of this southwestern part of the Sound
remarkably well, as it here sends out its feelers in every
direction, one of them almost reaching an arm of Hood's
Canal. What a paradise for yachting and picnic parties
this Sound will be when Tacoma and Seattle have
reached the size of San Francisco, and when Washington
will hold two or three million inhabitants — which it
can without the least crowding, or settling on poor
lands!

In some places, where earthslides have occurred, the
banks of the Sound are steep and palisade-like, but
usually the forest trees come right up to the edge of
the water. In this part of the Sound the scenery preserves its primeval aspect, human habitation being rare;
but occasionally an Indian hut may be seen, with a
family group consisting of a " warrior " taking his ease
on his back, while his wife chops the wood wherewith to

cook his dinner, and his mother mends his clothes. These dusky squaws have secured the right of doing masculine work which so many of their white sisters are now clamoring for; and they have husbands, too, which the latter usually have not: and yet they are not happy.

Only one town of any significance — Steilacoom — is seen on this route. Not far from it is one of the most beautiful scenic points on the Sound — a place where it widens out amid the islands in such a way that it seems the meeting-place of five large rivers, resembling a central square in a city into which as many streets lead. A few hours more, and we come to the capital of the State. Like the capital of Oregon, Olympia has not kept pace in growth with some other cities in the State, its population being about the same as that of Salem — five or six thousand; and if it is ever to become a commercial centre, it will have to rely on railways rather than on navigation, because its harbor is too much affected by the tide. The mile-long pier which stands on the sand in low tide has been the subject of many cruel jokes in rival towns. But Olympia is considered a quiet and pleasant place to reside in; and while Tacoma arrogates the title of "City of Destiny," and Seattle that of "Queen City of the Sound," Olympia likes to be called the "City of Homes." The houses are surrounded by gardens in which flowers bloom every month in the year and roses run riot, and from elevated points near by the scenic outlook embraces half-a-dozen snow-peaks, including those of the Olympic range.

It is on the route from Tacoma to Seattle and Victoria, however, that the Olympic range shows to best advantage. The Sound here is, as I have said, less winding and less puzzling to all but the pilot, but there are the same endless changes and suprises in the watery vista. At one place the channel is no wider than a river, so that one can count the pebbles on the shore; at another it widens out into a spacious lake dotted with islands; and in the upper part it expands so much that land for awhile is out of sight altogether, and we seem to be on the ocean. Here the water is not littered with the débris of saw-mills, as in many places below, but seals may still be encountered basking on logs in the sunshine. It must be admitted that the immediate bank-scenery of Puget Sound nowhere equals in grandeur and interest that of the Middle Columbia River; but the background of snow-mountains is even grander: the scenic frame is here more interesting than the picture itself. Tacoma, St. Helens, and Adams are to be seen, and just as we enter the bay of Seattle we catch our first glimpse of Mt. Baker, — another one of the North Pacific extinct volcanic snow-cones, eleven thousand feet in height. From the hill above Seattle a much more complete view of this peak, which stands like a sentinel just this side of the British boundary, is afforded; and here, too, the Olympic range shows to best advantage.

Unlike the other mountains of the Pacific Northwest, the dozen or more peaks which make up the Olympic range are not isolated volcanic cones, but form a range of jagged peaks connected below. They are covered with snow the greater part of the year, and rise in the two highest peaks, Mts. Olympus and Constance, to a height of 8150 and 7770 feet respectively. It is an odd fact that until a few months ago the region enclosed by this range, though appearing within stone's-throw of Seattle's thirty thousand inhabitants, was almost as unknown as parts of Africa before Stanley. A few trappers and prospectors for minerals had made spasmodic efforts to cross the mountain barriers, and hence arose rumors of the existence in this wilderness of Indians who had never seen a white man, of beautiful lakes full of fish, fine valleys suited for grazing and agriculture, gold, silver, iron, and lead ores, and bears and elks enough to make this a sportsman's paradise. But nothing definite was known until last June, when two parties that had gone out in the autumn returned in a deplorable condition, and reported on the correctness of the rumors. One of these parties consisted of Ex-Lieutenant-Governor Gilman of Minnesota and his son, and the other was sent out by the Seattle *Press*. Thus a new and valuable territory has been added to the new State.

In writing about Puget Sound it is difficult to get the mind away from the mountains, but I will only add that as the steamer enters Elliott Bay we get a most picturesque view of Seattle, framed in by Mt. Baker on the left, and Mt. Tacoma (here always called Mt. Rainier, of course) on the right; and that the view of the latter peak is quite as fine as at Tacoma. Like Tacoma, Seattle is built on the side of a hill sloping down to the water, and the harbor is excellent, affording room for several miles of wharfage. The business streets are again (as in almost all cities of the Pacific Coast) the only ones on level ground, while the residence streets run at right angles to them up hill. In one respect Seattle is perhaps the most modern of all American cities, as there is not a single horse-car line in the town, their place being taken by cable and electric lines, which do the work much better, quicker, and without cruelty to animals, of which all horse-car companies are inevitably guilty.

The first time I saw Seattle was a few weeks after the great fire in 1889 which consumed the entire business section of the city, with the wharves, and entailed a loss of eight to ten millions on its twenty thousand inhabitants. It was a most curious sight, — a city of tents built on the charred ruins of the former city, on the site of which it had literally grown up in a day, like a bed of mushrooms. Hotels consisted of large tents with the office in front, cots behind, and the kitchen and dining-room in other tents. Druggists, barbers, dry-goods dealers, grocers, etc., all had their business in tents; and as a sufficient number of these could not be obtained immediately, one could see here and there a "happy family," consisting, say, of a jeweller, milliner, and real-estate dealer, all in one tent. But the oddest sight I came across was a large tent filled with miscellaneous goods, displayed on improvised benches, and outside the tent was this notice in large letters: " POSITIVELY NO GOODS AT RETAIL."

It is possible that the reporters overdrew matters somewhat (contrary to their natural propensity) when they wrote of a theatrical manager who, when he saw his building on fire, forthwith rushed to an architect for plans for a new one; of a merchant who telegraphed for iron for a new store when he saw the flames had taken hold of his old one; and of wagons unloading stone for the foundations of a new building while the hose was still playing on the débris of the old one: but like an exaggerated perspective in a picture, such stories, after all, only show the situation in a true light, since the energy, pluck, and hopefulness shown by the Seattleites on this occasion have never been paralleled. When the anniversary of the fire was celebrated, on June 6, 1890, it was stated that during the year two hundred and sixty-five new buildings had been put up, together with sixty new wharves, with a frontage of over two miles — all of which, with other improvements, involved the expenditure of almost twelve million dollars. Sixty blocks, or one hundred and twenty acres, had been consumed, and in rebuilding this portion the streets have been made wider and straighter, and the buildings are of much better material and higher than formerly. The old ones would have been torn down anyway in a few years, so that, after all, the fire proved a blessing in disguise to the community as a whole. On re-visiting Seattle in June, I found that the new buildings were not in such an advanced stage as the newspaper accounts had led one to fancy; but there was no mistake about their being there, and their metropolitan dimensions, and their stone and iron constitution. The air was hideous with the noise of stone-cutters and carpenters, and the sidewalks were impassable for the piles of bricks and lumber. There were also a few direct traces of the fire in piles of charred timber, and in a few scattered tents where groceries, clothing, etc., were still being sold, the owners having probably lost too much to be able to rebuild at once.

Seattle enjoys almost exactly the same advantages as Tacoma regarding scenery, climate, shipping, coal, and lumber, and further details can therefore be dispensed with. Both these cities doubtless have a great future before them, and there is no ground for the fierce jealousy between them. But if the Seattleites do not wish to alienate the sympathies of tourists, they should cease naming the glorious Mt. Tacoma after an obscure English lord when we have such a beautiful American name for it.

Beyond Seattle the Sound widens out, and forty-seven miles to the north we come to the last of our cities this side of Alaska, — Port Townsend, the United States customs stations, at which all vessels that enter or leave the Sound have to report. It has most of the advantages of other Sound cities, and a population at present of five thousand. In the number of customs entries, Port Townsend claims to be next to New York. The climatic vagaries produced on the Pacific Coast by the " Chinook " wind, which comes from the Japan Current, are curiously illustrated by the rainfall at this city. As a general thing, the rainfall on the Pacific Coast may be said to increase steadily from San Diego's ten inches to Sitka's one hundred and eight. But, oddly enough, there is less rain in the Puget Sound region than in Oregon, the " web-foot " State. Tacoma has forty inches, and Port Townsend only sixteen. Similarly, it is observed that less rain falls in Vancouver's Island than in British Columbia in general. But when he gets into Alaska, the tourist is fortunate if he comes upon a rainless week even in summer; and in rainy weather its scenic wonders can only be half appreciated. It seems, therefore, as if Puget Sound had been placed where it is as a sample of Alaskan scenery and inland coast navigation; and a most excellent sample it is, for it is only when we get up as far as Sitka that the Alaskan salt-water river boasts of snow-peaks comparable to Mts. Tacoma Adams, Baker, St. Helens, and Hood, which adorn Puget Sound.

XV.

A WEEK IN ALASKA.

A GREAT SALT-WATER RIVER — THE GENUINE AMERICAN SWITZERLAND — HIGHEST SNOW-MOUNTAIN IN THE WORLD — THE EXCURSION SEASON — ISLANDS AND FORESTS — INDIAN TRAITS — ALASKAN VILLAGES — GLACIER BAY — AN ICEBERG FACTORY.

IF Long Island Sound could be continued for about a thousand miles, past the coasts of Maine, Newfoundland, and Labrador, as far as the entrance to Hudson's Bay, so that tourists might go all the way on fast river-steamers, with state-rooms on the main deck, and without the slightest risk of sea-sickness; and if this hypothetic "Long Island" could be broken up into several thousand, which, instead of being flat and sandy, were covered with forests of almost tropical luxuriance and with mountains of an infinite variety of shape, continually increasing in altitude until they culminated in two snow-peaks higher than Mt. Blanc, outrunners of the third highest mountain range in the world, and sending clear down and into the salt water numerous glaciers, compared with which those in Switzerland are mere pigmies, — if, in other words, the strip of coast which extends from Tacoma, Washington, to Glacier Bay in Alaska could be transferred to the Atlantic side,

231

it is safe to say that at least a score of large steamers, crowded with passengers, would be going up and down this salt-water river all summer long. The Atlantic Coast people, however, even if they possessed this scenic bonanza, would hardly be able to enjoy it comfortably, on account of the icy ocean current which sweeps down Davis Strait and chills and befogs Labrador and Newfoundland even in summer. Most persons in the East seem to imagine that Alaska must be in a similar, if not a worse, predicament; but they reckon without the warm Japan Current which does for Southern Alaska what the Gulf Stream does for the British Islands. Northwestern Alaska, indeed, shares with Northern Siberia the honor of having the coldest climate in the world; but the southeastern portion of the coast, as far north as Sitka, has a climate much warmer than that of Maine, though Sitka is some fifteen degrees of latitude north of Portland, Maine. It must be borne in mind how vast a country Alaska is, — as large, one writer has calculated, as the original thirteen States. A still more graphic way of realizing its extent is by noting that from California it is as far to the western extremity of Alaska as it is to New York; so that the central city of the United States is not Omaha or St. Paul, but San Francisco !

Fifty years hence, in my humble opinion, San Francisco, or the then metropolis of the Pacific Coast, will be not only geographically but in many other ways the centre of American life. The agricultural, scenic, climatic, and hygienic superiority of the Western to the Eastern Coast is too great not to affect the question of population and civilization. But long before that era Alaska will have universally established its claim

to that much abused-phrase "the American Switzerland,"—unless, indeed, the terms should be converted, and Switzerland come to be complimented as
"the European Alaska." Yearly the number increases
of those who ask themselves whether, instead of going
to Europe every summer, it would not be worth while
to try a Western trip. Before the Yellowstone Park
and Alaska were made conveniently accessible, this
Western trip could hardly have been recommended as
an equivalent for Europe; but now the scales are pretty
evenly balanced, and as soon as the St. Elias range shall
have been included in the regular round trip, and provided with guides, roads, and hotels, Switzerland will
have to "take a back seat"; for St. Elias rises twenty
thousand feet into the air, and can be seen from base to
top, with a snow-and-ice mantle reaching down to the
very level of the ocean, while the highest mountain in
Switzerland is only 15,784 feet high (to the spectator
only about twelve thousand, as he is already several
thousand feet high when he sees it), and has a snow-
mantle of only about seven thousand feet. Indeed,
considering that in the Himalayas and the Andes, the
only two ranges that tower above the St. Elias, the
snow-line is as high as fifteen thousand to twenty
thousand feet, it is clear that St. Elias must be the
highest *snow* mountain in the world.

Unfortunately, the present Alaskan round trip does
not include St. Elias, although the majority of the tourists would gladly risk the chances of sea-sickness by
making the additional two hundred miles from Sitka in
the open sea. Two mountains of the St. Elias range,
with their stupendous glaciers, — Fairweather and Crillon, both higher than Mt. Blanc, — are, however, vis-

ible to those who make the present tour; and although, like St. Elias, they are lamentably apt to hide themselves beneath and above clouds, even those who miss this wonderful sight find so much that is unique in the other attractions, that no one has ever been known to feel the slightest desire to "get his money back." Were the scenery much less inspiring than it is, yet would the trip be worth making for its hygienic value. Here, for two or three weeks, one can breathe a delicious mixture of ocean and mountain air, the latter just sufficiently impregnated with the fragrance of pine forests to prevent that enervating languor which an exclusive lung diet of ocean air is apt to breed. As regards the appetite for solid food, its average size may be inferred from Captain Carroll's favorite joke, — that, as the provisions are running short, he shall be compelled to take the turbulent outside passage back in order to curb the gastronomic propensities of the passengers.

The fare provided on these steamers is about as good as that on the average Atlantic steamers, but the daily salmon and a few other dishes become monotonous, and the passengers look in vain for "local color" in the bill of fare; *i.e.* for venison and bear steak, wild ducks and geese, salmon-berries, and some of the usual kinds of fish that haunt these waters. The fault for this omission is laid on the shoulders of the Indians, who are said to be too lazy to hunt and fish for more than they need for themselves daily. But as they willingly work in the mines for two dollars a day, it is probable they would gladly hunt and fish for the steamer stewards if enough were offered them. Yet, as just intimated, one needs no such special stimulants for the appetite, and one thing is certain, that the large number of invalids who cross the

Atlantic yearly, chiefly to get the benefits of a sea-voyage, would do much better to go to Alaska, for there they would be *sure* of gaining in weight daily, owing to the absence of sea-sickness. And another thing in favor of the Alaskan tour is, that one is certain to find pleasant companionship on the steamers. The passengers on Atlantic steamers represent all classes of society, and even of the tourists not all are pleasure-seekers in an æsthetic sense; but of the Alaskan passengers the majority are apt to be persons of refinement and taste, since the only magnet that can draw them there is the hope of enjoying fine scenery.

Most of the tourists, not feeling quite certain whether Alaska will come up to their expectations, go on the elegant new steamer which is provided with all modern comforts and makes the round trip in twelve days; but not a few regret afterwards that they did not take one of the old freight steamers, *Idaho* or *Ancon*, which require about a week more for the trip, and, as they repeatedly stop a whole day at interesting places, allow the passengers more time to explore the neighborhood, and go fishing, observe the natives, hunt for curios, etc. The fast steamer makes only six or seven stops in twelve days, remaining from two to six hours at each place; and for almost three days after leaving Victoria she makes no stop at all, thus resembling an ocean steamer, — a resemblance made the more suggestive by a series of rocky islands near Victoria that look very much like the coast of Ireland when first approached on the voyage to Liverpool.

The regular tourist season extends from the middle of April to the middle of October. Early in the year passengers will see more of the " midnight sun," but in

July and August fogs and rain are less common, although even during those months the warm winds blowing inland from the Japanese Current are very apt to condense into clouds and rain, — a wise arrangement which prevents the scenery from becoming monotonous to the tourists; and if any interesting point is thereby missed, there is always a chance of seeing it on the return trip, — unless, indeed, the captain should choose a different channel. There is an endless variety to select from, and the marvel is that any captain or pilot should ever be able to find his way through this labyrinth. For what the Milky Way is among stars, this island-studded archipelago is among terrestrial water-ways. Captain Carroll, however, finds his way as unerringly as the salmon which at some seasons splash about the ship, bound for the rivers of the interior. There is not a single lighthouse — only here and there a rude post. Fortunately the nights never become entirely dark, and even a dense fog does not arrest the steamer's progress; for the pilots have learned, by blowing the steam-whistle, to judge by the echo the distance from either shore; and the water is almost invariably so deep that danger is reduced to a minimum.

During our trip, which commenced on August 22, the fog was never dense enough to call for the steam-whistle; but the dense smoke, the result of forest fires and "clearings," which had prevented us from enjoying the Columbia River scenery and Mts. Hood and Tacoma, also hid from us the charms of the far-famed Puget Sound region with its background of Olympian and other snow-mountains. Gradually, however, as we passed along British Columbia towards Alaska, the smoke grew less dense and finally disappeared entirely.

Isolated columns of smoke were still to be seen frequently in the midst of the primitive forests, indicating Indian camps; but in Alaska, thanks to the frequent rains, forest fires cannot occur — a fact which will console the economically minded for the enormous wastes of timber in Washington Territory and Oregon. The visible wealth of Alaska, as Mr. Hallock remarks, lies in these forests: "There is a supply here of 5,700,000,000 feet at a low estimate, a very large part of which is at once accessible for shipment, as saw-mills and vessels can lie right alongside the timber at tide water all the way up the coast as far as it extends"; and Alaska with its islands is said to have a coast-line of twenty-five thousand miles, equal to the circumference of the globe.

Not only has Alaska the third highest mountain range in the world, but if the greatest landscape artist had been consulted, its members could not have been arranged in a manner more continuously impressive to the tourist. Beginning near Victoria with a moderate altitude and mere patches of snow on the sides, they daily grow higher and whiter until the climax is reached in the St. Elias group. When we were northward bound, the smoky atmosphere hid the distant peaks and left the impression that snow was rather scarce for the first three days; but on the return trip a shower had preceded us, clearing away this smoke, revealing snow in abundance, including, about thirty-six hours from Victoria, an undulating range with immense snow-fields that would not be without honor even in Switzerland; and this was before Alaska proper had been reached.

The whole of the second and third days the passengers could imagine themselves sailing along the Hudson River Highlands or Loreley Rock on the Rhine; but after that all comparison with Eastern rivers ceased, and the Columbia alone, with its background of snow-mountains, afforded approximate terms of comparison. The hour for sleep was postponed as long as possible, from fear of losing some of the grand sights. As one of the passengers remarked, it would be possible to make hundreds of Lake Georges out of this Alaskan salt-water river. The word "lake" is very appropriate, as the channel widens and apparently comes to an end, as in a few places on the Hudson, so that tourists frequently amuse themselves by guessing which way the pilot is going to turn next. In some places the channel is so wide that land disappears on one side; at other times so narrow that a woman could throw a stone on either shore.

Of the abundance and variety of islands which adorn this water-way, only those can form a remote conception who have seen the Thousand Islands of the St. Lawrence. But in Alaska, as one writer has remarked, we see not a thousand islands only, but "a thousand miles of islands," some as large as a State or a European kingdom, others just large enough for a house and garden; while many look as if future generations would inevitably call them "Picnic Islands," so cosey and inviting are they. Like the mountains that line the shores, all these islands are densely wooded and very few of them are flat. Indeed, a strip of flat land in this part of Alaska is such a curiosity that the tourist's attention is unconsciously attracted by it — reminding one of the young Tyrolean girl's exclamation on entering for the first time the monotonous plain between Munich and Stuttgart: "Oh, mamma, look out of the window. How beautiful! there is not a mountain in sight!"

Bare hill-sides are almost equally rare in Alaska, till

one reaches the glacier regions. Everywhere the forests extend down to the very edge of the water, and during high tide they actually seem to overlap or grow out of the water. Consequently there is no beach, its place being taken at low tide by ten feet or more of rocky wall adorned with mosses and other vegetable and animal growths, and sometimes almost as brilliantly colored as the walls of the Yellowstone Cañon. The forests above add to this an endless variety of green tints, indicating the different kinds of wood, the age of the trees; or, perchance, an isolated streak of fresher color betrays the path of an avalanche which carried away the old trees and made room for a new growth.

Some of the mountains are so rocky that they afford insufficient nourishment to the trees, which consequently die after a certain age, their gray, leafless skeletons suggesting the thought that after all forest fires have their use as a sort of scavengers. Still, these gray and green forests are less uninviting than those black and green charnel forests in which the fires have done their work incompletely; and they are the exception, not the rule, in Alaska.

For the first three days, as already intimated, these aspects of nature were the only new experiences and sights offered to the *Olympian's* passengers, no stops being made after Fort Townsend and Victoria till we reached Juneau (the largest town in Alaska), omitting Nanaimo, Tongas, and Wrangel. It is customary to stop at each place of any importance, either in going up or returning, the captain being guided in his decision chiefly by the necessity of passing certain dangerous places when the tide is favorable.

The most perilous of these places is Seymour Rapids,

some hours north of Nanaimo. As we approached these narrows, the water presented a most turbulently fascinating appearance, twirling around furiously in hundreds of little whirlpools, while large portions of the surface appeared to be several feet higher than the adjoining parts, as if a submarine earthquake had raised some places and thus made the water run down hill. The spectacle was as exciting as the Niagara rapids, and more sublime, because the fact of being on the water, and the knowledge that there were hidden rocks all about, added just that slight suspicion of danger which stimulates the feeling of sublimity.

In the narrowest part of the channel a regular waterfall was produced by the headlong plunge of the tide waters down some rocks near the eastern shore, while the other side was rendered equally dangerous by numerous rocks, thus leaving only a very narrow channel in the middle for the steamer to pass through. The *Idaho* and *Ancon* never attempt this passage while the tide rushes through it like a mountain torrent, but the *Olympian* plunged in boldly. In vain, however, did the engineer strain every muscle of his machinery; for more than an hour the noble steamer, though paddling away at a rate of almost twenty miles an hour, did not move a yard. Here was a lovely situation for timid souls, with plenty of time to speculate on the possibility of the shaft or rudder breaking, and to recall the fact that in this very place two vessels have already come to grief, one at a sacrifice of seventy Chinese lives! But the *Olympian* suddenly made a spurt, and the salt water-fall and the maelstroms were left behind.

On the fourth day we met the *Pinta* in a shallow, quiet bay, and exchanged greetings, mails, and provisions. The *Pinta* is the diminutive man-of-war which cruises these waters and keeps the Indians in subjection through the fear of having their villages bombarded. While the brass buttons of the officers exerted their usual magnetic power over the eyes of the young ladies, the other passengers were less romantically employed in watching the jelly-fish which crowded about the steamers, literally by the million.

The next incident of importance was our stop at the gold mines opposite Juneau, and subsequently at Juneau itself. Everybody went ashore to see the mines and the quartz mills, where a hundred or more machines reduce the ore to sand with a most terrific noise. The mine was said to be worth twice the price paid for Alaska, and it was evidently prospering, to judge by the additional buildings in course of erection.

At Juneau, which is a larger place than Sitka, the first thing that strikes the eye is the large number of "drug stores," almost every other building being labelled as such. Can it be that the Indian habit of leaving the heads and tails of salmon to decay in the street, in their part of the village, has such an injurious effect on the health of the Juneauites? or has the fact that the sale of whiskey is forbidden in Alaska a remote bearing on the subject? Certainly neither the whites nor the Indians look unhealthy.

Most of the Indian men were at work in the mines, but the squaws sat in rows on the pier or in front of their houses, offering for sale grass baskets, furs, blankets, small canoes and paddles, totem-poles, wooden spoons, masks, bracelets made of silver dollars, berries, etc. Each squaw seems to have the shrewdness and business instincts of a Jew and a Yankee rolled into one. In their own language they comment freely on the tourists, — tit for tat, — and appear to find their doings rather ludicrous, which, no doubt, they sometimes are. These squaws have obviously given their husbands elementary lessons in "woman's rights"; for the latter never dare to sell anything for a lower price than first asked, and if the wife says No, the bargain comes to naught. The squaws are also allowed to share the labor of the men on the water, and they are experts in paddling their own canoes. Their domestic accomplishments are less admirable. The interior of the house is as uncleanly as the blankets they wear, and it would not be pleasant to think of entering their huts were it not for the disinfecting smoke which pervades them. With a few exceptions, they have no stoves, the food being cooked over an open fire in the centre of the floor. The smoke seeks to escape through a hole in the roof, but, before escaping, it is utilized for curing strips of salmon that are hung on strings below the hole. In front of the houses other rows of salmon are suspended on sticks to dry in the sun; and before each hut lies a canoe carefully covered with mats, to protect it against the sun.

At Sitka we had an opportunity to see the Indians as influenced by missionary efforts. The Mission School contains over a hundred boys and girls. The girls do the cooking, and the boys are experts in carpentry. Their chairs and bedsteads are very neatly made, and are to be seen in most of the Indian huts. The boys wear a blue uniform, to give them a sort of *esprit de corps;* and the girls appear to give considerable atten- tion to their appearance, especially in the arrangement of the hair. Their gait is very ungraceful, owing, as some say, to the fact that their ancestors spent so much of their time in canoes. Among the half-breeds, and the Indians too, some have considerable beauty of figure and face; and were it not for the large mouth, many more would be pretty.

It is impossible to look at these Indians and not come to the conclusion that they are descended from the Japanese. The whole cast of the face is Japanese: the cheeks, the small, sparkling black eyes, with their scant lashes and brows, and the complexion, are unmistakably so; and the fact that, not so many years ago, some Japanese mariners were shipwrecked on the Alaskan coast, makes the Japanese origin of the American Indian all the more probable. Another Japanese trait of these Indians is their bright intelligence and their eagerness to adopt the customs of the white man. They learn very readily, and some of the pupils recited and prayed in English, while several squaws and Indian men prayed in their own guttural language. The singing of these children did not differ much in quality of tone or intonation from that in our primary schools.

Besides these Indians, there is little of interest in Sitka itself besides the old Russian castle and the Greek church, in which it is odd to see pictures of saints in these out-of-the-way regions. The church itself does not deserve the amount of attention it has received, except from an antiquarian point of view; but the charms of Sitka harbor have hardly been exaggerated even by those who compare it to the Gulf of Naples. The arrival of a steamer is always a great event for the Sitkans, natives and whites, who assemble on the wharf to greet her arrival and cheer her departure; and the local weekly paper, the *Alaskan*, was enterprising enough to get out an extra in a couple of hours, with the passenger list; and this edition the young ladies bought by the dozen and mailed to their friends as conclusive evidence that they had been so near the north pole.

In speaking of Sitka before Glacier Bay I have followed the map rather than the steamer's course; for Sitka is already some distance on the home stretch, and before arriving there the steamers visit Lynn Canal, which leads up to the Chilcat country, famous for its furs, blankets, salmon-canneries, and glaciers; and then Glacier Bay, which runs almost parallel to Lynn Canal, and, with the Muir Glacier, represents the climax of the present Alaskan tour. Lynn Canal contains a large number of glaciers, each of which would make the fortune of a village and a dozen hotels in Switzerland, and conspicuous among them are the magnificent Eagle and Davidson Glaciers, which would be the "lions" of Southern Alaska were they not slightly surpassed in grandeur by the Muir Glacier, which, Jumbo-like, therefore gets all the attention of the visitors.

As the steamer enters Lynn and Glacier bays, the scenery becomes truly Arctic, as well as the climate, and overcoats are in demand. Vast snow-fields are visible in every direction, and the frozen rivers or glaciers which represent their drainage all creep down to the water's edge, in some cases presenting a front of several miles. As the steamer moves on, the panorama constantly changes, showing the mountains and glaciers from every point of view without involving the slightest fatigue on the part of the tourists; and as soon as one ice-river is out of sight, another shows its edge, and gradually stands revealed in all its grandeur. One never gets over the surprise that the snow-line should be so low — that the snow in the crater-like dug-outs on the mountain

SITKA.

sides should be so near the level of the ocean in mid-summer.

On entering Glacier Bay, another Arctic surprise awaits the tourist. Icebergs of all shapes and sizes begin to float about the steamer, some just large enough to fill the steward's depleted ice-box, others, the size of a steamer, compelling the *Olympian* to moderate her speed. As the great glacier is in sight two hours before the steamer reaches it, though headed directly for it, the passengers have ample time to admire the exquisite blue and white tints of these icebergs, and note their odd forms and resemblances to the hull of a steamer, various geometrical figures, a bundle of logs, a fairy grotto, or a sphinx, etc. Some of them are entirely covered with scores of gulls, which fly away with harsh cries as the steamer approaches.

It appears incredible that the surface of the glacier which lies a few miles ahead should be more than two hundred feet above the water; it seems no more than twenty; but the apparent height constantly increases until the steamer brings up suddenly within a few hundred feet of the icy wall. Then there is a chorus of ohs and ahs, and the Bishop of Rochester (England), who is one of the passengers, dogmatically pronounces it the grandest sight in the world.

Imagine a wall of solid ice, two hundred and twenty-five feet high, extending for about a mile to right and left, the upper portions white and broken up into the most fantastic crags and pinnacles, like the rocks of the Yellowstone Cañon; the lower portions of a deeper and deeper blue, according as the increased pressure from above and from the sides has squeezed out the air and changed the solid snow into pure ice, producing near the centre a grotto of more than celestial blue. Imagine, furthermore, that there are eight hundred feet more of this wall under the water, that even if it is true that the Muir Glacier moves thirty or forty feet a day, instead of only two or three, like those of Switzerland, the portion of ice now visible to the eye represents snow that fell perhaps hundreds of years ago, and has been slowly creeping down with the ice-river ever since — and the meaning of the word "sublime" will perhaps become clearer than any metaphysical definition could make it.

Every ten or fifteen minutes the spectator is startled from his reveries by an explosion, followed by an aggravated multitudinous echo, and caused by the fall of a portion of the ice-wall into the bay, where it floats away as an iceberg. As it splashes into the sea, the water flies up as in a geyser, and a wild wave dashes over the rocks, tosses about the steamer, and threatens to land it high and dry on the beach.

After this spectacle has grown familiar, the boats are lowered, and every one goes ashore to climb up the side of the glacier and get views of its rugged surface, resembling a stormy ocean suddenly frozen with all its white-caps. Here also can be seen the dozen or more tributary glaciers which combine to make the Muir, and the semicircle of snow-mountains whose sides they adorn. The amateur photographers have brought their apparatus along, and take groups of the passengers with this picturesque background; and then the steamer's whistle summons all back to embark for Sitka.

As the steamer slowly gets ready to depart, one notices what in the excitement had previously escaped notice, — the grooved and polished rocks, at least a thousand feet up the mountain side, indicating how high the glacier must have been formerly. A century ago Glacier Bay was not navigable, and according to Indian tradition the Muir Glacier has receded five miles in three generations ; but this need not alarm tourists, as it still has a reserve to last a few thousand years longer. On leaving Glacier Bay we were so fortunate as to see the giauts Crillon and Fairweather outlined against a perfectly clear sky, illuminated by one of the most gorgeous sunsets I have ever seen, and the glories of which did not fade till ten o'clock. It is a superb mountain group, bearing a distant resemblance to the Mönch-Eiger-Jungfrau group, as seen near Mürren, which Mr. Tyndall does not stand alone in regarding as the finest iu Switzerland.

XVI.

ACROSS THE CANADIAN PACIFIC.

THE dense smoke from forest fires, which, by obscuring the grand mountain scenery of Oregon and Washington during July and August, so often makes summer travel in those States an illusion and a disappointment, also extends into British Columbia, as far east as Banff, the Canadian National Park, sometimes called the Yellowstone Park of Canada. Tourists who, on their return from Alaska, wish to proceed to the East via the Canadian Pacific Railway, will therefore do well to postpone this trip till after the middle of September, unless there have been some heavy rains earlier to put out the fires and lay the smoke. Rain on the coast means snow in the mountains, and no one need be told that half the beauty, grandeur, and apparent height of the three great mountain chains which this railroad traverses, depends on a new cloak of magnifying snow.

And an autumnal trip has this further advantage, that the foliage along the banks of the upper Columbia River will wear its most brilliant tints of red and gold, which constitute one of the greatest charms of this tour, contrasting delightfully with the snow-capped peaks on every side.

Although Vancouver is really the Pacific terminus of this Canadian railroad, the project of making Victoria the terminus by building bridges over the chain of islands which in some places almost connect the mainland with Vancouver's Island, having been abandoned, Victoria practically remains the starting-point; for a boat leaves this city early in the morning to connect with the daily east-bound train; and most tourists make it a point to spend a day in the capital of British Columbia before starting, not only because Victoria is interesting on account of its fine location, but because here many Americans for the first time get a glimpse of English life. For Victoria is English to the backbone, — as English as Montreal, or more so, because the similarity of the climate of Vancouver's Island to that of Southern England (due to the effects, respectively, of the Japan Current and the Gulf Stream) enables the English in this Pacific city to surround their houses as at home, with fine lawns and trees, and gardens in which flowers are in bloom all the year round, snow being almost as unknown as in Southern California. Built on gently undulating ground, — such as is characteristic of old England, — the very location of Victoria differs from that of the " American " cities on the Sound, with their sloping hills and precipices. Nor are the streets laid out with the geometrical regularity so universal in the United States. The ladies on horseback, the nu-

merous churches, the animated streets on Saturday evening, the abundant beef markets, the pirated American
novels in the book-stalls, the substantial appearance of
the houses and many other things remind one of the
fact that here we are in America indeed, but not in the
United States. But the most utterly utter anglicism
in Victoria is the fact that if you want to leave a valise
or parcel at the steamship office or elsewhere, you get
no check or receipt for it, but have to rely on the re-
ceiver's memory to see that no one else carries it off. At
the present rate of progress it will take another century
or two to get the idea of a numbered brass check, so
simple, rapid, and convenient, through the British skull.

After inspecting the sights of Victoria, including
Chinatown and the naval station at Esquimalt, we seek
our cabin on the elegant steamer which leaves very
early in the morning for Vancouver. The parting
whistles wake us up, and for a while we gaze at the
scenery from our bed, through the window. The shores
are here more mountainous and higher than in Puget
Sound, and gradually, indeed, the scenery becomes so
Alaskan in character that we jump out of bed and dress
hastily at this unseemly hour, lest we miss some fine
effects; and well it is that we did so, for straight ahead
are some superb mountain forms which look coal-black
in the dim, semi-foggy atmosphere. The island of Vancouver (three hundred miles in length, with mountains nine thousand feet in height, and still largely
unexplored) gradually disappears in the distance, and
the city of Vancouver, on the mainland, comes into
view. Its location reminds one again of Tacoma or
Seattle, and in other respects, too, this brand-new city
seems much more American than Victoria. While

Victoria, as a town, was incorporated almost thirty years ago (1862), and has grown steadily to its population of twelve thousand, Vancouver is a "boom town" of the most ultra-American fashion. In 1886, its site was a dense forest, and to-day it has a population of ten thousand — a growth almost equal to that of Tacoma, and for similar reasons, — Oriental trade, lumber, fisheries, etc. Subsidized steamers run hence every few weeks to Japan, China, and Australia; and this circumstance alone would suffice to make of Vancouver a city which will run a close race with Seattle and Tacoma.

A European could hardly be made to believe that this city of ten thousand had grown up in four years in the midst of a gloomy forest of firs. What strikes the observer is not so much the number of the buildings as their appearance, — solid, substantial granite and brick buildings four to five stories high, and many of them of real architectural merit and individuality, — buildings such as are usually only seen in cities of one hundred thousand inhabitants. But this anomaly will disappear in a few years with the growth of the city, together with the still more striking anomaly presented by the numerous blackened stumps which still stand everywhere between the superb stone buildings, as no one has had time yet to remove them. Usually clearings are made for wheatfields by farmers, but here the forest was cleared away for a metropolis — and in the eager hurry the stumps were left standing.

A striking peculiarity of Vancouver is the very large size and number of windows, both in public buildings and private residences, — evidently suggested by the necessity of getting as much light as possible during

the many cloudy days which this mountainous region
is responsible for; but that sunshine also is abundant is
attested by the fact that pumpkins and even tomatoes
ripen in the gardens.   English influence is shown in the
astounding number of churches already built, and others
in process of erection.   Everybody carries a prayer-book
on Sundays, and all the stores are closed.   Finally, mention must be made of the fact that the Canadian Pacific
Railway has built here a magnificent hotel, equal in every
respect to the fine Tacoma Hotel built some years ago by
the Northern Pacific Railroad, and to the new Hotel Portland in Oregon's chief city.   The scenery embraces the
Cascade range, with Mt. Baker, the Olympic mountains,
and the peaks of Vancouver Island ; and the city has
good wharfage, water, and electric light.   With such
advantages it will continue to eat its way rapidly into
the dense surrounding forest.

The Frazer River, almost as widely famed as the Columbia for its abundant salmon and its superb scenery,
enters the Sound about ten miles from Vancouver, at
New Westminster, which had hoped to be the terminus
of the railway, but now has to content itself with being
the headquarters of the salmon-canning and lumber
export trade.   It is connected by a branch road with
New Westminster Junction, a station on the transcontinental road, and is reached at 13.30 o'clock by our train
which had left Vancouver at 12.45.   The Canadian
Pacific Railway has very sensibly adopted the custom
of naming the hours from noon to midnight, 13 to 24
o'clock.   Passengers unused to this method need only
subtract 12 from those figures to feel at home; and after
a day or two, 20 o'clock will seem as natural to them as
8 P.M.   Nor is this the only thing in which this Cana-

dian road could teach our American roads a useful lesson, as we shall see later on.

After leaving Vancouver, and before reaching Westminster, the train for some time runs along Burrard Inlet, on which is situated Fort Moody, another town which had hoped to be chosen as terminus, and actually did enjoy that privilege for a short time. The shores of the Inlet are beautifully wooded, and some of the trees are of enormous size. At the crossing of Stave River a fine view is obtained of Mt. Baker, looking forward to the right, and the bridge over the Harrison River, where it meets the Frazer, also affords a picturesque view. For the next fifteen or sixteen hours the train follows the banks of the Frazer River and its tributaries, and this is one of the grandest sections of the route. At the first the Frazer is a muddy, yellow river, about the size of the Willamette above Oregon City, but more rapid and winding, and an occasional steamer may be seen floating along with the current, or slowly making headway against it. In some places the railway runs so close to the precipitous bank of the river that a handkerchief might be dropped from a car window into the swirling eddies fifty feet below. At other places it leaves room — and just room enough — for the old wagon road between the track and the river; but it would take a cool driver, with much confidence in his horses, to remain on his wagon here when a train passes. At last the road itself becomes frightened and crosses the river on a bridge, whereupon it winds along the hill-side above the opposite bank, at a safe distance. This road was made during the Frazer River gold excitement in 1858, when twenty-five thousand miners flocked into this region, and wages for any kind of work were ten to eighteen dollars a day. To-day the metal no longer exists in what white men consider paying quantity; but Chinamen may still be seen along the river washing for remnants, their earnings being about fifty cents a day. There is also a "Ruby Creek" in this neighborhood, and some Indian habitations, and salmon-fishing places. Shortly before reaching Yale, which for a long time was the western end of the road, there is a slight intermission in the scenic drama, represented by some rich, level, agricultural lands — as if to give the passengers a moment's rest before the wonders of the Frazer Cañon begin to monopolize their bewildered attention till darkness sets in and drops the curtain on the superb panorama.

Yale, which is so completely shut in by high, frowning mountain walls on every side that the sun touches the village only during part of the day, has lost its importance since it ceased to be a terminus, and seems at present to be inhabited chiefly by Indians and half-breeds. The train is invaded by a bevy of half-breed girls with baskets of splendid apples and pears, which could not be beaten for size and flavor in any of our States, and indicate a possible use for these mountain regions in the future. And now the train plunges into the midst of the series of terrific gorges which constitute the Frazer Cañon, and which make this railway literally the most gorge-ous in the world. Here were appalling engineering difficulties to overcome, which no private corporation without the most liberal government support could have undertaken. Yet the builders had to be thankful even for this wild and rugged cañon dug out by the Frazer River, without which the Cascade range would have been impassable. The palace cars of

FRASER CAÑON.

the Canadian Pacific, which contain all the best features of the Pullman cars, with home improvements, have a special observatory, with large windows, at the end of the train, whence the cañon should be viewed; but to see it at its best one must sit on the rear platform, so as to see at the same time both of the wild and precipitous cañon walls, between which the river rushes along as if pursued by demons. At every curve you think the gorge must come to an end, but it only grows more stupendous, and the river, lashed into foam and fury, dashes blindly against the rocks which try to arrest its course. These rocks, ten to thirty feet wide and sometimes twice as long, form many pretty little stone islands in the middle of the torrent, and are a characteristic feature of the cañon scenery. Numerous tunnels, resembling those on the Columbia River, are built through arches seemingly projecting over the river. The train plunges into them recklessly, but always comes out fresh and smiling on the other side, although it seems that if the bottom of the tunnel should by any chance drop out, the train would be precipitated into the river below.

Once in a while the river takes a short rest, and in these comparatively calm stretches hundreds of beautiful large red fish can be seen from the train, in the clear water, struggling up stream. With their dark backs and bright red sides they form a sight which is none the less interesting when you are told that they are "only dog-salmon," which are not relished by whites, though the Indians eat them.

The train stops for supper at North Bend, and here we are once more impressed with the fact that although we are in America, we are not in the United States.

At our own stations, as soon as the train stops, there is a grand rush for the dining-room, the waiters dump half-a-dozen small dishes before each passenger, who attacks them nervously, with one eye on the door and his ears pricked up for the bell. It would be useless to extend the dining-time more than fifteen or twenty minutes, for in five minutes most of the small dishes are empty and in ten or twelve minutes not a soul is left at the tables. though the *restaurateur* has called out repeatedly, " Plenty of time," " Departure of the train will be announced."

How differently they manage things on British soil! There passengers sit down, unfold their napkins leisurely, while the waiter-girl brings on the soup. There is a regular *menu*, of so many courses, each of which is brought on separately. The conductor, after disposing of his share of the feast, waits at the door till the last passenger has of his own free will left the table, picking his teeth, and then calls out " All aboard." Time, forty-five minutes; and at other stations similar scenes are enacted, with never less than half an hour for a meal. Yet the train is always on time.

It must be admitted that it is not very difficult to be on time when the average speed for the first day is only seventeen miles an hour. There is danger from the boulders which may roll on the track from the steep cañon sides, and occasionally you see a sign along the track telling the engineer to " Go Cautiously — Four Miles an Hour." All the dangerous ground, however, is covered by walkers, who go over the track an hour before each passenger train.

During the night east-bound passengers will inevitably miss the fine scenery along the Thompson River, with the Thompson and Black cañons; but it should be stated that the time-table in both directions has been so arranged that the best part of the route is traversed in the daytime; and that consequently no radical change will perhaps ever be made. Passengers who are willing to get up at six may still see part of the Thompson River and get some fine views of Shuswap Lake as the train skirts its shores. Here, obviously, would be the place for lovers of sport to get off, for vast flocks of ducks and geese rise from the water as the train rushes past. About ten o'clock the train arrives at Craigellachie, which is notable as the spot where the rails from the east and west met, and where the last spike on this great continental road was driven in, on November 7, 1885.

Scenic wonders now succeed one another with bewildering rapidity throughout the day. This second day, in fact, represents the climax of the trip, and the attention is not allowed to flag for a second. However much such a confession may go against the grain of patriotism, every candid traveller must admit that there is nothing in the United States in the way of massive mountain scenery (except perhaps in Alaska) to compare with the glorious panorama which is unfolded on this route. Within thirty-six hours after leaving Vancouver we traverse three of the grandest mountain ranges in America, — the Cascades, Selkirks, and Rockies, — all of them the abode of eternal snow and glaciers, and all of them traversed through by cañons which vie with each other in terrific grandeur.

Before the Selkirks are reached the train passes the Columbia or Gold range, through the Eagle Pass, so called because it was discovered by watching an eagle's flight. Eagle Pass is a poetic and appropriate name, and yet I think it would be well to re-name this mountain pass and call it Mirror Lake Cañon, because that would call the attention of tourists to what is its most characteristic feature, which may otherwise be overlooked. There are four lakes and many smaller bodies of water in this valley, in whose placid surface the finely sloped mountain ridges and summits of the pass are reflected with marvellous distinctness, so that here, as in the Yosemite Mirror Lake, the copy is more lovely than the original. Some of the mountain sides reflected in these mirrors are naked rocks, others are covered with living evergreen trees, and others still with dead trees. In the mirror these dead forests look hardly less beautiful than the living ones; but in the original the eye dwells with more pleasure on the green forests which here, and almost everywhere in British Columbia, grow with the rank luxuriance of a Ceylon jungle. The soil under these dense tree-masses, consisting of decayed pine and fir needles, a foot deep and always moist, makes a paradise for lovely mosses and ferns. Here, also, is the home of the bear, and one would not have to walk far in this thicket to encounter a grizzly, black, or cinnamon bruin.

On emerging from the Mirror Lake Cañon, a great surprise awaits the passengers. The Columbia River — to which they had fancied they had said a final farewell when they were ferried across it on the way from Portland to Tacoma — suddenly comes upon the scene again, as clear and as picturesque as ever; and even at this immense distance from its mouth still large enough to require a bridge half a mile long to cross it. A few hours later the train again crosses the Columbia, at

Donald, where the river has become much smaller than it seems that it should in such a short distance. To get an explanation of this circumstance, it is interesting to glance at the map, and notice what an immense curve northward the Columbia has made in this interval in order to find a passage through the Selkirk range; and in thus encircling the snowy Selkirks it has, of course, added to its volume the contents of innumerable glacier streams and mountain brooks. Its real sources are southeast of Donald, on the summit of the Rockies, separated by but a short distance from springs which run down on the eastern side and find their way through the Mississippi into the Gulf of Mexico. Thus do extremes meet. It would be difficult to find anything so curious in the course of any other river as this immense, irregular parallelogram which the Columbia here describes from its sources to Arrow Lake.

Fortunately, railroad builders are not quite as dependent as rivers on deep cañons for getting over mountain barriers; hence our train is not obliged to follow the Columbia in its great sweep around the Selkirks, but proceeds comparatively straight across this range towards the Rockies proper, *via* the Albert Cañon, at an elevation of 2845 feet, in which the train makes a brief stop to enable passengers to look down into a flume in which the river, narrowed by the walls to twenty feet, rushes along three hundred feet directly beneath them.

The snow-peaks of the Selkirks are now looming up on all sides, and the atmosphere becomes more bracing and Alpine as the train slowly creeps up the mountain side, doubling up on itself in a loop. The Glacier House is reached before long, and here every tourist who has time to spare should get off and spend a day or two, since next to Banff, in the National Park, this is the finest point along the whole route, scenically speaking, while the air is even more salubrious, cool, and intoxicating than at Banff, owing to the nearness of the glacier. It would be difficult, even in Switzerland, to find a more romantic spot for a hotel than the location of the Glacier House. High peaks rise up on every side, so finely moulded, so deeply mantled with snow, and presenting such various aspects from different points of view, that we forget our disgust at the fact that, as usual in the West, these grand eternal peaks have been named after ephemeral mortals, — Browns, Smiths, and Joneses. The Grizzly and Cougar mountains are more aptly named, as these animals will long continue to abound in the impenetrable forests which adorn these peaks below the snow-line. Looking from the hotel towards the glacier, to the left is a peak which looks like the Matterhorn, the most unique mountain in Switzerland; and what is still more striking, at its side is another, smaller peak, which is an exact copy of the Little Matterhorn.

The greater part of the Selkirk region is still entirely unexplored; and good mountain climbers who scorn to reascend the Swiss peaks, which have long since all been measured, named, and labelled, may here have their pick of first ascents. But they will miss the conveniences of the Swiss Alps, — well-informed guides, and hotels with all modern conveniences. Not even a satisfactory map has existed heretofore, and an Englishman, W. S. Green, who published a book called " Among the Selkirk Glaciers " (1890) was obliged to make his own map which is added to his volume. It is tantalizing to read of Alpine paradises, " which no being higher than a bear had entered before" Mr. Green and his companion, and of "a perfect ocean of peaks and glaciers," etc., which they could see on elevated points. Who knows but that a hundred years hence there will be as many visitors to the Selkirks every summer as now crowd into Switzerland?

The Glacier Hotel will always remain a popular point, because it is so near a great glacier of almost Alaskan dimensions. It is only about a mile thence to the foot of the glacier, which has the moraine of huge boulders, the gaping crevasses, the stream at the end, and all the other accessories of ice-rivers. At noon, on a warm day, when the ice melts rapidly, the roar of the glacial stream can be distinctly heard far away; but as the sun sinks lower, the water flows more scantily, and at night the brook is silent or merely whispers.

The principal difference between the Swiss Alps and the Selkirk range lies in the aspect of the mountain sides below the snow-line. These, in Switzerland, are green meadows dotted with browsing cows; while here they consist of superb forests of giant cedars, with bears in place of cows, and presenting one unbroken mass of dark green, except where an avalanche has tobogganed down and opened what seems at a distance like a roadway, but is found to be a battle-field strewn with the corpses of cedars three and four feet in diameter.

The most imposing view of such a mountain forest, unbroken by a single avalanche path, is obtained from the snow-sheds just above the hotel. Sitting outside these sheds and looking toward the left, you see a vast mountain slope covered with literally millions of dark green trees. Why has none of the world's greatest poets ever been permitted to gaze on such a Selkirk forest, that he might have aroused in his unfortunate readers who are not privileged to see one, emotions similar to those inspired by it? But I fear that neither verse nor photographs, nor even the painter's brush, can ever more than suggest the real grandeur of such a forest scene. This mountain is not snow-crowned in September, but its wooded summit makes a sharp green line against the snow-peaks beyond and above. From this summit down to the foot stand the green giant cedars, as crowded as the yellow stalks in a Minnesota wheatfield. But in place of the flat monochrome of a wheatfield, our sloping forest presents a most fascinating color spectacle. The slanting rays of the sun tinge the waving tree-tops with a deeply saturated yellowish green, curiously interspersed with a mosaic of dark, almost black streaks and patches of shade, due to clouds and other causes, and the whole edged by the dazzling snow.

If we descend and enter this forest, a cathedral-like awe thrills the nerves. Daylight has not the power to penetrate to the ground hidden by this dense mass of tree-tops rising two hundred to three hundred feet into the air — except that an occasional ray of sunlight may steal in for a second, like a flash of lightning. And the carpet on which this forest stands! In America we rarely see a house, even of a day-laborer, without a carpet: why, then, should these royal trees do without one? The carpet is itself a miniature forest of ferns and mosses, luxuriating in riotous profusion on an ever-moist soil, the products of thousands of generations of pine needles. Nor is this carpet a monochrome, for the green is varied by numerous berries of various kinds, most of which are red, as they should be — the complementary

THE SELKIRK GLACIER.

color of green. But there are also acres of blueberries as large as cherries; and if you will tear off a few branches of these and bring them to the young bear chained up near the Glacier Hotel, he will be very grateful, and you will find it amusing to watch him eating them.

There is music, too, in this Forest Cathedral, which is heard to best advantage from the elevated gallery occupied by the snow-sheds. It takes a trained ear to distinguish the steady, rippling *staccato* sound of a snow-fed mountain brook from the prolonged *legato* sigh of a pine forest, swelling to *fortissimo*, and dying away by turns. In the romantic spot we have chosen, these sounds are blended, the music of the torrents being caught up by the sloping forest as by a huge sounding-board, and increased in loudness by being mingled with the mournful strains of the tree-tops, as orchestral colors are blended by modern masters. Those err who say there is no music in nature. It is not in "Siegfried" alone that the *Waldweben* is musical, that leaves sing as well as birds, while the thunder occasionally adds its loud *basso profundo*.

The æsthetic exhilaration which we owe to these poetic sights and sounds is intensified by the salubrious breezes which waft this music to our ears. Born among the clouds and glaciers, they are perfumed in passing across the forests, warmed by the sun's rays in passing over the valley; and every breath of this elixir adds a day to one's life. It is not surprising that mountains should make the best health resorts; for do they not themselves understand and obey the laws of health? They keep their heads cool under a snow-cap, their feet warm in a mossy blanket, and their sides covered with a dense *fir* overcoat.

In comparing the Alpine scenes of British Columbia with those of Switzerland, I should have noted one more advantage in favor of the former, namely, the rows and groups of giant cedars through the spaces between which glimpses of the snow ridges and peaks, and of the green slopes leading up to them, are caught. This always adds a lovely frame to the picture, and gives infinite variety. Even the stumps and fallen trees in the foreground, whether they are the result of an avalanche or left there by the builders of the railroad, add an element of wildness and desolation which harmonizes better with Alpine scenery than meadows, cows, and dairy huts.

But we must not linger too long at the Glacier House and amid the Selkirks, for another range of the Rockies, equally grand, awaits us beyond. I have mentioned the curve on which the snow-sheds are built, just above the hotel, whence such a fine view of peaks and forests is to be obtained. We who have been able to stop over a day have had time to enjoy this view at leisure. But those who are unable to interrupt their journey would have missed one of the finest sights in America had it not been for the most commendable wisdom and liberality which prompted the builders of the Canadian Pacific Railroad to construct a second track outside of the snow-sheds, which is used in summer, so that every passenger can, for a moment at least, feast his eyes on this incomparable scene. Of all commendable features of the Canadian road which I have had occasion to praise, this one most merits imitation on some of our "American" railways, unless an exception be the delightfully convenient "Time-Table," in form of a forty-four page booklet, which is given free to passengers, and which contains brief notes on all the stations and principal scenic points, while the hour at which the train arrives at each is printed in the margin, both for east-bound and for west-bound trains.

On passing the snow-sheds it is interesting to study their appearance and note with what an apparently lavish waste of timber they have been constructed. But it must be remembered that timber is more than abundant here, and that the trees that had to be cut down to make room for the track more than sufficed for all the sleepers, sheds, and other protective bulwarks against snow, landslides, or avalanches. The log-remnants, lying about on both sides of the track, will soon be covered with mosses and ferns and add a new element of loveliness to the scene. And there is another way in which the railway atones to the vegetable kingdom for the damage caused by passing through the forests. As the train speeds along, its suction whirls into the air, like snowflakes, the light-winged seeds ripening along the track; and thus it becomes a great distributer of herbs and flowers.

Twenty minutes after leaving the Glacier House the train reaches its highest point on the Selkirks, — 4275 feet. Then the descent begins, and we leave the vicinity of the glaciers, though the snow-peaks that give rise to them continue for hours to gladden the sight. What had seemed more or less isolated peaks near by, are now seen to be merely the highest points of a vast conglomeration of mountain ridges, which are thrown into ever-new groups as the train winds along the mountain sides. In rapid succession several bridges are passed, built over brooks several hundred feet below. To the right, far below us, is a long,

narrow valley, painted a mellow golden yellow by the
setting sun (it sets here at three); and winding through
it is the Beaver River, which from this height looks as
small as if it were seen through an inverted spy-glass.
Glimpses of the Rockies are now caught, and at 16.45
o'clock Donald is reached, where we once more cross
the Columbia, which starts out hence for its grand
curve around the Selkirks. The river here is about as
large as the Rhine at Schaffhausen, and yet the passengers discover to their amazement that even here it is
navigable, and that if they wish to make a hundred-
mile trip, which is said to equal in grandeur any part
of the Columbia River, they need only stop over at
Golden City, two hours beyond Donald, and take the
small weekly boat which runs from that station up the
river, charging six dollars for the round trip. Golden
City owes its name to a former mining excitement, but
its present appearance suggests that Golden Fizzle
would be a more appropriate name.

For the greater part of the two hours which the train
requires to go from Donald to Golden City it passes
along the bank of the Columbia River; and there is,
perhaps, no part of the whole route where grandeur and
beauty are so admirably united as here, especially in the
autumn. The grandeur lies in the snowy summits
which frame in this Columbia valley — the Selkirks on
one side, the Rockies on the other. The beauty lies in
the river itself and in the young trees and bushes along
its banks, dressed in fall styles and colors, some as
richly yellow as a golden-rod, others as deeply purple or
crimson as fuchsias or begonias, the yellow predomi-
nating. These colored trees occur in groups and streaks
along the river, and in isolated patches on the mountain

sides, where they might be mistaken for brown mosses or lichen-covered rocks. There may be as beautifully colored trees in our Eastern forests, but they are not mixed, as here, with young evergreen pines, nor have they a framework of snow-mountains, like these, to enhance their beauty. High up on the ridges there is another variety of trees of a beautiful russet color set off by a deep blue sky. Talk of color symphonies! Here they are — miles of them — long as a Wagner trilogy, and as richly orchestrated! Even the masses of blackened logs and stumps — if one can set aside for a moment all thought of pity for the poor charred trees, so happy before the fire in their green luxuriance, and of the sad waste of useful timber — enhance the charm of this scene by contrast.

I have said that the time-table of the Canadian Pacific Railway is so arranged that the finest scenery is passed in daylight, in both directions; but of course there must be exceptions, and, as a matter of fact, as long as the road crosses the three great mountain ranges of the Cascades, Selkirks, and Rockies, there is hardly a mile which does not offer something worth seeing. Consequently, as darkness again closes in soon after leaving Golden, east-bound passengers must resign themselves to lose sight of the Kickinghorse Cañon, the Beaverfoot and Otter-tail mountains, the large glacier on Mt. Stephen, etc., — which is all the more provoking as they have to sit up anyway till midnight, when Banff is reached; for of course, every tourist who is in his right senses and not a slave to duty gets off here to spend a few days in the Canadian National Park.

It was Goethe, I believe, who spoke somewhere of the pleasure of arriving at a place famed for its beauty, in the darkness of night, thus reserving for the morning hours, when our senses are refreshed by sleep, the first impressions of the scenery. Passengers who have not " read up " on the subject, would little imagine, as the midnight coach takes them to the Canadian Pacific Railway Hotel, as it is called, that they are in some of the finest mountain valleys in the world, and that the hotel itself is as picturesquely perched on top of a hill as any castle on the Rhine. But no castle on the Rhine boasts a view comparable to that which is spread before them in the morning. The best place to enjoy it is in the open rotunda built behind the hotel, just over the precipice. Far below, the clear and rapid Bow River winds along in graceful curves, forming on the left a series of turbulent cascades terminating in a fall which is visible from the rotunda, though of course at this distance less effective than from the river-bank. Below the falls the river hastens on in the direction of the Peechee Mountain, which forms the boundary wall of the valley east of the hotel and, with the wide ridge on the right, is the most interesting sight in the whole Park. This ridge seldom presents the same appearance on successive days, and hardly two photographs of it are alike, owing to the fact that the melting snow, after a storm, constantly stripes and mottles it in different patterns. Though the ridge, which is several thousand feet wide, seems to be absolutely perpendicular, the snow still clings to it and paints it white, except in one section, near the summit, where a black, snowless streak runs across horizontally, dividing the snow-wall into two sections.

To the right of the hotel are some sharp-pointed peaks inclining over each other, somewhat like the

CANADIAN PACIFIC HOTEL AT BANFF.

Three Brothers in the Yosemite Valley, " playing leap-frog"; and to the left is the massive Cascade Mountain. The most important excursions for those whose time is limited to a day, are a trip by boat up the Bow River, as far as Vermilion Lake, in the morning, and a drive to Devil's Head Lake in the afternoon.

The Bow River excursion, which is made on a little steam-launch whenever a party is ready for it, has only one drawback, — the ugly, bristling corpses of charred pines on both sides of the river, the effects of a recent most deplorable forest fire. Arrangements have been made with lumbermen for the removal of these charred trunks, but it will take years to finish the job, as there are thousands of them. Fortunately there is already a new undergrowth, and in a few years the vigorous young trees will have covered up the stumps. In many places, however, the green trees have been spared, and in these sections matchless views of the surrounding mountains may be obtained through the loveliest green foregrounds. Winding about as it does, the Bow River shows all the mountains included in the Park, and many others, with endless changes of the point of view and grouping. Among the most imposing peaks two will be specially impressed on the memory, — Mt. Edith, a sharp, bare, rocky formation, apparently inaccessible, and the extremely interesting Copper Mountain, shaped like a heart, whose two sides, as seen from the upper Bow River, are surprisingly symmetrical. In the centre is a rocky projection of a regular shape.

There are a few shallow places where one can see logs and dead trees lying at the bottom; but generally the small river is wonderfully deep, so that it seems more like the arm of a lake than a mountain stream.

Below the falls, however, it becomes too shallow and turbulent for navigation, and this suggests the theory that the cascades and falls were caused by a landslide, or rather a rockslide, which blocked up the river and deepened the part above this obstruction.

The water of the Bow River comes direct from the Rocky Mountain glaciers and springs, and is, therefore, as clear as a crystal, and if you want a delicious drink, you need only dip your cup into the water and help yourself. What a boon such a copious mountain stream, free from the faintest suspicion of microbes, would be near a large city! There are fish in this water, as a matter of course, and wild ducks can be seen swimming about on it every day, from the hotel rotunda. The part of the river below the falls is also well worth a visit. The Spray River, almost as wide as the Bow, and even more turbulent, enters the Bow just below the falls; and for those who are fond of listening to the music and the babble of brooks, a finer spot than this could not be found. Below the bridge, over the Spray, is a mountain side rapidly crumbling away, and here a stone avalanche may be heard and seen every five minutes. All around are groups and groves of straight, slender mountain poplars, with smooth, pale olive bark and golden autumn leaves. There is something fresh and delightfully healthy in the appearance of these young mountain trees, suggestive of trout bred in icy brooks. It is impossible to walk a hundred steps without being arrested by the really thrilling beauty of these tree-groups, — the blackish green pines encircling the poplars and birches, whose leaves are resplendent in the deepest dyes, representing their transition from fresh, light green, through a dozen shades of greenish yellow, till a deep golden yellow is attained as the climax. While the leaves are mostly yellow, the numerous kinds of berries — bunchberries, mountain-ash, sweet-brier, etc. — are red, and one of the most exquisite bits of color is contributed by the scarlet leaves of the wild gooseberry. The berries of the sweet-brier are much larger than in Oregon, though the bushes are only a foot in height, while in Oregon they are eight to ten, and with their thousands of roses or berries form a most lovely sight.

Forest symphonies like these are also to be seen in abundance on the way to Lake Minnewonka, better known as Devil's Head Lake. An excellent carriage road has been constructed by the government, the distance being nine miles. For the most part the road runs along the foot of precipitous palisade-like mountains, in measuring which the famous Hudson River palisades might be used as a yard-stick, or standard of measure. These mountain sides are beautifully striped and mottled with snow, in a manner that seems to be peculiar to this region, and is repeated on a still grander scale on the steep cañon walls which form the sides of Lake Minnewonka. Before reaching the lake, a most imposing range of the Rockies — a wild jumble of snow-peaks — is seen on the right, beyond the river. Altogether, this drive to the lake is one of the finest in the world, and the lake itself forms a fitting climax. It is a curiosity among mountain lakes, being fourteen miles long and only one to two miles wide, both its sides being steep and beautifully formed mountains. It might in fact be described as a cañon filled with a lake — as the Yosemite Valley is supposed to have been at one time. Its average depth is only forty feet, but owing to its peculiar oblong shape and its vertical sides, it is greatly subject to mountain "draughts," which are likely, without a moment's notice, to assume the form of wild and sudden squalls.   In the morning the surface of the lake forms a perfect mirror of the surrounding peaks, and at certain hours and states of the wind it is tinted with the most exquisite shades of green, blue, purple, and violet.   In this surface iridescence it resembles Lake Tahoe; but in another respect there is a remarkable difference between these two lakes; for although Tahoe has an altitude of almost two thousand feet above Minnewonka, and is also surrounded by snow-mountains, its waters never freeze, even though the snow on its shores be ten feet high; while the Canadian lake does freeze to a depth of two to four feet in February, and then forms an admirable surface for ice-boats and for skating.   The lake is full of large trout which are still quite abundant, as they were not fished for till about four years ago.

The government is so proud of this lake that it has appointed a keeper to prevent it from being stolen. He keeps an inn on the end nearest to Banff, and he says that so far the best catch made by a tourist in one day was eighteen trout, weighing seventy-eight pounds. The Vanderbilt party, in 1889, caught one weighing twenty-eight pounds, and in 1888 the keeper said that he and the cook caught one weighing fifty-three pounds, which was probably served *cum grano salis*. (Please remember that I am merely repeating what was told to me.)   The incident will probably recall to the reader the story of the heathen whose budding faith was nipped when a missionary told him the story of Jonah and the whale.   "When it comes to fish stories," he

DEVIL'S HEAD LAKE.

remarked subsequently to a friend, "no one can be trusted." I must add, however, in justice to the keeper, that a fifty-three-pound mountain trout, abstractly considered, is not impossible. Very large hooks are used to pull these lake trout in, and though they cannot be young, their firm pink flesh is of delicious flavor and not at all toughened by age. The keeper sneered at those tourists who come from the Canadian Pacific Railroad Hotel, and fish from noon to five o'clock, — a time when no self-respecting trout will bite, — and then go away growling that there are no fish in the lake. He also said that there was at present no road around the lake, except an Indian trail, but that a road was projected, as was the placing of a small steamboat on the lake.

Besides the drive to this lake (which passes through the village of Banff, about a mile from the hotel), there are other excellent roads in several directions, notably those to the Lower and the Middle and Upper Sulphur Springs. The Canadian National Park bases its claim to the attention of the travelling public on the curative properties of its sulphur springs quite as much as on its scenic attractions. On approaching the Lower Springs, the fumes bring back memories of Yellowstone Park, as do the curious, gray, brittle stones and the aspect of the soil. Bathers can have their choice of a subterranean plunge in a dimly lighted grotto or cave, which might have been the abode of a mountain nymph, or in an open pool, framed in by the bath-house on one side, and on the other by rocks, from which the plunge may be made. The temperature of the grotto is 80°; of the open pool, 92°. In the latter the hot water bubbles up from a hole in the bottom, and the boys dive down, put an arm into it, and bring up a handful of very coarse-grained quicksand. Hours can be agreeably spent here, and the sulphur odor is not unpleasantly noticeable; but after the bath one smells for hours like a walking parlor-match. In front of the bath-house is a fountain, the water in which is so strongly impregnated that soap cannot be used in washing in it: yet the ice which forms on it in winter is pure from all mineral matter. Animals are fond of this water. I saw a dog drink it (in Oregon I saw a dog drinking sea-water, for that matter), and the keeper of the bath-house says that the cows and horses often come up from the valley to drink it, although there is abundant pure water below.

The Middle and Upper Sulphur Springs are farther up the same mountain — appropriately named Sulphur Mountain. The carriage road, three and one-half miles long, passes through a dense jungle of young pines, no thicker than birches, crowded like Chinese in a tenement house, and therefore looking lugubrious and unhealthy. Most of these will have to be smothered in the struggle for existence, before the strongest ones can get breathing-room enough to develop into full-grown trees. The silence of a mountain forest reigns here, rendered audible by the faint, distant babble of the Bow and Spray rivers. We pass by the road which leads off to the Middle Springs, and soon reach the Upper Springs, around which half-a-dozen bath-houses are grouped, whose favorite sign-board, or trade-mark, is a pair of crutches suspended from a tree, with this notice attached: "I came here with these, and left without them." A few yards above these huts the water can be seen gushing out of the mountain side in a strong current, and so hot that one can hardly hold his hand in it — 110 to 116°. These baths are supposed to be good for rheumatism and skin and blood diseases. I met an old miner here who has hunted gold on four continents, and who entertained me with stories of his adventures in Alaska, and how he "blew up" Mr. Muir for making such a fuss over Glacier Bay, where the glaciers were mere pygmies compared with some that he had come across on his prospecting tours in the interior. He had offered to guide Mr. Muir to these, but the professor seemed to be afraid of the hardships and perils, and refused to go; whereat our miner was still so indignant that he threatened that if he had more skill in using the pen, he would write to the Eastern papers and expose him as a fraud. He said that he was going back to Alaska as soon as cured, because he believes there is untold wealth in that country, and added that if any "literary feller" from New York wanted to accompany him, he would guarantee him material for a book that would make Eastern people's hair curl.

From the Upper Springs the hotel can be reached by means of a short-cut footpath through the dense woods, following the flume which carries the sulphur water down to the hotel. It is used, of course, only for special bathing purposes; but all the water seems here, as in the Yellowstone Park, to be impregnated with traces of sulphur: for if you wash with soap and leave the water in the basin over night, curds will be found in it in the morning; and in the men's wash-room there are yellow streaks in the marble basins, where the water runs into them. Sulphur water is supposed to be good for the stomach, but I have on several occasions found it to be just the opposite.

The Central Pacific Railroad Hotel has electric lights in every room, and is well managed, and its terms reasonable. For those who have to study economy, there are smaller inns and a sanitarium not far from the hotel, with a few stores and a row of tents.

Summing up on the Canadian National Park, we may say that it has not so many natural wonders as the Yellowstone Park, — no geysers, steam-holes, gold-bottomed rivulets, paint-pots, nor anything to place beside the Yellowstone Cañon and Falls. But the Minnewonka Lake may fairly challenge comparison with the Yellowstone Lake, and the mountain scenery is grander in the Canadian Park, and the snow and glaciers are nearer, though not so near as at the Glacier House, where the air is in consequence cooler and more bracing in summer than even at Banff. As the Canadian Park is only twenty-six miles long and ten wide, while the Yellowstone Park is about sixty-two by fifty-four miles, the former can be seen in much less time than it takes to do justice to the latter.

When we get ready to leave Banff we have to take the midnight train, so there is no chance to say good by to the mountains. But we have seen so much of them since leaving Vancouver, that we have felt almost tempted to cry out to Nature, "Hold, enough — less would be more!" Now we get ample opportunity to ruminate in peace over our crowded impressions. When we get up we are on the prairie; we go to bed in the prairie, after traversing a territory larger than a European kingdom; again we rise on the prairie, and again go to bed on it; and not till Lake Superior is approached does the scenery once more become interesting. There is little local traffic west of Winnipeg, towns being few and far between. A dining-car is attached to the train, and on the following day is replaced by another. The train makes a bee-line for Winnipeg, as there are no more "loops" to climb mountain sides on, no more puffing engines pulling in front and pushing behind, no more noisy bridges and trestle-works to cross. We are moving along at the rate of half a thousand miles a day, yet the view is always the same, varied only by the sight of buffalo tracks, — the autographs of departed herds, — a few coyotes, and some begging squaws with their pappooses at the stations — only this and nothing more, except the prairie itself, on which it is said a rider who sets out on a day's journey can see before starting the place where he will be in the evening. The train stops a few hours at Winnipeg, where some of the passengers use this first opportunity to branch off to the United States; then on we speed again over the prairie. There is an occasional stretch of dark, ploughed soil in the distance, which causes you to look twice to make sure that it is not the ocean; and when finally the train suddenly plunges into a tunnel, you are almost as much startled, after all this prairie monotony, as if an Atlantic steamer on the way to Liverpool took you through a tunnel; in fact, you are at first disposed to fancy that this tunnel had been artificially created by the engineers as a practical joke on the passengers. It is only a prelude, however, to the Lake Shore scenery, which, with the wild rocks and cliffs on one side, and an occasional glimpse of the lake on the other, forms one of the most fascinating fifty miles of the whole road. Instead of going along this north shore of Lake Superior in a wide curve, passengers have the option of taking the steamer from Port Arthur to Sault Ste. Marie, and thence rejoining the transcontinental road.

As a general thing, it is no doubt wiser to take the Canadian Pacific Railway westward than eastward, as the scenic climax is on the western side. However, it is quite possible to avoid the feeling of anticlimax on going east, if we conclude the trip with the Thousand Islands and the Rapids of the St. Lawrence, together with Montreal; or with Niagara Falls and the Hudson River. The Pacific slope no doubt is scenically far more attractive than the Atlantic; still, there are some things in the East which even California would be proud to add to her attractions.

XVII.

THROUGH YELLOWSTONE PARK

LIKE all the other transcontinental railroads, the Northern Pacific has its grandest scenery on the western half of its course. On the eastern section, between Livingston and St. Paul, the train traverses monotonous prairies, suggestive of the ocean, but less exhilarating, on account of the dust, and less uncertain and exciting, and with only a few prairie dogs, herds of cattle, grain-fields, and ugly little villages to vary the view from the car windows. But on its western section there is the magnificent scenery of the Cascade Division, with Mt. Tacoma, or, for those starting east from Portland, the romantic Columbia River route. As both of these have been described at length in preceding chapters, we can here pass at once to what is the climax of the Northern Pacific route — the Yellowstone Park, although reference must be made in passing to the rare beauty of Lake Pend D'Oreille, the shores of which the train skirts for hours. At Livingston the tourist leaves his comfortable Pullman and takes the branch road, which in a few hours lands him at Cinnabar, where stages have to be taken, as no railway is allowed within the limits of the Yellowstone Park.

This little branch railroad reminded me of some of the so-called "passenger trains" in Southern Europe. For slowness it would certainly get the first prize at a national exhibition of time-tables. "Gentlemen," I once heard a conductor exclaim, as he entered the waiting-room of a railway station in Southern Germany, — " Meine Herren, hurry up with your beer; it is time to start." But local color varies. On the Yellowstone Road the train was stopped for ten minutes in one place to leave a box of merchandise in the middle of a field, and to dispose of a bucketful of buttermilk which a nut-brown maiden had brought there for the trainmen and passengers; and shortly afterwards the train was again stopped, apparently because the engineer had espied a couple of prairie-chickens on the hillside. He pursued them with his revolver, bagged one of them, and after that the train stubbornly proceeded to its destination, notwithstanding the polite request of one of the passengers to the conductor to stop until he had caught a string of trout in the adjacent Yellowstone River. A week later, when I returned over the same road, the train stopped for a quarter of an hour at one place while the conductor, engineer, and brakeman amused themselves with a game of base-ball.

The gateway through which the train enters the fertile Paradise Valley and the National Park is bounded east and west by lofty mountains, on which, however, only a few specks of snow remained in the first week of August. Indeed, throughout the Park I saw much less snow than the guide-book had led me to expect; but for this an uncommonly warm summer may have been responsible. Yet even without snowy summits the Yellowstone mountains are picturesque, and must appear sublime to those who have never been in Switzerland. In ruggedness and grotesqueness of outline they are unrivalled, and the colors are often unique, the rocks being sometimes so white that they present the appearance of slightly discolored snow, such as is seen in the lower portions of glaciers; and this partly atones for the absence of real snow.

After a dusty stage ride, lasting several hours, and very much uphill, the passengers are landed at the Mammoth Springs Hotel, where a fair supper and good beds await them. Although this hotel is conveniently located near the foot of the remarkable many-storied, snow-white terrace-mound, built by the calcareous deposits of the hot springs, and adorned with the most brilliant colors, its site is nevertheless badly chosen; for there is no view from either the front or back windows, or from the piazza; whereas, if the building had been erected only a few hundred yards to the front, visitors might have enjoyed an extensive and delightful mountain view on all sides. This error is possibly responsible, to a large extent, for the fact that fewer visitors than had been expected make this large hotel their home for a week or two. With the exception of that at the Upper Geyser Basin, all the Yellowstone Park hotels are placed in like manner, though in each case a picturesque situation might have been found within a short distance. Perhaps the builders calculated that visitors, after their wearisome stage ride of forty or fifty miles and a subsequent brief inspection of the geysers, would hardly look upon the hotels as anything else than a place for providing them with meals and beds.

Having been apprised of the disadvantages to which those who take the regular round trip by stage in five days are subjected, I concluded to see the Park in a more leisurely manner, and hired a saddle-horse for a week at the rate of two dollars and a half a day, to which one dollar and a half a day was added for taking care of the horse at the several stations; thus making the expense about the same as it would have been if I had taken the regular forty-dollar coupon ticket, which includes fare and hotels for five days. They seem to have great faith in human nature in Wyoming; for I was allowed to take away my horse without leaving a deposit, and even without being asked my name! On entering the Park, an officer rode up and requested me to register, explaining that all persons entering privately were asked to leave their names, and state how long they intended to stay, as a precautionary measure against violations of the laws relating to hunting and forest fires. These regulations, with others, are printed on linen and conspicuously posted along the road every few miles, so that no one can plead ignorance of the law. Scattered throughout the Park are also hundreds of signs reading "No Hunting," "Extinguish your Fires," with others indicating good places for camps. In the Geyser Basins the principal springs and geysers are also marked by sign-boards, though not so liberally as might be desired. There should be more of them near the road to indicate the most remarkable spots. At present the "paint-pots" and the Gibbon and Tower falls are very apt to be missed by tourists. Some of the sign-boards of the Geyser Basins need renovating.

MINERVA TERRACE - YELLOWSTONE PARK.

At Norris one of these attracted my attention; and after getting my eyes within six inches to decipher the obscure inscription, I read the word "DANGEROUS!" These danger signals ought to be much more frequent. The very day when I was at Norris, a lady broke through the crust near one of the springs and was badly injured.

Norris Geyser Basin is directly south of Mammoth Hot Springs, and is the place where the tourist, if lucky, gets his first view of a geyser. If the reader has never looked at a map of the National Park, he may get an approximate idea of its topography by bearing in mind that the principal curiosities are so placed as to form a parallelogram. The road first leads south from Mammoth Springs to the four geyser basins, — Norris, Lower, Midway, and Upper; then east to the Lake; then north to the Falls and Grand Cañon, and over Mt. Washburn, to Yancey's; and thence back west to the Mammoth Springs. The patrons of the stage line, however, miss the Lake and Mt. Washburn, and are obliged to return by the same road a great part of the way. This must be very fatiguing, as the road between Mammoth Springs and Norris is most dreary and uninteresting, being generally lined on both sides by melancholy wastes of blackened tree corpses — a veritable forest cemetery. Now that fires are carefully guarded against, a vigorous undergrowth of young trees is perceptible, which in time will obliterate these and the many similar stretches of charred timber.

The hotel at Norris was destroyed by fire about the middle of July, 1887, and I arrived just in time to be the first occupant of a room in the new hotel. In the ruins of the old hotel were still to be found heaps

of roast potatoes, hams, and other meats, and groups
of molten beer and wine bottles twisted into peculiar
shapes. Beer and wine, by the way, may be had at-all
these hotels, although no bars are allowed within the
limits of the Park. The water throughout this part
of the Park is strongly flavored with sulphur and other
mineral ingredients, and is apt to disagree with some
people. After supper I went up the road for a mile
to see the Geyser Basin. The distinguishing characteristic of the Norris Basin is the many steam-holes,
which send out uninterrupted columns of steam, with a
deafening roar. I have read of canary-birds who were
silenced forever after hearing a mocking-bird imitate
and surpass their song. I wish all locomotive engineers
could be sent to the Norris Basin; perhaps that would
make them stop competing as to which of them can
make night most hideous with steam-whistles. Besides
these steam-holes there are simple hot springs, sizzling
" frying-pans," mud geysers, and " paint pots," in which
paste of various colors is boiling and blubbering. A
bench has been placed beside one geyser which every
seven minutes sends up a mass of liquid mud, splashing
and spluttering, and darting out arms in every direction, like a hideous polyp, until the frenzy has reached
its climax and forced some of the mud over the border;
whereupon the agitation subsides as gradually as it
came on, and the liquid mass disappears down a fathomless hole, where it compresses the steam until it has
gained sufficient volume to drive the nasty intruder
once more out of its hole.

While I was watching this ludicrous spectacle, some
of the workmen who were building the new hotel passed
by and invited me to follow them and see the " Mon-

arch " geyser spout. We occupied a place on the hill-side where there was no danger that the wind would drive the steam and hot water into our faces, and waited. The liquid eruption was due at eight, but the Monarch long refused to give us an audience. The workmen, meanwhile, discussed the news of the day, — the accident to the lady, already referred to, the moral character of the new dish-washer, and the death of a popular saloon-keeper, " a splendid fellow, who never refused a man a drink whether he had money or not." The Monarch awaited this opportunity to make the transition from the ridiculous to the sublime, and, pre-cisely at nine o'clock, with hardly any warning, he shot up a hot stream into the air a hundred feet or more, and kept it there for several minutes, the moon furnishing just enough light to see the stream of water amid the steam. *Après nous le déluge* appeared to be his motto; for we found it difficult to reach the road again because of the inundation he created during his brief activity. One of the workmen told me he waited for the erup-tion every evening, and that he had discovered some springs not known previously, including one sourer than a lemon (probably sulphuric acid). The number of hot springs in the Park seems, indeed, to be count-less. Every day the tourist comes across them repeat-edly, often most unexpectedly, and it seems probable that some of the greatest wonders of the Park remain to be discovered on the forest-clad hill-sides.

Among the most curious of the springs are the groups of little ones, with openings no larger than peas, lining the banks of the brooks and roadside, and so hot that one has to exercise caution in riding across them.

I should have stated that perhaps the prettiest sight

on the road from Mammoth Springs to Norris is the frequent patches of dense grass, ordinarily of a pale yellowish green color, but if seen from above, facing the sun, of the richest yellow, suggestive of lakes of liquid gold. More beautiful still are the golden rivulets which form the outlets of some of the hot springs in the Lower and Upper Geyser Basins. As the "Fountain," the principal geyser of the Lower Basin, was at rest when I saw it, I devoted most of my time to admiring these streamlets with their golden beds. All the gradations in color, from red through blood-orange, and orange to pale yellow, are here to be seen, the color fading out gradually with the distance from the spring. Quite as beautiful as the colors themselves are the exquisite waving golden lines and honey-comb figures which adorn the bottom of these rills, the reflections of the wavelets and ripplets on the surface of the water. In some places these dainty figures are replaced by rows of silky yellow fibres gently undulating with the movement of the water. The bottom of these rills is not hard, but consists of a soft pulpy mass, in some places several inches deep. This is fortunate; for otherwise some of those irrepressible idiots who write their names even on the bottoms of the white basins into which the water flows from the geyser craters would not hesitate to mar also the beauty of these fairy brooks.

The hero of Midway Geyser Basin is the "Excelsior," which, however, has been quiescent for several years. It forms an immense pool, which, with some others and their overflow, converts the Basin into a place of most dismal, forbidding aspect. It is close by the Firehole River, which is lined by hot springs, one of which has the aspect of a pigmy water-fall, the spray being represented by the steam. When one considers the number of these mineral springs, and the fact that the Excelsior has been known to vomit sufficient hot water to convert the Firehole River, a hundred yards wide, into "a foaming torrent of steaming hot water," one wonders no longer that this river, like several others in the Park, notwithstanding that its water is usually cool, rapid, and clear as a crystal, is destitute of fish. Were it not for this occasional excess of hot mineral water, there would be scores of places where a tourist might go through the unique performance of catching a trout, and boiling it in an adjacent spring, without moving from his place. As it is, those who wish to try this curious experiment have to do so at the Gardiner River or the Yellowstone Lake.

Few of the unfortunate tourists who are hurried through the Park on the Wakefield stages have an opportunity to see a geyser in activity till they arrive at the Upper Geyser Basin. Here more than a dozen geysers of the first magnitude are congregated; and although some are very irregular, and others only play at long intervals, there are several which every one who remains a few hours can see. A blackboard in the hotel gives a list of the geysers and their intervals of performance, and the hotel is so placed as to command a view of almost the whole basin, so that, whenever one of the irregular geysers starts up, the guests may be at once informed, and hasten to the scene. Fortunately, one of the finest geysers in the basin is "Old Faithful," only a hundred yards from the hotel, and so-called because it spouts once in sixty-five minutes, almost with the regularity of a clock. The "Grand," "Castle," "Beehive," and "Splendid" geysers are also certain to play for the benefit of those who spend a day at the Upper Basin. But the grandest of them all, the "Giant," wakes up only once in a fortnight; and unfortunately I arrived just eight hours too late to see it. But there was no room for disappointment, as the other geysers afforded more than enough excitement and wonder for a day.

Even if these geysers were extinct, it would be worth a visit to this Basin to see the fanciful, lofty craters built up by the calcareous deposits of the hot springs. No two geysers appear to be quite alike in their style of playing. Some have more steam mixed with their water than others; some shoot up a constant stream; others, an intermittent one, somewhat like the various forms of rockets. The stream of the Castle looks almost like a water-fall flowing upwards and vanishing in mid air; and the Splendid afforded the spectacle of two lovely rainbows.

Besides these exciting geysers, which represent the sublime, the Upper Geyser Basin has some of the loveliest pools or springs in the Park, as representatives of pure, placid beauty. Chief among these are the "Morning Glory" and the "Gem,"— pools of fathomless depth filled with diamond of the purest water, lined inside with the richest, deepest colors, and with a "horrid" black hole at the bottom, suggesting the entrance to the nether regions. Into one of these pools a stupid boy once threw a stick, and his poor dog jumped in after it and was boiled to pulp in a few minutes. In another was found the bare skeleton of an elk, possibly driven into it by pursuing wolves,— a fine subject for a ballad.

From the Upper Basin I might have gone straight to

the Lake; but as the road is a mere trail on which a horse cannot run, and the distance is therefore too great to cover in one day, I returned to the Lower Basin, whence it was only about thirty-five miles to the hotel camp at the Lake. With many tourists it seems to be a moot point whether it is worth while to visit the Lake; and as few used to go there, the accommodations until recently were of a most primitive kind. There were two men at the camp, and three tents — one for cooking, one for eating, and one to sleep in. An Englishman and his wife were the only guests besides myself. The lady naturally desired the sleeping-tent to be made up into two separate rooms, and the "landlord" finally submitted to the extra trouble this involved, though afterwards he was overheard commenting to his assistant on "them fussy English." When the English lady got up in the morning to wash, she found the towel had already been used by her husband and myself, so she asked for another. The assistant replied he had already put out a fresh towel for that date, but after a moment's hesitation he decided to make an exception in her favor, and produced a second.

For the season of 1890, however, a new hotel was opened, and boats placed on the Lake; and the tourist who omits it makes a great mistake. Not only does it rank among the curiosities of the world, being the only lake of its size at so great an altitude (7788 feet above the sea; or, as the guide-book graphically puts it, if Mt. Washington could be sunk in it with its base at sea-level, "its apex would be nearly half a mile below the surface of the lake"); but its intrinsic beauty would insure it renown at any altitude. Snow there was none on the surrounding mountains when I saw them; but, like all mountains, they gain immensely in picturesqueness and apparent loftiness by being seen across a sheet of water. And a beautiful sheet of water the Lake is, aside from its surroundings; but it is treacherous, and there is a violent thunder or wind storm almost every morning at eleven. About six o'clock in the morning I distinctly heard the mysterious rushing sounds in the air referred to in the guide-book as unexplained. I suppose they are due to the sound of the waters dashing against the beach and borne on by the wind, gradually accumulating loudness. Or the sounds may be due to the movements of the capricious and fitful wind among the tree-tops. I repeatedly heard a gust of wind approaching in that way with a magnificent *crescendo* and climax which a modern orchestra could hardly equal.

Everybody knows that the Yellowstone Lake is as brimful of trout as the Columbia River is of salmon. But a general notion prevails — even among those who dwell in the Park — that they are all unfit to eat, being infested by worms. This is an error. About half the trout are as sound as any other fish, and can be readily distinguished from the diseased ones. In the middle of the Lake it is said that all are sound, — a statement for the truth of which I cannot vouch. Our Englishman caught a dozen in the river just after it leaves the Lake. The cook assorted them, threw away the bad ones, and fried the others, which proved to be as good fish as I ever ate. The next day, on the way to the Falls, I stopped for a short time to catch a few of the numerous two-pounders that I saw swimming near the shore. Further down the Yellowstone the trout are smaller and less abundant than near the Lake, so that there is some sport in catching them; but where I stopped it was very much like fishing in a reservoir filled with hungry hatched fish. All I had to do was to select my fish, place the bait before his nose, and pull him in. I took along half-a-dozen which I knew to be sound, but at the Falls hotel I was informed that their French cook refused to touch the Lake trout. As the hotel itself furnished trout for supper caught below the Falls, where they are admitted to be sound, I did not argue the point with the cook, who was busy providing for an excursion party of fifty.

If the Yellowstone region contained nothing but the two falls at this place, and the Grand Cañon, it would have been worth while to reserve it as a National Park for all time. The two falls, though only half a mile apart, are utterly different in character; as the smaller, upper one plunges into a quiet, small basin in a secluded idyllic retreat, while the lower plunges three hundred and fifty feet down an abyss which is formed by the stupendous walls of the Grand Cañon, of which several miles lie before the eyes of the dazed spectator. The best place to enjoy the grandeur of the Falls and the Cañon is not at Lookout Point, as is generally believed, but at the edge of the Falls. Seen from a distance above, these Falls present a unique sight. The water flows on like any other rapid current until suddenly it appears to vanish in the air. On approaching the edge of the Falls, this illusion resolves itself into a scene which Niagara can hardly equal. As the water plunges into the pool below, it is dissolved into clouds of vapor that put to shame the steam columns of the biggest geysers. The breakers which wildly dash against the sides of the pool indicate the turbulence of the water beneath this spray and foam. Some of the spray is carried by the wind to the abrupt walls of the Cañon, where it nourishes mosses and lichens, which add one more color to the numerous tints that adorn these rocks. These tints bewilder by their variety and richness. The same strong mineral waters that have painted such exquisite brook-bottoms in the Geyser Basins here undertook a kind of fresco-painting on a scale of the most sublime grandeur.

Near the summits of some of the rocks may be seen some curious caves. Other rocks terminate in turrets and pinnacles suggesting mediæval architecture; and some of the rocky walls are adorned with a mosaic of brown, red, yellow, and white, as elaborate as the floor of St. Mark's in Venice. Some of the turrets, when you climb up to them, appear so woefully weather-beaten that it looks as if you could kick them over; but you cannot. The torrent, at a dizzy depth below, in which the green water struggles wildly for supremacy with the white foam, enlivens the scene; and in one place a turn of the river-bed, near a streak of painted rock, gives the impression of two water-falls side by side, one green, the other red; one in motion, the other frozen.

From the Grand Cañon the coupon tourists return to the Mammoth Springs and Livingston, while those who travel independently can enjoy the ride over Mt. Washburn, with its extended views of the Rocky Mountains, its fertile sides fairly crammed with flowers of the richest colors and strangest varieties, and its solitary trail through the depths of a primeval forest, frequently blocked by fallen trees, on which one may not meet a human being in eight hours, nor hear any sound but the melancholy moan of a poor tree against which a

FALLS OF THE YELLOWSTONE.

dead trunk has fallen, and is wounding it with every movement of the wind. The dismal delight of this ride is as indescribable as the exciting sport of trouting that may be enjoyed at Yancey's, whence it is but a short distance back to our starting-point, the Mammoth Springs Hotel.

After spending a week in the National Park on horseback, I came to the conclusion that what the Park chiefly needs now is a railroad, — not a steam railway, which would frighten the game and set fire to the forests, but an electric railroad. Great as are the wonders of the Yellowstone Park, the intervening distances are so great and the scenery often so commonplace, that nothing would be lost, and very much gained, by having an electric road. Dust and fatigue could be thus avoided, and more time devoted to the wonders of the Park in three days than at present in a week.

XVIII.

THE GRAND CAÑON OF THE COLORADO.

IT is unfortunate for travellers that the masterpieces of American scenery are not all grouped along one or two of the transcontinental railways. As it is, each line has its own lions, and to see them all one has to cross the continent more than once. Some of the principal features of the Canadian Pacific, Northern Pacific, Union Pacific, and Southern Pacific railways have been commented upon in preceding pages, and it remains to notice the lion of the Atlantic and Pacific or Santa Fé route, which is nothing less than the Grand Cañon of the Colorado River, which Captain Dutton considers "the sublimest thing on earth." It is one of the sublimest things on earth, beyond a doubt; yet how many readers of this book, all of whom are of course highly educated persons, are able to tell, without consulting their geography, where the Grand Cañon of the Colorado is? In Colorado, of course, nine out of ten will say. But Colorado has only the honor of giving birth to the smaller rivers which unite to form the mighty Colorado, and which are fed by the snow of the Rocky Mountains. As Major Powell graphically puts it: "When the summer sun comes, this snow melts, and tumbles down the mountain sides in millions of cascades. Ten million cascade brooks unite to form ten thousand torrent creeks; ten thousand torrent creeks unite to form a hundred rivers beset with cataracts; a hundred roaring rivers unite to form the Colorado, which rolls, a mad, turbid stream, into the Gulf of California," about two thousand miles from its sources. Only about six hundred miles of the lower part of the river are navigable, on account of the earth fissures, or cañons, through which it has eaten its way for five hundred miles. Some of these cañons are in Utah, but the two largest and most famous — the Marble and the Grand — are in Arizona. The longest of the cañons is two hundred and seventeen and one-half miles long, and is separated from another one of sixty-five and one-half miles only by a narrow valley.

Lieutenant Ives says of the Grand Cañon region: "The extent and magnitude of the system of cañons in that direction is astounding. The plateau is cut into shreds by these gigantic chasms, and resembles a vast ruin. Belts of country, miles in width, have been swept away, leaving only isolated mountains standing in the gap; fissures, so profound that the naked eye cannot penetrate their depths, are separated by walls whose thickness one can almost span, and slender spires that seem tottering upon their base shoot up a thousand feet from vaults below." Or, as Major Powell puts it, the tributary streams, like the Colorado, "have cut gorges of their own; and they all have wet-weather affluents, that run in deep cañons. It is a cañon land."

Previous to Major Powell's bold expedition down this subterranean river, about twenty years ago, it was practically a *terra* (or rather *aqua*) *incognita*. For a party of scientific men and artists to venture in a few frail boats down this sun-forsaken river, shut in for over five hundred miles by precipitous walls rising sometimes over a mile and a half on both sides, not knowing how soon they would be dashed to pieces on the rocks below a water-fall, or sucked into a suffocating tunnel, or starved to death by losing their provisions, was surely one of the most heroic deeds on record, comparable to Columbus's expedition on the unknown, illimitable ocean in search of a new world. It was a Jules Verne novel realized; and I know of no romance more fascinating in its narrative and more poetic in its descriptions of scenery, than Major Powell's account of this expedition, which is unfortunately buried amidst the government reports of geological surveys. At least four hundred rapids, eddies, whirlpools, falls, and cascades were encountered, and many were the hair-breadth escapes. They were chilled at night, and in the daytime the thermometer sometimes rose to 115°, in this river dungeon, amidst a forest-like gloom; but still they had to go on, for return was impossible, as they knew very well before they started. Sometimes the water hurried along their boats with the speed of railroad trains. The rocks on both sides would roll the water into the centre in great waves, and the boats would go leaping and bounding over these " like black-tail deer jumping the logs " which strew the forests. Indians have come to grief here. In the onomatopoetic description given by one of them, " The rocks h-e-a-p high; the water go h-oo-woogh, h-oo-woogh; water-pony [boat] h-e-a-p buck; water catch 'em; no see."

THE GRAND CAÑON OF THE COLORADO.

I cannot resist the temptation to quote two more brief passages from Major Powell's pages, describing portions of the Marble and Grand Cañons. " The walls of the Cañon, twenty-five hundred feet high, are of marble, of many beautiful colors, and often polished below by the waves, or far up the sides, where showers have washed the sands over the cliffs. At one place I have a walk, for more than a mile, on a marble pavement, all polished and fretted with strange devices and embossed in a thousand fantastic patterns. Through a cleft in the wall the sun shines on this pavement, which gleams in iridescent beauty." " In other regions the rocks, when not covered with soil, or more vigorous vegetation, are at least lichened, or stained, and the rocks themselves are of sombre hue, but in this region they are naked, and many of them brightly colored, as if painted by artist-gods ; not stained and daubed with inharmonious hues, but beautiful as flowers and gorgeous as the clouds. Such are the walls of the Grand Cañon of the Colorado where it divides the twin plateaus."

No one can read even these few extracts without feeling convinced of the truth of Captain Dutton's remark that the Colorado Cañon is " a great innovation in modern ideas of scenery, and in our conception of the grandeur, beauty, and power of nature "; and without wishing to see a portion at least of this Cañon. The Atlantic and Pacific Railroad is at present the only one which brings tourists into its vicinity ; and the station to get off at is Peach Spring, about eighteen hours' ride from Los Angeles, and situated twenty-three miles south of the Grand Cañon. The region between Los Angeles and Peach Spring presents many attractive features. First comes the city of Pasadena, with its large hotel, charmingly situated near the foot of the mountains, the sides of which present a peculiar wavy appearance. In some places they are curiously furrowed and crevassed, as if the very mountains had split themselves up into town lots during "boom" times. The surface is bare in the autumn except for a few trees near the rocky summits; but in spring the lower slopes are covered by millions of fragrant flowers, springing as by magic from the dust. Other picturesquely situated villages follow, some of which are destined no doubt to become flourishing towns. At present they are a curious compound of unfinished buildings, tents, and Mexican mud or adobe houses.

As the train proceeds in a northeastern direction, towards Barstow, the region of alternative ocean and mountain breezes is gradually left behind, and an arid desert of cactus, sand, and rocks is traversed. The sun's rays, no longer tempered by the ocean and mountain refrigerators, have it all their own way, and the wind is powerless in their clutches. For although a strong breeze is blowing, it feels like a blast from a hot furnace, so that one hesitates whether to keep the car windows open and desiccate, or closed and suffocate. Peach Spring I found to be an Arizona village consisting of five saloons, six dwelling-houses, a "stage" office, and an Indian camp in the background. It is so called, apparently, because no *peach* grows within a hundred miles, and because the only *spring* in the neighborhood is four miles from the depot, whence the water is pumped to the station with an engine fed with coal that is brought there from the station. Mr. Farlee, the man who has this coal contract, also undertakes to convey tourists to the Grand Cañon. He is an intelligent man, whose enterprise has built a fair road, twenty-three miles in length, generally along or in a dry river-bed, which, after every freshet, calls for extra labor in clearing away the rocks wildly strewn about by the strong current. As there is no possibility of missing this road, I secured a pony of Mr. Farlee, and started alone for the Cañon ; and on the whole way I saw no soul except an Indian, who rather suspiciously went behind a tree near the road as I approached. Being weaponless, I met any possible scalp-hunting propensities on his part by a cordial "Good morning," which he as cordially echoed. The Indians of this neighborhood are lazy, and, with few exceptions, refuse to do any work even for good pay. Their filthiness, also, is great; and no wonder, considering that the nearest spring is four miles away and monopolized by the railroad company.

A mile or two beyond this spring is another one, where the horse may be watered. During the remaining eighteen miles there is only one spring, and if the traveller misses that, he has to suffer agonies of thirst, unless he has wisely provided himself with a flask of tea or lemonade. The brisk, hot breeze which sometimes blows only aids the physiological desiccating process, and the result is a temporary dipsomania, in the frenzy of which one would gladly give a gold coin for a glass of lemonade. Nothing but forbidding cactus and a few similar tough and spiny plants can resist this heat; hence the whole region seems barren, and the few animals one may chance to see — a hawk, butterfly, rabbit, or cata-mount — but add to the desolation of the scene. There is not a sound in the air, and the silence is as absolute as on an Alpine snow-field, or in mid-ocean during a calm. The slightest sound made in urging on the weary horse is echoed by the hill-sides though they are several miles away.

The mountain scenery is unique and grand, and becomes more so the nearer we approach the Grand Cañon. For the road is a regular *descensus Averno*, taking us deeper and deeper down between the mountain walls; and when we reach the end of it we are almost a mile nearer the sea-level than we were at Peach Spring.

At a spot about a mile from the river Mr. Farlee intends to erect a large hotel. Sandstone, granite, and other fine building-material lie about in profusion, and only need to be hewn and piled up architecturally. At present there is nothing but a very primitive hut, with accommodations for about a dozen persons. The inn is run by one man, whose special duty it also is to keep his end of the road in order; and a lonely life he must lead in this solitary hut, twenty miles from any other human habitation. When there are no guests to take care of, he fills his canteen with water and starts up the valley, to roll the stones out of the road. In the evening he wraps himself in his blanket and goes to sleep, with the starry firmament for a roof, regardless of possible disagreeable neighbors, such as centipedes or rattlesnakes. He says he sleeps in the open air two-thirds of the time, and has not been ill for thirty-five years. Yet the heat in this part of the Cañon (which is so deep that stars are often visible in the daytime, and at night I saw a million more stars than ever before) must be a terrible strain on his system, as it sometimes rises to 120 ° in the shade, with not a breath of air.

I shall never forgive this man, or his employer, for having nothing sour in the house except a spoonful of very bad vinegar — no pickles, lemons, or even a grain of lemon sugar, which, by the way, every traveller in hot regions should always carry with him.   So I had to content myself, on arrival, with tea and water.   The water is good, although superstitious people might hesitate to drink it, as it comes from a brook — Diamond Creek — which seems to be bewitched.   Just in front of the hotel a portion of this creek, about half a mile in length, disappears every day towards noon, although above and below this place it flows on merrily and abundantly.   About ten o'clock at night the water suddenly returns to the deserted portion of its bed.   Mr. Farlee has repeatedly dug down many feet to find the subterranean brook-bed, but in vain.   It almost seems as if the water, after leaving the cool and deep Diamond Cañon, were afraid of being absorbed by the superheated air in the open space in which the hotel is situated, and therefore concealed itself underground.

I still felt so desiccated, after my four cups of tea and about ten glasses of lukewarm water, that I made the man in charge of the hotel promise to wake me at 10 P.M., as soon as the mysterious creek commenced to run again.   He did so, depositing a bucket of the water at my bed, and it was delightfully cool and refreshing.   A breeze had sprung up, and the night air was tolerably cool; but the man slept out of doors all the same.

Possibly there may be a poetic Indian legend accounting in some such manner for the fact that even the broad Colorado River has in this region dug its way into the bowels of the earth so deeply that it now runs more than a mile below the summit of its precipitous banks.   Yet, after all, there lies more poetry and sublimity in the scientific account of the manner in which the soft water has, by infinitesimal degrees, worn its channel through these hard rocks, and even through the lava, with which Major Powell thinks this river-bed has been filled more than once: "What a conflict of water and fire there must have been here!   Just imagine a river of molten rock running down into a river of melted snow.   What a seething and boiling of the waters; what clouds of steam rolled into the heavens!"   But it must be frankly admitted that those who visit the Grand Cañon, with anticipations at fever heat from reading Powell's exciting and poetic description of his adventurous trip down the Colorado, will be somewhat disappointed at first sight of this river.   It is about a mile from Farlee's inn, and is reached by following Diamond Creek, which empties into it.   On comparing the mud color of the Colorado with the crystalline purity of this creek, one realizes to what the latter might owe its name.[1]   Rapid the Colorado is, and broad, and its walls do rise to the height of a mile, but they slope and recede towards the background, and in vain does the tourist look for the "granite prison walls" rising abruptly from the edge of the water, and almost meeting above so as to shut out the daylight, their sides adorned with floating clouds and with the water-falls and cascades of tributary streams.

Yet in truth it is foolish to look for all these things here — to expect that all the wonders of Mr. Powell's long and perilous tour should be concentrated in one place for the convenience of tourists.   The fact is, that the most sublime portions of the Cañon are at present inaccessible except to those who are willing to undergo the

---

[1] It is said, however, that the creek owes its name to the fact that diamonds were once "planted" here, to deceive investors.

same dangers and hardships as Major Powell. One can readily believe the legends of parched travellers wandering along the brink of this Cañon for days, and "perishing with thirst at last, in sight of the river which was roaring its mockery into dying ears." Powell himself once spent four days wandering along the river, trying to get down. Diamond Creek seems to afford the only entrance to the Grand Cañon. The Atlantic and Pacific Railroad entertains a project of building an eighty-mile branch road from Flagstaff to the Cañon. Such a road would offer many attractions, as it would pass by some of the ancient cliff dwellings and the snow-capped San Francisco Mountains. It would, however, arrive at the top instead of at the bottom of the Cañon, which would thus lose some of its cathedral grandeur. Possibly the tourists might be let down to the river by means of a miner's shaft, in which case a ride of a few miles down the river on a boat (or " water-pony," as the Indians call it) should be added to the programme. But this would be at the Marble Cañon. For the Grand Cañon, Peach Spring will probably remain the stopping station ; and for their partial disappointment in the Grand Cañon itself, tourists will be amply repaid by a visit to the Diamond Cañon, which is reached by going up Diamond Creek, a few miles from Mr. Farlee's inn. Here they will find what they longed to see, — perpendicular, awe-inspiring walls, not, indeed, a mile, but more than half a mile, in height (twenty-seven hundred feet), topped with fanciful pinnacles and domes, and producing a feeling of gloomy sublimity as refreshing to the soul as the coolness of this granite prison is to the body.

Diamond Cañon and the Grand Cañon may be visited on the day of arrival at Farlee's inn. Leaving the afternoon of the second day for the return to Peach Spring, no visitor should fail to ascend Prospect Point, which forms one of the banks of the river, in the morning. It is an hour's hard climb from the inn, but it repays the toil a hundred-fold. From the summit one obtains several picturesque glimpses of the yellow Colorado, afar down, where it seems a mere brook ; and of course the surrounding mountains do not appear in their true size and grandeur until one sees them from this elevated point of view. These mountains all have a curious family likeness. Their basis is always formed by a striated, vertical layer, reddish or brown ; then follows a story or layer which slopes like a roof, suggesting human architectural efforts, but on a scale of infinite grandeur ; and above this are several more distinct strata towering straight into the skies. It is the constant sight of these superb and unique mountains, on the way from Peach Spring, that partly prevents tourists from being as deeply impressed as they would otherwise be at first sight of the Grand Cañon. "They get their belly full before they reach the river," as Mr. Farlee forcibly remarked.

After leaving Peach Spring, east-bound tourists may, if they have time, stop over at several places of interest which will claim a day each, — cliff dwellings, San Francisco Mountains, Pueblo villages, Sante Fé, etc. If they lack time, the car window still affords many pleasant sights which charm, even after the Grand Cañon, including the Cañon Diablo, two hundred and twenty-two feet deep, which the train bridges in the midst of a plain. Beyond Albuquerque the evidence multiplies that water is more abundant, and New Mexico has many picturesque and healthful spots, with wooded hills and green meadows, which only await the arrival of pioneers to be soon converted into populous and flourishing districts. Small pine forests make their appearance, and one readily understands why they are locally known as "parks," so clear are they of all underbrush and rubbish. In Kansas, bits of local color present themselves in the shape of immense herds of cattle, the three guardian angels of one of which (alias cowboys) race with the train quite successfully for a short distance. But while all these incidents and scenes are apt to be soon forgotten, the Grand Cañon remains stereotyped in the memory, where fresh copies can always be produced at will. "Great as is the fame of the Grand Cañon of the Colorado, the half remains to be told," as Captain Dutton remarks in his "Tertiary History of the Grand Cañon," the eighth chapter of which, "The Panorama from Point Sublime," is one of the most valuable essays on natural æsthetics ever written, and should be read by all who make the Great American Scenic Tour.

Presswork by Berwick & Smith, Boston.

Typography by J. S. Cushing & Co., Boston.